The Red Notebook

The Red Notebook

Michel Tremblay

translated by Sheila Fischman

Talonbooks

Copyright © 2004 Leméac éditeur / Actes Sud
Translation copyright © 2008 Sheila Fischman

Talonbooks
P.O. Box 2076, Vancouver, British Columbia, Canada V6B 3S3
www.talonbooks.com

Typeset in Adobe Garamond and Tribute and printed and bound in Canada.

First Printing: 2008

The publisher gratefully acknowledges the financial support of the Canada Council for the Arts; the Government of Canada through the Book Publishing Industry Development Program; and the Province of British Columbia through the British Columbia Arts Council for our publishing activities.

No part of this book, covered by the copyright hereon, may be reproduced or used in any form or by any means—graphic, electronic or mechanical—without prior permission of the publisher, except for excerpts in a review. Any request for photocopying of any part of this book shall be directed in writing to Access Copyright (The Canadian Copyright Licensing Agency), 1 Yonge Street, Suite 800, Toronto, Ontario, Canada M5E 1E5; tel.: (416) 868-1620; fax: (416) 868-1621.

Le cahier rouge by Michel Tremblay was first published in French in 2004 by Leméac éditeur in Montreal. Financial support for this translation provided by the Canada Council for the Arts and the Department of Canadian Heritage through the Book Publishing Industry Development Program.

Library and Archives Canada Cataloguing in Publication

Tremblay, Michel, 1942–
 [Cahier rouge. English]
    The red notebook / Michel Tremblay ; translated by Sheila Fischman.

Translation of: Le cahier rouge.
ISBN 978-0-88922-588-6

    I. Fischman, Sheila II. Title.

PS8539.R47C33213 2008   C843'.54   C2008-903034-6

My thanks to Jean-Claude Pepin whose copious documentation on the 1967 World's Fair was very helpful.

To my transvestite friends.

And as they were surprised at such generosity, a radiant Madame told them: "Not every day is a holiday."

>Guy de Maupassant
>*La maison Tellier*

But the crystalline piece of the figure it forms while it turns with others in the kaleidoscope: what does it know?

>José Carlos Somoza
>*The Detail*

Life isn't what we have lived but what we remember and how we remember it.

>Gabriel García Márquez

Prologue

September 1967

In my black notebook I endeavoured to describe in as much detail as possible the difficult period I lived through last year, to explain myself to myself in an attempt to understand what was going on, with the result that my life changed drastically, and for the better. In this brand new red notebook that I've had in my possession for more than a year and a half and in which I've not yet written a word, I would like to recount two days that marked this summer, now nearly over, the summer of Expo 67, which all of Montreal had been looking forward to as the promise of an earthly paradise, with its events of all kinds—cultural, athletic, social, merely recreational—spread over a period of several months and concentrated on two man-made islands right in the middle of the St. Lawrence, pulled from its bed to house the theme pavilions of every country in the world. The opening up to others that it represented as well, for us who have been brought up with an appalling inferiority complex and who could not until then imagine being the centre of attraction for anything. And in the end, prosperity, because this fair would no doubt put Montreal on the map, at any rate according to Mayor Jean Drapeau, that high-flying sly old fox.

And I would also like to use those two exceptional days to illustrate what my life has become, which is now the farthest thing from ordinary. It was ordinary during my time at the Sélect, but not at all when I was at the Boudoir. Since my early days on the Main, and especially since Expo 67, I've seen so many odd and interesting things, I've witnessed so many events that were so different from anything I'd ever known, so amazing and in the company of such unusual people that several times a day I'll tell myself that I have to make up my mind to tell every detail of the tale. Those two crazy days that I'll try to recount here are a perfect example ...

On Tuesday, July 25 of that year, I was wakened by the throaty voice of Michèle Richard who was guaranteeing to anyone who'd listen that tonight she'd be the loveliest one at the ball. Good for her. What I wanted was to sleep a little longer. A lot longer even. It had been a long night at the Boudoir, difficult and eventful for a plain little Monday—rowdy clients and Madame unwilling to budge as she so often is since Expo opened, we wonder why business is so great. Nothing is ever good enough or fine enough for her—for her house, for her regular clients, for the strangers passing through; the "girls" are often treated roughly, harshly (Marlene had the gall to complain, in June, and now Marlene's not at the Boudoir), crises are frequent, solutions rare and the atmosphere of the place suffers. But I'll come back to that later. For the moment, I've just awakened on the morning in question, it's the prelude to a series of events that would make this a singular day in the summer of Expo.

So. Michèle Richard—everybody was happy for her—would be the loveliest one at the ball … It was probably a practical joke by Mae East, an incurable insomniac, who, exasperated at her inability to sleep, had got up before anyone else and decided to make those of us who were still asleep sweat, by forcing us to listen to a song we all—including her—hated. Mae East is like that: when she's upset, everybody else has to be as well, and when by chance she's in a good mood she can't stand gloom and insists on smiles that we'd rather not offer and bursts of cheerfulness that we don't feel. She was furious, she felt like letting off steam by laughing at Michèle Richard, so the rest of us had to join in, from deep in our sleep if necessary.

(Here, a small clarification: when I talk about my drag queen friends in this beautiful brand new red notebook, I'll try to use the feminine all the time—as they do among themselves in any case—except for Jean-le-Décollé of course, who is without a doubt the only drag queen in history who still uses a man's name. He wants to be treated like a woman, a cliché of a woman in fact, but you have to address him in the masculine, which is strange when you're dealing with a bundle of rags that is obviously feminine. Anyway ... you get used to it.)

He was the first to react to the record. That harsh voice of Michèle Richard, the voice of someone who swallows every kind of smoke and Scotch—the Duchess of Langeais, the funniest drag queen in town, says of her voice that it's the result of a marriage between an effeminate longshoreman and a hairy, mannish, well-bred lady—rose up in the big apartment on Place Jacques-Cartier, at once husky and strident.

"Mae, if you don't stop that record right now you won't be the loveliest, you'll be the biggest wreck tonight and nobody's going to want you! Mind you, that wouldn't be such a big change ... "

Mae East's reaction was immediate. A tremendous din of dishes breaking could be heard in the kitchen.

Jean-le-Décollé again, "And add a dollar to the broken objects fund. I'm sick and tired of paying for your bad moods! If you've made a mess, clean it up!"

When I got to the kitchen, with my hair uncombed and bathrobe not done up properly, Mae hadn't cleaned anything yet. A shattered cup lay on the table in a puddle of steaming coffee. Mae East was leaning against the stove, mouth swollen and wig askew.

Anyone who's never seen a drag queen who's just got out of bed, without her dream creature's tricks and still swathed in the escapades and excesses of the night before cannot imagine what was before my eyes. It was both pathetic and funny, pathetic because you'd want to take that haggard thing in your arms and tell her to tidy herself up a little before she faces the world and funny in the sense that it's always surprising—for me at any rate—to see how much my friends don't give a damn about what they look like in private, while they'd never allow themselves to go out for a quart of milk without extravagant makeup and hairdos. When the three of them—Mae East, Nicole Odeon and Jean-le-Décollé—are around the breakfast table you might think you were watching a horror show because of the faces smeared with whatever ran during the night, whether red, green or brown, and puffy from lack of sleep. A conversation among three clowns who've forgotten to take off their makeup and a spic-and-span midget—me—who wouldn't dare go to sleep before she'd removed her makeup with linden-scented cleansing milk. I'm so used to it that I can't even fall asleep unless my pillow smells of linden flowers. It's a fragrance I discovered by chance, a range of products that don't cost too much—toilet water, cleansing milk, body milk, etc.—when I was rummaging through containers of cosmetics at reduced price in Ogilvy's basement, and it quickly became my personal scent, a fragrance that follows me everywhere, that even precedes me, according to my work-mates. Fine Dumas, my boss—Madame, to her friends—claims that she knows when I'm there, when I've just left, when I arrive. She says that linden flowers announce me, declare my presence, that it's become something like a second identity. I've often asked her if it smelled too strong—she's always replied that in a whorehouse nothing ever smells too strong. What she wears—arrogantly, because it's expensive and chic—is Chanel No. 5, but it often turns bad on her skin, especially when it's as hot as it's been this summer, and no one dares to tell her. I feel sorry for the poor fool who would dare to tell Joséphine Dumas that she smells bad!

So I was most likely preceded by the not very refreshing smell of linden flowers from the night before when I sailed into the kitchen, because without raising her head, Mae East said, "Hands off that record, Céline, or you'll end up a foot shorter. And God knows you can't spare an inch!"

It's very rare that my physique is mentioned in the house and I was surprised. No one in my circle ever mentions that I'm a midget and I'm grateful. Or at the Boudoir: Fine Dumas chose me mainly for my intelligence and resourcefulness, she says, but also for my unusual appearance, I'm sure of it. The girls were quick to accept me—true, it was after a period of frowns and snickers hidden behind hands, but that, I'm used to—and before long I'd become what the boss called a feature of the house: apparently I attract customers, they come to the Boudoir almost as much to see me as to do certain things with the girls. All that—my role at the Boudoir, what I do there, how I feel about it—I'll come back to later.

For now, I'll return to the kitchen in our apartment, because that was where the memorable day began.

When my third roommate, the so well-named Nicole Odeon, an inveterate movie fan who was in on all the Hollywood and Paris gossip, saw the film *Les demoiselles de Rochefort* a few months ago—in France, if you please, with a super-rich Frenchman who was crazy about her for the duration of a romantic crossing of the Atlantic: bound for glory on a ship, she came back with her tail between her legs, by plane, at her own expense—she decided that we were going to live in an atmosphere like the one Jacques Demy had created for his film. If *The Umbrellas of Cherbourg* had moved her deeply a few years earlier—apparently she would sometimes sing "I'll Wait for You" to clients who were to her liking—*Les demoiselles de Rochefort* finally drove her crazy. Painters, each one sexier than the last, showed up one morning with their brushes, their gallons of paint, their ladders and their overactive muscles, they slaved away for several days like Snow White's seven dwarves, and we now live surrounded by colours that would give the most proficient chameleon a headache. The kitchen, for instance, is painted blood red, the cupboards lemon yellow. With a hangover it's rather violent—besides being terrifyingly ugly—and you should hear the comments by Mae East and Jean-le-Décollé on certain mornings when, to recover from the night before, they mix themselves a Bloody Caesar the same colour as the kitchen walls. Nicole thinks it's cheerful, the rest of us think it's scary!

Jean-le-Décollé: "When I walk into that kitchen I'm afraid the walls will murder me! I'm sure there's a knife hidden somewhere!"

Mae East: "What we need to go with your ketchup and mustard, Nicole, is a huge hotdog in the middle of the room!"

Needless to say, a few days later we found one, made of china, on the centre of the table. It's still there in fact. It's what I was looking at while Mae was talking to me.

"Really, that's all I needed! When disaster strikes it won't let go, right? After a stupid sprain that nearly cost me my job, *that* had to happen! Some people don't have any luck."

I knew it was pointless to ask questions, I had to wait for answers to come on their own, at their own rhythm. I unscrewed the Italian coffee maker, filled it with water and the coffee that smells so good and costs so much. I even had time to screw it back together and set it on the stove before Mae East said another word. I understood then that it was serious, probably the thing that every self-respecting hooker is most afraid of: a venereal disease—which the Duchess of course calls venerable. The clap or syphilis, a little dose, a big one, a severe one, a mild one—it doesn't matter, they're all the same. For these ladies it means first and foremost a serious loss of earnings—for a few days or a few weeks. A temporary but serious write-off. In a worst-case scenario, if Fine Dumas reacts badly, it's an unpaid vacation that looms, which can be ruinous too, because when the girls are on vacation they don't just hang around, they spend. Not to mention the humiliating ridicule of their colleagues—it seems worse among drag queens than among prostitutes, they're meaner to one another and less supportive—and it's harder to get one's reputation back because the rumour mill on the Main runs faster and more efficiently than anywhere else.

I leaned against the stove, next to Mae.

"Is it what I think?"

"It's the first thing we always think about and we're nearly always right … Yeah, it's what you think all right."

"Have you seen Doctor Martin?"

"Hardly. There hasn't been time, I just realized it when I woke up. A nice present for the day after the party. But the worst thing is I maybe didn't get it yesterday and I've maybe already passed it on to loads of clients without knowing … "

"Are you absolutely sure?"

"Do you want a look at the green pearl at the tip of my tool?"

"Mae! I'm fixing the coffee!"

"And I'm fixing a wonderful end to my summer! A venereal disease in the middle of Expo is like running out of gas in the middle of the Atlantic: your plane won't last long!"

She was slumped on a chair across from Nicole's hotdog.

"If she doesn't take that thing off the table it's going to end up in a thousand pieces on one of her goddamn red walls! And I'll make her eat them!"

I poured each of us a mug of coffee after I'd cleaned up the pieces of the one she'd just smashed. Instant, of course, unspeakable dishwater she'd stirred up for herself that I'd sworn I'd never touch again when I left the Sélect where I'd been a waitress for two years. To think that I drank it for years—in fact for the greater part of my life it was the only coffee I knew—until I replaced it with tea for a while out of sheer disgust … But among other things, and to my delight, Jean-le-Décollé had introduced me to the pleasure of Italian coffee, and now I can't do without it and I can never thank him enough.

As Mae East hadn't made up her mind to talk yet, I took the liberty of breaking the silence.

"Does it hurt?"

"It burns."

"That means it's just gonorrhea. That's not as bad as syphilis … "

"Just because it's not as bad doesn't mean it's funny!"

"I never said it was!"

"You're smiling!"

"What? I am not smiling. Absolutely not!"

"I saw you smile, Céline, don't contradict me!"

When she turns paranoid like that there's nothing to be done. Mae East is pigheaded and trying to make her change her mind or persuade her that she's wrong is a total waste of time. So I smiled.

"Okay, fine, I'm smiling! Now are you happy? If you want to be even happier, just decide that I'm glad you're sick, happy that you'll spend the rest of the summer sitting on your livelihood, moping around and watching the rest of us get rich."

With that I slammed my cup on the table—not too hard, I didn't want to break it, one a morning is quite enough—and made my way as quickly as my short legs would let me to the door that opens onto the hallway.

"Deal with your own problems if you don't want sympathy, Mae! Don't talk about your gonorrhea, keep it to yourself. Try to make us believe that you've decided to take a holiday!"

For some reason I thought that she'd stop me in mid-speech, apologize, blame it on the bad luck she'd been hit with, try to make peace ... But oh no, she was sure she'd seen me smile before I really did, and there was no way to convince her she was wrong.

Still it was odd, people who start by pleading for your sympathy, then get in your face if you give it to them. Pride? Lack of self-confidence? Regret at showing weakness? Shame at seeing yourself reduced to begging for help? Why tell me about her disease if she was just going to turn down any offer of help?

I was there in my thoughts when I opened the front door to bring in my newspapers—after I'd gone down the four sets of stairs that are so steep for my short legs. The apartment is gorgeous but a little high up for my liking.

It's true that we're having an extraordinary summer. In every sense of the word. There's been hardly any rain during this tremendous party that Montreal has been offering itself for three months. The weather is glorious, just hot enough, and so far there haven't been too many sweltering days or sticky nights. At Expo everything is going fantastically well, better than expected. Besides all that, foreign visitors like our city, they think we're friendly—they should pay a visit to the Boudoir around 2 a.m. if they want some flagrant examples—Montreal is bursting with fireworks every day, she's inundated by compliments, beaming with contentment, and starts over again every day with obvious happiness. What more can one ask of life?

For a while I kept an eye on Place Jacques-Cartier. It could stand a touch-up, some cleaning and polishing. It's just pretty now, when it could be beautiful.

One of the first changes I made when I moved into this apartment a year and a half ago was to subscribe to three papers—*La Presse*, *Le Devoir* and *Le Journal de Montréal*. I was shocked at my roommates' ignorance of what was going on in the world and I wanted to try to stir their appetite for knowledge. I myself was far from knowledgeable but compared with them, I could be a Nobel laureate! They knew that a world's fair was in the works in Montreal because, more and more, street prostitution was being banished, and the Boudoir was filling up as the sidewalks of the Main were emptying, but of what was going on, of its importance, of what it represented for their city and its inhabitants—including them, after all—they had no idea and not the slightest curiosity. Except of course on the subject of the money they might make, so they could buy taller wigs, vertiginous heels and, in certain cases, more effective forms of artificial paradise from which they would never come back. So you can imagine what they knew about the state of the world.

Most of the people I work with at the Boudoir don't know the name of the prime minister of Canada or the premier of Quebec. As for the mayor of Montreal, they know who he is because he was already there when they were schoolchildren.

But the three working girls I live with now have a chance to leaf through three newspapers every morning, even if they don't always take advantage of it. It's true that they spend more time with the women's pages and the arts sections than on the serious articles that analyze wars, famines and disasters of every category. At least it takes them out of their own inbred little world which they never leave. (More than once I've caught Jean-le-Décollé laughing at the caricatures in *Le Devoir*, which is better than nothing, isn't it? And more and more often he offers to go down the four flights of stairs to pick up the papers.)

It's true that I went a bit too far with *Le Devoir*. It's too intellectual for the four of us but even so, I sometimes read a whole article.

I knew before I worked there that the world of the Main was closed and cut off from reality, but not to what extent. A microcosm of internal wars and petty-mindedness large and small keep it wrapped up in itself, concentrating on its own not-always-clean navel, busy with its own crises and minor woes that often take on an exaggerated importance, that come close to the ridiculous, a product of the unrestrained imagination of its inhabitants and the prevailing paranoia. Don't get me wrong; I love the Main, I love its festive atmosphere, its non-stop party side, its resistance to the established order, the way it thumbs its nose at so-called normality, and it would be hard for me now to do without it, but I often worry about its frivolous nature and those with whom I've dared to talk about it—Fine Dumas, the Duchess, even Jean-le-Décollé all tell me I should enjoy it, not analyze it. I'm not there to be Lady Bountiful, they tell me, I'm there to earn as good a living as possible, taking advantage of the windfall that Expo 67 represents.

I bent down to pick up the three papers ... and the first thing I saw was a huge photo of General de Gaulle. The entire front page of the *Journal de Montréal*: "Vive le Québec libre!" On the front page of *La Presse* as well: the general, arms raised in a *V*: "Vive le Québec libre!" *Le Devoir* too, of course. We'd heard something about it at the Boudoir the night before, but it was more like a rumour, a story told by drunks. So it was true. He really had said it. In front of everybody.

I loved his insolence. I've never paid much attention to politics, I'm not interested, I don't believe politicians, not one. It seems to me they're all inveterate liars and they bore me, on both sides, red or blue, both so-called liberals and avowed conservatives. They take themselves too seriously not to be suspect. I haven't voted yet because I'm too young and I don't know if I ever will, even if I suspect that it must have some importance ... But this foreigner who comes and sows discord right in the middle of a world's fair, who dares to utter a slogan unhoped-for by one part of the local population and reviled by the other, this arrogant giant with upraised arms standing on the city hall balcony, in front of dignitaries, as ready to insult as to please, to get involved in something that's none of his business—what nerve and what a treat! I don't know why, but I could have kissed him!

But I couldn't linger very long over this event.

Another piece of news, important in a different way, was waiting for me when I read the papers that morning.

Michèle Richard had changed her tune. Now it was the catchy song of the summer that was imposed on the living room, the excruciating "J'écoutais la mer" that you heard everywhere, the typically loathsome tune, the one you wished you'd never heard because it stays in your brain like a disease, for which, alas, there's no cure, the musical phrase that wakes you up in the middle of the night and keeps you awake, that makes you white with anguish, that's so exasperating it drives you crazy. Mae East had kept the record changer up, so we were doomed to listen to that unbearable noise for hours unless someone put a stop to it. I decided to do it in spite of the likely consequences and I took the 45 RPM off without bothering to put it back in its sleeve while Michèle, all smiles, seemed to be taunting me. "Even if you don't want to listen to my song, you'll hear it anyway!"

I was amazed that there were no protests. Mae must have been in the shower and the other two, who would finally be able to get back to sleep, would be grateful to me without deigning to show it.

If the kitchen is ugly, the living room is staggering. The walls are periwinkle blue, the panelling and ceiling lilac, the curtains salmon pink and the carpet peacock blue. Maybe Scheherazade would feel at home, but not me. Nicole thought it was restful, but as far as I was concerned, I felt as if I were lounging in a box of fondants. Our living room could cause tooth decay, I'm positive! Especially because, for lack of funds, we had to keep the same old furniture that we had before our major cleanup, indescribable horrors from the 1930s inherited from Nicole's parents—massive, heavy, covered with cut velvet that was too stiff and trimmed with red acanthus leaves and vine leaves against a brown background. Here, Scheherazade wouldn't spend three minutes. We had a choice then between a mustard-and-ketchup kitchen and a candy-box living room. A salty and sweet apartment.

I set the papers on the dance-floor size coffee table that still displayed some vestiges of the party the night before: a half-empty bottle of champagne brought home from the Boudoir most likely; a box of poor-quality condoms; and a sample of a phenomenon that's appeared recently at the Boudoir, the new craze for drag queens and hookers that for some reason is called a "joint." But I haven't succumbed yet. Everyone tells me I should. I have to admit it smells good. Actually it was surprising to find one that wasn't even started, untouched by anyone. Mae, Nicole and Jean must have left it, too stoned to remember it was there. But they'd probably be thrilled to find it after breakfast ...

I opened my three papers on the coffee table to read what they said about General de Gaulle's declaration. But a second piece of news at the very bottom of the front page of *Le Devoir* and *La Presse* immediately attracted my attention.

The headline in *Le Devoir*: "Rioters Ransack Detroit" and *La Presse*: "1800 paramilitary enter Detroit where black rioters ransack and set fire to the city (photos and news, page 29)." So while visitors from all over were coming to Montreal, which was finally open to the world and for the first time showing a semblance of personality and strength of character—on the same day a visiting foreigner had come to encourage it to free itself from the ties that bound it to a country that didn't respect it—black Americans exasperated by three hundred years of injustice have to ransack a city to attract some attention to their misery. And even so, that story comes after de Gaulle's "Vive le Québec libre!" While in *La Presse*, they don't even rate an excerpt from an article, you have to go to page twenty-nine to find it! As for *Le Journal de Montréal*, not a word, just the general's big smiling face. Surely it's not up to me— a one-time waitress at the Sélect who's now the hostess in a very distinctive brothel in Montreal's red light district—to show journalists how to make up their papers, that's not my job—

besides, I've just written that I'm not interested in politics—but the glaring difference in importance of the two events struck me even though I'm just an ignorant night-worker without much education. General de Gaulle's declaration is no doubt of the utmost importance for those who think like him, for the separatists, the RIN, for the pride of French Canadians and even for the opponents of the independence movement who'll be able now to boo the president of France all they want: I understand all that, I'm not an idiot, but haven't the black Americans suffered more than we have, and for longer? Isn't the Detroit fire with its twenty-five dead and a thousand injured more important than some Frenchman, regardless of his high position, who came to encourage his "cousins from America," whom he'll shamelessly make fun of as soon as he turns around and leaves them to their problems, after people have finished talking about him, about his courage, about his gall, in all the papers of the world (if by chance they even mention it)?

Again, I don't want to make a big fuss about it, I don't know enough, but I suddenly feel as if I'm part of a very tiny society that is remote and cut off from everything. Earlier, I wrote that the Main is closed in on itself, that it has no interest in the outside world, and the proof was there in the papers that morning that Montreal wasn't much better, focussed as it was for three months on a little world's fair that may not leave behind the slightest trace, and that the city imagined to be more significant than it really was. Blacks are murdered by soldiers in Motor Town, the city where the gap between rich and poor is among the biggest in the United States, and what ends up on the front page of our papers? The face of General de Gaulle!

I was very upset. How many people across Montreal thought the same thing when they picked up their newspapers this morning? Surely I'm not the only one! I never read foreign newspapers but I promised myself that I'd try to find a copy of the *New York Times* that afternoon. I was curious to see if it would talk about General de Gaulle's declaration from the balcony of Montreal's city hall.

I was gloomy for a good part of the day. Michèle Richard bellowed her greatest hits ("Quand le film est triste," "J'entends souffler le train," "Les boîtes à gogo") not to mention the ones we'd already heard that morning. Jean-le-Décollé, when he saw Mae East's stubborn expression and sensed that trouble was brewing, slipped out, claiming he had a date, which didn't fool anyone; Nicole Odeon disappeared into the bathroom—which we call her dressing room because it's where she spends most of her time—to put her face on, which took hours and was far from convincing when the butterfly finally emerged from the cocoon.

I left the three papers on the coffee table and went back now and then to re-read some articles (Claude Ryan, in *Le Devoir*, was trying to understand what the general had meant. Honestly!) and study the smug expression on the French president's face, proud of the effect he'd created, a modern-day prophet, saviour of his New World cousins. No flattering photo of the rebellious blacks of course, but an American soldier arrogantly brandishing a machine gun on page two of *La Presse*.

I couldn't explain clearly what shocked me most: the ridiculous layout of the papers that emphasized the least important story from the day before, in my opinion anyway, or knowing that after my own protests, after spending the day seething and cursing the journalists, I would, like everyone else, go back to the daily grind, to the air-conditioned Boudoir, to Fine Dumas's unctuous and self-interested expressions, to the foreign clients' demands, to the Duchess's ranting—should she deign to show her face, to Mae East's dose that mustn't be allowed to develop into something more serious. I was obviously helpless in the face of the great worldwide social movements. After all, a midget on Place Jacques-Cartier isn't going to make any difference in a conflict like the one shaking Detroit that could lead to a revolution in the United States, but it may have been precisely that helplessness, the impression that I was the only person offended by the front pages, that had me so exasperated. Because as I've already said I knew that in a few hours, at nightfall, I would forget it all and plunge headfirst back into the illicit little world of the Main. My world. That I now never leave. And that cuts me off from everything.

I promised myself that I'd go through the papers every day. Maybe the next day, after the general had left, things would return to normal, the important events would take back the space they deserved. After the party, the revolution.

Wrong. The next day I'd have forgotten all of it. Like everyone else.

Around four in the afternoon—this time, Michèle was trying to persuade us that "l'argent ne fait pas le bonheur," as if she believed it!—Mae East, with a grim look on her face, came to see me in my room.

"Okay."

I looked up from the latest Françoise Sagan which I've been devouring over the past few days. I find the woes of the French bourgeoisie hilarious. I'm never moved by them. I've never had any contact with them, but I always take a malicious pleasure in their marital escapades and their financial problems. It's amazing how important money can be in French novels.

"Okay what?"

Mae, unlike most of her colleagues, doesn't wear a wig. She merely bleaches blonde her mass of hair whose original colour she's long ago forgotten—most likely it's starting to go grey—which she pulls up into a chignon, a beehive or a variation on a French twist, a pile of hair that's generally complicated, that doesn't always work, but is surprisingly often flattering. This time she'd settled for a simple ponytail that flapped against her back and gave her the girl-next-door look that Americans are so fond of. Not the clients of the Boudoir though. Those tourists from Nebraska or Arkansas haven't come to Montreal to get it off with the girl next door, they want the slut next door! And every night, Mae East is happy to oblige.

"Doc. Martin. I'm going to see him."

"At last, a decision! Surely you didn't think that you'd be spared!"

She sat at my dressing table, ran my brush through her hair while I set my book down on my bedside table.

"Hardly. I just didn't feel like talking about it this morning. I was too pissed-off. I'd just realized what it was ... If the guy who gave it to me had been there ... "

"You all say that!"

"We'd do it to them too! Bring back the guy who left a girl with a dose and I'm telling you, you won't recognize him and he'll be out of circulation for a good long time! He'll be in no shape to pass anything on to anybody!"

"Want me to go with you?"

"What?"

"To the doctor's. Do you want me to go with you ... Isn't that what you came to ask me?"

"That would be so nice of you ... You see, I don't want to be alone in case he tells me it's something else ... "

"It won't be something else ... "

"You never know."

What could I say? It's true that you never know. During the year and a half I've been working at the Boudoir I've seen even girls who were careful catch things nasty enough that they had to retire, to take a leave for several months—unpaid, needless to say—though they never think of the future and spend every cent on useless doodads and on makeup they'll never use. They borrow from Maurice's shylocks at usurious rates, never meet deadlines, get beaten up, Fine Dumas chews them out or kicks them out, they try going back to the street, get arrested ... Some life!

"But you know, Mae, you could've decided before ... It's after four, we have to be at the Boudoir by eight, you know how Fine hates it when we're late ... "

"I can't imagine it will take four hours. A shot of penicillin takes two seconds!"

"Last time with Babalu, Doctor Martin didn't have anything ... "

"That was during the gonorrhea epidemic in London, it's not the same thing ... I don't think there was one girl who didn't get it!

Don't scare me, Céline, I want to be back at work in three days max; I can't afford a holiday in the middle of Expo!"

She knew though that was what would most likely happen. A forced holiday. At her own expense. Right in the middle of an economic boom for the local drag queens. Which was, I imagine, the reason for the line on her forehead that I hadn't seen before, that made her look like a sulky little girl. At that moment no native Nebraskan on a spree in Montreal would have wanted her.

"Are you ready? I'll call a taxi."

"Mae! It's three blocks away!"

"I don't feel like walking. I'm burning! Anyway, I'll pay so don't complain!"

"Even with my short legs I'm sure that if I left now, I'd get to the doctor's before you!"

She gave a hint of a smile which relieved me a little. Then she went to the phone.

On my way through our *Thousand and One Nights* living room, I found Nicole Odeon deep in one of the newspapers still open on the coffee table.

"Find something interesting, Nicole dear?"

A moment of social awareness, maybe? You never know …

She waved *Le Journal de Montréal* in front of her.

"Can you believe how ugly this man is? And just think, some woman somewhere in France gets it on with that every night!"

"The ones you get it on with every night aren't always better, Nicole … "

"No, but at least it's never the same ones! Looking at that every night would be torture! I hope at least he didn't bring her along … That will give her some breathing room, poor woman!"

Slut's logic.

While the people around me are fairly discreet about my appearance, I've been less concerned about it for a while. Surrounded now by individuals even more thin-skinned, more ill-treated than I am, who often use self-mockery as a kind of protection, a carapace, the only way to deal with the world, since I've been at the Boudoir I have learned and adopted the salutary state of mind we know as carefree. Not the fake kind you can identify in a second, that in the end attracts only pity for the person who is trying to create an illusion; no, being genuinely carefree because of genuine well-being, fleeting or not, being genuinely content to be oneself which leads to absolutely not giving a damn about what other people think of us.

I can almost say that I feel good about myself for the first time in my life. And that I can finally think positively about my very unusual body. My mother always told me to try everything to be overlooked or, if that was impossible, to be forgiven for my unattractive physique, through acts of kindness and—I think it's the right word—through every kind of sycophantic behaviour. Of course she didn't say sycophantic, she didn't know that word, but she taught me to belittle myself in front of others, to flatter them, serve them, let them have all the room because I didn't deserve any respect, because of my oddly-shaped body. I listened to her for too long not to be mad at her still. And to curse her for making me waste so much time. I've always wanted to go unnoticed, while my only chance of survival was to look people right in the eye and say to them, "So what?"

It's a little like what I'd done without realizing it when I started waitressing at the Sélect, in my first real fit of independence, of assertiveness—being the midget who dares to take a job that isn't intended for people like her. But it's only now, surrounded by social misfits for whom disguise is the only way out and black humour the balm that soothes every pain, when I descend the Boudoir's staircase in my green sequinned gown and my blood red shoes like Dorothy's in *The Wizard of Oz*, that I fully understand the meaning of the word *carefree*. I stand barely five feet in heels, but no one has more presence than I do, or more presence of mind, and you can see it in my behaviour. And anyone who dares to say a word, watch out!

My friends from the Main have shown me how to anticipate blows, to dodge them, forestall them, use them to make others laugh before they laugh at me, and it saves my life with steadfast regularity. I owe a particular debt of gratitude to the Duchess of Langeais who always says that the first one to laugh is the winner! She has spent her life laughing and making others laugh, and her devastating wit and her pithy retorts have made her one of the most loved, most hated and most respected characters of the Main. I am not yet a fighter like her but at least I now know where to concentrate my strength, and that makes my existence easier.

The little hostess at the Boudoir with the sense of humour that's so remarkable, who hides her bowlegs under brightly coloured lamé and sequins, is more ambitious than you think, and with a little bit of luck she may go far!

Or so I was telling myself while I waited for a taxi with my friend Mae East—the Mae West of Pointe-Saint-Charles. She was a pitiful sight, poor dear: squeezing her legs together because her crotch was sore, while she smoked a cigarette that made all of Place Jacques-Cartier stink. From a distance we must have looked like a mother and her little girl. Mae West, the real one, the one who meows like a cat in heat when she talks and sings in her strident voice words that she doesn't bother to enunciate, is very tiny apparently, hardly any taller than me, and she perches on very high heels so people will think that her height is normal (in fact that's why you never see her in a short dress in any of her films); Mae East, on the other hand, is over six feet tall, wears shoes the size of a dromedary's foot and dresses, verging on indecent, that graze her asshole. She's much in demand at the Boudoir, especially by Asians, and I thought to myself that I didn't want to be present when Fine Dumas found out that for a while she'd have to get along without one of her biggest earners. Especially after all her warnings, notes and practical advice that have been flooding the girls' notice board on the floor where the rooms are since Expo opened. She even took the trouble to write in purple ink on mauve paper posted prominently above the notice board, "Forewarned is forearmed!" Mae East was the first victim of negligence in a while and I was afraid that she'd have to pay a heavy price. Fine would want to make an example of her and since she doesn't mind terrifying her girls now and then, she would use the opportunity to vituperate, to fulminate, to punish and condemn, waving her cigarette-holder like an avenging weapon.

At last the taxi arrived, Mae mashed her cigarette with her shoe rather elegantly—a little like heroines in old black-and-white French films. Viviane Romance. Or Simone Signoret. (Here I must point out that the individuals around me are constantly inspired by and often copy what they have seen in movies, and that everyone— sometimes, I confess, including me—borrows their gestures, their way of speaking, their dress from French and American movie stars. We're constantly going back and forth between Bette Davis and Arletty, between Viviane Romance and Barbara Stanwyck, between the European-style femme fatale and the tougher, colder American one.)

Mae opened the door of the taxi. I have my own way of climbing into a car. I haul myself up the way children do, bracing myself on the seat with my arm before I lift my leg, and often I find myself facing the seat before I climb up and settle in. I've found a line that lets me avoid taxi drivers' sarcasm, a quip that I used again this afternoon and that even brought a smile from Mae.

Before the driver opened his mouth, I said, "Don't think I'm on my knees because I've been drinking! I'm actually standing up!"

He laughed, winked at me in the rear-view mirror when I settled myself on the leatherette seat and, as they always do, mentioned my good sense of humour. I felt like telling him it wasn't a sense of humour, it was a sense of survival!

But he came down to earth when Mae gave him the doctor's address.

"It's next door! You could have walked! Bother me for three blocks! Jeeze!"

Mae held on to my shoulder as if to protect me.

"It's because of my friend, she has trouble walking."

I jabbed her with my elbow but didn't dare protest because the driver apologized profusely. I was content to give her a withering look. I hate being used as a cover or to attract pity. She knew that, though. I attributed it to her "venerable" disease and decided just to drop it—again.

Doctor Martin is old, crabby and ugly. The Duchess has said of him that he'd been present at the birth of Adam, that he'd been in a bad mood and had scared him.

As Mae and I arrived towards the end of his office hours, we didn't have long to wait. Now and then a couple of hookers, real women, took a worried glance in the direction of his office. We didn't know them so we didn't have to start one of those fake cheerful conversations in which embarrassment at meeting in such a place is mixed with worry about what's going on between your legs. Year-old copies of *Photoplay* and the *Nous deux* lay on a round table in the middle of the room. Mae East plunged into an account of the tumultuous life of Susan Hayward while I read a stupid, icky story intended to inspire dreams in housewives yearning for romance but that only infuriated me.

Mae's turn came. As she was his last patient of the day, Doctor Martin agreed to leave his office door open and I could hear their whole conversation. He began—gently, I admit—with the usual rebukes about being careful, the risks of her trade, the importance of prevention and so forth. But my friend was in no mood for sermons and put the doctor in his place with a little monologue of her own: brief, well-phrased, well-structured and, most of all, needing no reply, "Listen up, Doc, I could hear the Sermon on the Mount at Sunday Mass and I stopped going to Mass so I wouldn't hear it, so save your spit! I know my job better than you do and I know the dangers too, and I'm in no mood to have my nose rubbed in my crap because I made a mistake, okay? Now—do you want your ten bucks or don't you? Because if you don't there's another doctor somewhere in the city of Montreal who'd be real happy to give me a little shot of penicillin for that price! All I want you to tell me is when I can go back to work. And in my opinion, I'd say maybe two days' rest oughtta do it!"

But the doctor was in no mood to be yelled at either and Mae, I suppose, was paying for all the nasty diseases he'd seen since morning. For the sarcasm too, and the insults he'd put up with from unhappy hookers who'd tried to chastise him for their mistakes instead of blaming themselves. Mae's speech maybe wasn't a reply, but it served as one for the doctor.

"Listen to me Mademoiselle ... " He rifled through her file to look up her name. "Mademoiselle East! I wasn't the one who chose that profession and I'm not the one who'll suffer the consequences! You are! And you're going to do what I tell you to do with no arguments! After a large shot of penicillin, because we aren't going to take any chances with what's going around, *galloping* around these days behind the scenes at the fair! If you knew what I know, you might change your profession for a while! You and your colleagues, real women and fake, should be twice as careful in the next three months! But I don't get the impression that you will! You're too busy counting your money to bother protecting yourselves. So live with it! It's going to hurt, it's going to burn, maybe for a long time, and you're going to put up with it because the green stuff that's oozing out of what you call so delicately the tool of your trade is not good news and I want to see you again tomorrow afternoon at the same time! Without fail! If not I'll call the authorities to report a suspicious case of venereal disease! Did you hear what I said,. Mae East? Whose real name according to your file is Jean-Claude Bergeron? It isn't Mae East who's sick, it's Jean-Claude Bergeron! Jean-Claude Bergeron has a serious case of gonorrhea, he ought to be worried about it and thank the doctor who's going to take his ten dollars and not declare it to the authorities! Now turn your back to me, drop your drawers, bend forward and bite your lips, this is going to hurt! And if you want to take your business elsewhere, I'll have you know that not all doctors are as sympathetic and understanding to working girls as I am!"

Madame often says it, drag queens are hard to shut up. This time though, Mae East stood there facing Doctor Martin with her mouth wide open and couldn't come up with a word. She even looked my way in the hope that I hadn't heard everything. The doctor too, but proud of himself and hoping the very opposite. I gave the doctor a thumbs up to show my appreciation and approval. He smiled. Mae didn't. With a shrug, she pulled down her drawers. She seemed to be on the verge of tears. The same state I'd found her in that morning, in the kitchen.

So now it was true that she wouldn't be the loveliest one at the ball that night.

She let out a loud, "Shit, that burns!" while the doctor was sticking an enormous needle into her right buttock. She slapped the table with the flat of her hand. I couldn't help wondering if he would use a smaller needle for me ... A small dose of penicillin for a small woman, a great big dose for a giant like Jean-Claude Bergeron!

I had just learned his real name and it's funny, but right away he was less interesting. He lost a lot of his originality, his mystery. A transvestite called Mae East is funny. But a Mae East called Jean-Claude Bergeron isn't. A Mae East has no past, is born from nothing, comes from nowhere; not so for a Jean-Claude Bergeron. I tried to picture him in a schoolroom or at Sunday Mass, listening to that Sermon on the Mount—and all I saw was a little boy dressed as Mae East! A tiny little Mae East, thin and pimple-faced, who was dreaming—while the priest held forth—about Ronald Coleman or Gary Cooper. As if Jean-Claude Bergeron didn't exist any more, as if he'd been erased from the surface of the earth and it was Mae East in the end who'd always been there. But don't all transvestites claim that? That the woman has always been there, omnipresent, invasive, inescapable?

For the first time I wondered what the real names of the other girls in the Boudoir might be. I'd have to conduct a little investigation.

Mae was rubbing her butt as she left the doctor's office.

"A dose, a sermon, a needle that burns like the fires of hell … The only thing that hasn't happened today is losing my job at the Boudoir! And maybe that's exactly what's waiting for me!"

We walked home, me slightly hobbling on my little legs, her limping and holding her butt. A taxi was out of the question.

Now we had to give Madame the news!

Elegiac Interlude in Tribute to the Sélect

I haven't been back to the Sélect much since I left there. First of all, I don't like playing the client in a place where I've worked. It doesn't seem right, I always want to give them a hand if they're busy—an old habit that goes with the territory—or fold paper napkins with them if the restaurant is empty even though they don't ask. And then, because the time in my life when I earned my living there seems so long ago now, practically unbelievable ... Little Céline who scurried around more than anyone else to meet the customers' needs because she wanted to prove that she could be a waitress in spite of her physical handicap—with hot plates spread along her arms, out of breath, sweating and often impatient—is someone I don't recognize any more.

I think she's naïve, she's touching, sometimes I even miss her. Because the world she lived in was so much simpler than the one I first plunged into a year and a half ago, with all its conspiracies and everyday dramas that you have to pretend to take seriously when most of the time they're ridiculous, and most of all with its characters, who it's true are colourful, fascinating, hilarious and entertaining, but also intrusive and hard to put up with.

Which doesn't mean that I'd want to go back, to end up in the company of Nick and Lucien in the kitchen that smells of stale grease, or see again my gang of hairy artists who spend the night reinventing the world, or even Aimée Langevin who, the last I heard, hadn't yet managed to convince anyone that she is a talented actor—no, of course not, I much prefer my present life.

But I do sometimes daydream ...

It's 5 p.m., I've just arrived at the restaurant, I've hung my raincoat in the employees' cupboard that smells like the kitchen because it's part of it, a simple wood compartment tucked in between the fridge and the door, I chat with Madeleine who has decided, now that her day shift is over, to fill the sugar containers before she leaves. I've told her five times already to never mind, I'll look after it, her day is over, her children are waiting for her at home—nothing works. With a cigarette in her mouth, right eye closed to avoid the smoke, she unscrews the lid of a sugar container, working confidently, stirs the contents with a knife to remove any sugar from the glass, pours in what's needed, screws the lid back on, puts the sugar bowl back in its place, satisfied with a job well done. She scrubs the Arborite table with vinegar and water and moves on to the next, serious and absorbed.

Jeannine rushes in, nearly late. Quickly takes off her coat, she's going to tell us a good one …

I sit at the waitresses' table, holding a cup of tea (my time at the Sélect corresponds with the time in my life when I switched to Orange Pekoe because the restaurant's coffee was so disgusting), I rest my head against the back of the leatherette booth, I listen to Jeannine's confidences—more or less complicated variations on the same disappointments in love transferred from one man to the next, an endless yet simple pattern that she doesn't realize is there because she never thinks about it, she's content to suffer it and then complain it isn't fair that she has such a hard time or so much bad luck.

Madeleine winks at me from the other end of the restaurant. I smile back. And for a few fleeting seconds, over too soon, I feel good.

That simplicity is what I miss, I think, the absence of responsibilities, my life cut into two parts that never mingle: on the one hand, work, on the other hand, everything else—private life, problems, anxieties. Now, on the Main, I live with my fellow workers, the Boudoir follows me right into my living room, problems never stop at my doorstep, they sweep in everywhere, they're the very fabric from which my life is made. I sometimes think that transvestites are their own problems! And I, the only girl in the group, am the hostess in the apartment on Place Jacques-Cartier just as I am at the Boudoir. It's never boring, that I admit, but it isn't restful either.

It's nearly always the voice of Fine Dumas that pulls me out of my daydreams. I open my eyes, I'm sitting in the main room of the Boudoir with its velvet and plush. It's 4 a.m., I've dozed off. Sometimes I'm relieved to wake up, other times I'd rather go back where I was, surrounded by the smell of fried potatoes and the warmth of the girls at the Sélect.

"You can go to bed, Céline, we aren't busy tonight. I don't think we'll see daybreak this morning ... "

Somewhere deep in my memory little Céline is taking the bus to De Lorimier Street. Here, in my real life, Jean-le-Décollé or Nicole Odeon or Mae East takes her arm and steers her into a nearby bar where she has no desire to go but lets herself be dragged, too tired to resist.

Never though, never in my life will I think about my family, and if such a memory should touch me, I'll brush it aside and move on to something else.

Part One

A Surprising Plan

Close to a year ago Fine Dumas had a stroke of genius. You could even say that she had, with unprecedented impudence and disconcerting ease, gone beyond the limits of what until then had been allowed in Montreal and she'd made the unthinkable possible. In the midst of repression by both the municipal and the provincial police, who wanted to present to foreign eyes, especially the eyes of hypocritical Americans, a friendly Montreal, sanitized and sexless, for the duration of the World's Fair—don't forget that the city of Montreal had refused to allow a show business promoter to open a strip club on the Expo site!—Madame had imagined, in the heart of the Main, something that until then had never existed in our beautiful city and no one, ever, would have thought conceivable: a brothel featuring transvestites!

Now it goes without saying that the Boudoir's back of the shop does not exist officially, it is nonexistent, a foreign body whose name is passed on in whispers, and is never mentioned in the papers—the protection must come from very high up—even though everyone knows that it has been running for nearly a year. The Boudoir represents a breach in municipal bylaws, an unusual project that someone, somewhere, thought would be lucrative enough to let it through. Because money is the name of the game at the Boudoir! Everything here costs way too much for the usual crowd on the Main; not one client of the other establishments in the neighbourhood would dare to even take a look: the admission price alone is way too steep. What goes on here is an unending subject of gossip, assumptions and rumours of all kinds though when all's said and done, we're just a good old brothel disguised like so many others as a nightclub livened up with, let's say, somewhat livelier activities behind the scenes. But our girls—and this is what sets us apart and makes us so interesting—are men.

How did Fine Dumas manage to ride roughshod over the law so dramatically? The very outrageousness of her project? Its originality? Its expected yield?

That too is a matter of speculation. And I've heard a few versions of what might have happened, the most mind-boggling and amusing being that Fine Dumas is in a position to blackmail Mayor Jean Drapeau. They claim that she turned up at city hall out of the blue one day, as a good neighbour, and left a few hours later with a lease in her hand and a smile on her face. I have to say, that's the version I like best because it's the most outrageous. (Though Madame often tells us that she could blackmail even the biggest big shots in town.) People also claim that our beloved mayor has recently opened a fancy restaurant where opera singers perform to help out his mistress, a well-known French singer—so why shouldn't it work for the Boudoir too? Then again, we might well wonder what relationship exists between Mayor Drapeau and Fine Dumas!

The fact remains that a few months before Expo opened, the Boudoir was already a hit. Fine Dumas, who knew her people, knows how to treat her "partners," and a number of "benefit evenings" in aid of "charitable works" were held before the official opening. The charitable works in question had names that I'd never heard anywhere and were often weird, the benefits were handed out in more or less equal piles at daybreak, and those who left with money didn't seem to be the least bit needy or to lack anything at all. Madame, suddenly chosen queen of the night, spent lavishly, knowing that the wind would promptly bring money back to her coffers once Expo got underway ... I saw thick envelopes passing from hand to hand; cases of champagne leaving the Boudoir in the middle of the night to be piled into very pricey cars; and, I can't name them because I'm sworn to secrecy, certain Montreal personalities, female and male, sometimes sneaking in backstage to taste the forbidden fruits that until then, so they claimed, they'd kept away from.

For a while then, banging a transvestite became the thing to do. Before it cost too much. Because people knew that prices would go up as soon as Expo was open. Which was of course what happened.

In the dead of night transvestites—talkative, indiscreet, crude individuals if ever there were—talked about things that would make your hair stand on end, but that too is subject to speculation even though, as they say, where there's smoke there's fire. If a tenth of what was said backstage at the Boudoir were true though, there would be enough fuel to feed the scandal sheets for years to come. But whom can you believe and to what extent? I live now in a world in which the truth is sometimes hard to distinguish from the fantasies of the creatures who live in it. At the same time though, that's one of its charms …

More proof that Fine Dumas enjoyed exceptional protection: Maurice, Maurice-la-Piasse, indisputable king of the Main, terror of the hot districts of Montreal and personal enemy of Madame, hasn't said a word! He lets it all happen without batting an eye, without ever sticking his nose inside the Boudoir—though he always gets involved with everything, especially when money is involved! (But I've often seen Tooth Pick, his partner in crime, leave the house with a rather well-stuffed brown envelope …) Had someone in a higher position forced Maurice to take only puny dividends from the Boudoir because he hadn't thought of it himself? Was he reduced by force of circumstance to the role of Fine Dumas's "partner" in this very lucrative operation?

And did it mean that Fine Dumas had both Mayor Drapeau and Maurice-la-Piasse by the balls? Nice if true, but not really credible. The mayor must have access to the means to bring people like Madame down to earth, and Maurice, as everyone knows, is trigger-happy—actually it's Tooth Pick who is quick on the draw when something isn't to his liking. If all that is true, the only reason would be that the profits generated by the Boudoir are quite out of the ordinary. And from what I've seen circulating night after night for more than three months now, that wouldn't be surprising.

In her great wisdom though, to avoid attracting too much attention or because it's the way she has always operated, Fine Dumas hasn't succumbed to megalomania or the gargantuan: the Boudoir is a small business with a rather low turnover of girls (there are six but they make enough racket for fifty); it only operates after nightfall; doesn't need a doorman or a bouncer; every night at eight is scrubbed, polished and lacquered by a mysterious army of household fairies of whom no one's ever seen the tip of a feather duster—only I know that they're Gaspesian, hard-working and no doubt very well paid, because they're absolutely discreet—and it operates like a small-town family business with one head who makes all the decisions and, whatever happens, does everything. Madame is at once the director of the establishment, its soul and its accountant, and I'm convinced that if she were capable of doing my job she'd do that too.

But since the Boudoir is a beast with two heads—one official and harmless though a little unusual, the other, the back of the shop, more interesting for both clients and owner—it needs constant, dual surveillance. So Fine Dumas has pride of place over the legitimate part, certified by tons of permits placed very prominently above the cash register which needless to say registers only lawful beverages, alcoholic or not, while I, behind the scenes if I can put it that way, starting at eight o'clock, monitor the comings and goings—sometimes hilarious, sometimes pathetic—of those ladies and gentlemen. Perched on my high heels that I finally got used to after months of hobbling and blisters, with a menu in my hand and a smile on my lips, I sometimes think that Madame hired me because she couldn't be in two places at once.

To legitimize its existence, the Boudoir puts on a drag show that actually isn't all that interesting because none of the artistes has any talent. Their dancing may be nearly tolerable, but all, without exception, sing badly and make worn-out jokes that weren't getting a laugh from the population of Sodom and Gomorrah. Someone who didn't know its hidden assets and the other side of the scenery could legitimately wonder why they'd paid so much for such a lousy show. But clients like that, people who'd come to see a genuine show, were few and far between, given the Boudoir's reputation, and if someone inadvertently complains about the quality of the performers, Fine Dumas gets on her high horse, gives them a refund, acts insulted and shows the louts to the door. We may be lousy but we've got our dignity!

Past the front door, which opens directly onto the west side of the Main somewhere between St. Catherine and Dorchester and not far from the French Casino, it looks quite good: Fine Dumas didn't skimp on the gold and the red, the indirect lighting and the Venetian mirrors. The actual club is small, intimate as Madame says, the stage tiny—what goes on there doesn't need to spread out—the bar, jewel of the establishment with its gleaming brass, dark oak and fake Italian marble, makes you want to loll around, to confide in the barmaid, to drink too much and then go upstairs—the aim of the operation. There, the bar, is where the boss stays, on a raised revolving stool with a comfortable back from which she towers over everything like a libidinous Buddha who doesn't want to miss a thing. And take my word for it, she never does miss a thing. Ever. Nothing escapes her gaze, that of a bird of prey. You can always tell what's going on of interest by following the direction of her cigarette-holder.

The name of the barmaid is Mimi-de-Montmartre even though she's never laid eyes on France and her real first name is George. She's a well-endowed peroxide blonde in her forties who has known better days and who takes her role very seriously. Expert at mixing combos and cocktails of every kind, she knows how to lead people to drink. She can concoct a Between the Sheets or a Cucumber Dream for you in the time it takes to say it, while pretending to be fascinated at what you're telling her, and she knows how to cut back on the alcohol when the client starts to lose the notion of what's going on around him because she's taken too good care of him. She makes a lot of money and because of that is unfailingly grateful to Fine Dumas, her benefactor, her angel, her idol. She would throw herself in the flames for her and maybe already has.

Only one other girl—the Boudoir's waitress—works on the floor. She too has an unlikely name: Greluche. I don't know her real name because she refuses to tell me. But Greluche suits her fine because she's a ditz to her fingertips: as skinny as the barmaid is fat, as nervous as the other is lethargic, as rude as the other one is kind, as unseemly as the other would like to be chic, she wears—not all that well—clothes that look as if they've come straight from Barbie's old wardrobe. She's the terror of the Boudoir, its bulldog, and Fine Dumas uses her to lay down the law. No need for bodyguards, Greluche is there to make sure the house rules are respected. To the letter. No special favours. Carrying at arm's length a tray covered with drinks of every sort, she can insult a table full of clients she's unhappy with while she's serving the next table, and she never makes a mistake over orders or price. She's as abusive as she is enthusiastic and puts some life in the Boudoir when the girls aren't there or when they're too "busy" upstairs to play their roles as artistes.

Behind the stage where things that were mostly depressing took place, you come to my domain, to which access is next to the door to the men's room. The ladies' is at the end of the bar, and it hides nothing. At the end of a short corridor that's too ornate, to be honest, a small staircase with just a few steps can be made out through a bead curtain that for some reason depicts pink flamingos against a sunset whose reds and oranges have been over long ago, leading to the much talked-about and somewhat forbidden special pleasures that the clients have come for, in the company of hookers who are, to say the least, different and who are said to be as funny as they are good at their job. But who most likely will only survive for the duration of Expo. The Boudoir is one of the hidden benefits of this world's fair, one of the little secrets passed on cautiously and in veiled terms that you have to take advantage of before they disappear into the mess of sanitized souvenirs of a World's Fair that tried to be too tolerant. Never would the idea of picking up a drag queen on the Main have crossed your mind of course, or of recommending one to a passing stranger, but it's still something else when the experience is introduced as a "unique discovery to be revealed in the particular context of unexplored experiments and avenues," as proclaimed on the small card that is the only advertising Fine Dumas allows herself and which she holds out to the clients with a smile as soon as they arrive ... The dream alibi. The perfect screen.

My domain resembles a caricature of a European brothel, the kind you see in old movies. It's indescribably silly, but Fine Dumas knows her men, knows their tastes, or rather their lack of taste, and their habits, and she made no mistakes in the layout of the distinctive pleasures and delights that they come here for. A product of the calculating imagination of its owner, it doesn't leave out a single cliché and shamelessly, with superb confidence, announces what to expect: everything is peachy pink, sky blue, sea green, falsely feminine, skilfully veiled and sparingly lit. It has thrown together haphazardly, without a complex, *The Thousand and One Nights*, *Alice in Wonderland*, the Kama Sutra and an Italian epic film—a mass of staggering platitudes that's hard to believe, but that succeeds in a way I'd call scathing, because I sense in it a hint of a brothel-keeper's ill-concealed contempt for her clients' stupidity. It's so ugly it's scary, but the returns are fantastic. Even the room fragrance, chosen with the same amount of care, gives the gentlemen an urge to spend. That, I think, is what surprises me most, though I can't exactly convey it in words: how had Fine Dumas been able to come up with everything necessary to give men an uncontrollable urge to spend? A lot. In the company of men dressed as women.

In the middle of the waiting room sits a genuine old whorehouse sofa, round and bright red velvet like one in a painting by

Toulouse-Lautrec, a wheel of cloth and wood that was once comfortable but now is prickly to the legs in places where the fabric is so badly worn that it tears and that breaks your back because the frame barely holds together. But Madame loves it, apparently she's been dragging it around with her since her early days at Betty Bird's during the war.

So it's a rather decrepit house that we offer our clients, a cheap copy of clichés that we owe to the movies, in contrast to the bar which claims to be modern—and it works! They arrive, they look around, curious, seem delighted with the old-fashioned, faded aspect of the place, maybe because they already see in it the decadence they've come looking for, then ask right away to see the girls.

While you might expect to see in my lair the swaying hips of cancan dancers or beautiful, scantily clad women, with hair that falls down their backs, on their way to a sponge bath in a basin of warm water, what you see first of all is me in my green sequined gown, my red shoes and what I call my stage makeup, standing very erect in the doorway, greeting clients with a menu and a smile. The Boudoir's watchdog is a nice little midget, polite, at times funny, and good company.

The menu was my idea. The girls say that it's a holdover from my old job as a waitress, but I think it's original: the client—male or female, by the way—there are more women than you might think—can leaf through the catalogue of services offered by the house without being obliged every time to watch a parade of the girls who are available, as is the practice in other houses. As well, it has the advantage of discretion because the clients never meet the whole household at the same time (except of course those who insist on it, who want to, who want a bigger cast for their party, which we happily go along with because it's so lucrative). So I really am the hostess of the Boudoir, not just the matron who controls traffic and handles supplies. Everything goes through me, I always know who is free, who isn't, who is on stage and who'll come next, so I can advise the client on the range of possibilities, offer advice, ask him about his preferences, describe the specialties and, every time, make him think that he's made an excellent choice. Just like a restaurant.

They're sometimes bewildered when they study the menu, leafing through it with a frown; the photos are flattering of course, even though it's hard to make some of the girls look good—but they end up willing to play the game. After all, this is supposed to be the first time they'll have sex with men dressed as women! What's most surprising is that I often have the impression that the appearance of the creature in question, her beauty, whether she's sexy or not, is relatively unimportant. The proof is that Greta-la-Vieille, who often looks downright alarming because of the horrible way she decks herself out, is as popular as Babalu, the jewel in our crown, the loveliest of our six wonders.

After all, our workers are former fake-female streetwalkers who scarcely a year ago were hauling themselves around, winter and summer, on St. Lawrence Boulevard between St. Catherine and Dorchester, in search of some poor fool who's too stupid to realize that he wasn't dealing with a woman ... So these are men with no particular talent and no experience with whorehouses or show business, who are asked to behave like professional women while also trying to persuade people that they can sing or dance! Which takes nerve! They slave away and in my opinion deserve to be paid a lot more than they get.

Which means that everything always goes wrong at the Boudoir and that's probably what Fine Dumas is aiming at: a kind of chaos that's more or less under control, where anything can happen at any moment; a hint of subversion, of resistance, in a six-month-long party that's too polished, too clean, too well-planned; where people forget that entertainment can be found elsewhere than in theme pavilions, cultural shows and traditional meals. I don't know that she thinks of her need for subversion—maybe she just had a brilliant idea for making money—but I have boundless admiration for her daring.

Legends of the Boudoir

I—The Kidnapping of Fat Sophie

The performances at the Boudoir—if we can use that name for a series of amateur acts executed without much conviction and sometimes with obvious hostility by people who have no business on a stage—are intermittent, elastic in length and unpredictable, to put it mildly, depending on the mood, condition, availability and good will of the "artistes." After all, they only serve as an alibi for the establishment's existence, an excuse for what goes on backstage, an appetizer or tidbit before the main course.

Some nights, when the clients are in short supply and you can hear all the way up to the rooms Fine Dumas's crimson nails hitting the fake marble bar like a tap-dancing regiment of metal spiders, the Boudoir revue *Expo Follies* (with two l's to look English), can go on for hours because the girls, not busy at their real livelihood, feel like having some fun to pass the time. They're not so nervous when they go on stage, tell dirty jokes or crank out their repertoire, which is sometimes brief and depressing, do impersonations, or execute a few dance steps, and it's at those moments, I think, when no one can see and therefore judge them, and they don't feel obliged to deliver goods that they're well aware they can't, that they're most interesting. In the midst of chaos, nonsense, the uncertain, there is sometimes a pearl, a moment of grace or sincerity, a true story or the same old tale from childhood, a moment of pure beauty that transforms them and makes them, for the duration of an improvisation or a song, great artists.

Greta-la-Vieille, for instance, who's from New Brunswick, can either make you die laughing or break your heart with "Évangéline," depending on whether she's in the mood to butcher it because the clients at the bar aren't listening or don't understand French, or lapses into the heart-rending homesickness of the

Acadians and tells of their rootlessness. The Évangéline of Greta-la-Vieille, when it's delivered with sincerity, is truly magnificent. As for Greta-la-Jeune, her adoptive daughter who has never been outside Montreal, now and then, especially when she's had too much to drink, she'll give you her totally original and absolutely devastating interpretation of the kitsch masterpiece "Padre don José"—original because the singer is convinced that she's mocking herself by piling on the melodrama that the hokey old song recounts, devastating because from the very heart of that exaggeration emerges a kind of false truth that is more true than the real truth, that could make the most biased cynic understand the protagonist's woes and even draw tears. The simple ballad then becomes something grandiose. The same for Babalu's "Babalu," which is shocking or brilliant depending on the mood of the performer.

In two words or a hundred, I'm afraid that our show isn't very different from the much maligned freak shows that have been offered for years at presumably disreputable places like the Auberge du Canada near where I live, or the Café Monarch on St. Catherine where for a shot of hard liquor or a beer you can go on stage and make a fool of yourself.

Which prompts me to tell how Fine Dumas was able to pull off another coup: stealing Fat Sophie, our pianist-accompanist, from the Auberge du Canada. Right in the middle of a show.

The Auberge du Canada is an institution in the underground world of Montreal, in the secret city, the seedy parts swarming with a strange and outlaw crowd—one of those sleazy places that everybody knows about, talks about, but where they claim they don't go or just dropped in once to keep someone company, or didn't know what they were embarking on, and left stunned, shocked, even scandalized. A little like our Boudoir, but not as chic, not as fashionable. Those who claim to be the most scandalized, however, often have eyes that proclaim the opposite and a cheerful voice that betrays a guilty pleasure at having witnessed something shameful and unique that they can't keep to themselves, and that they relate with cheeks flushed and heart pounding with excitement. They've gone slumming and they want to share it.

The Auberge du Canada, located on St. Paul Street, not far from the Théâtre des Saltimbanques and close to our place, is the headquarters for society's rejects, those tired of life and those who've given up interest in anything at all, abandoning themselves to the listlessness of warm beer, to raw drunkenness, to painful wakenings, to the trap of the eternal new beginning. It was Jean-le-Décollé who first spotted the place one boozy night when, wanting to drown his sorrow over a broken heart—a client he'd got attached to, the idiot, who'd quickly put him in his place after the first expression of genuine affection—he'd wandered the streets of Old Montreal searching for a panacea that he knew didn't exist but that he was trying hard to find anyway.

Ever since, he's repeated to anyone who would listen that at the Auberge du Canada, he'd found not oblivion but talent.

The shows put on there two or three times a week—self-styled amateur contests—featured the clients themselves, who were offered a round of drinks if they dared to go on stage and croon a tune or trip the light fantastic. It was a place to spend part of an evening disparaging the artistes who came cheap but could be lucrative if they were grotesque enough to encourage drinking. The performance would switch with no transition from hilarious to monstrous, from pitiful to pathetic, with toothless singers digging into their memory in search of some old love song learned in childhood or some trivial recitation inherited from their mother that would earn them a free beer: an extra fifteen minutes of oblivion in the grey zone of their present-day existence, featuring dancing girls with a shady past and no sense of rhythm who didn't understand that people did not admire them because they thought them still beautiful, and instrumentalists who were never without their accordion or fiddle or mouth-organ, in the hope that some day they would be discovered despite the fact that they'd never had anything to offer.

But that's not what I want to talk about—I haven't spent much time at the Auberge du Canada and I don't intend to—I want to talk about Fat Sophie whom we adore and without whom the Boudoir's *Expo Follies* would never have happened because too often the "artistes" weren't in the mood or were too busy earning their meagre wages backstage.

Jean-le-Décollé hadn't stopped talking about Fat Sophie since the night he'd gone to the Auberge du Canada. It was when Fine Dumas was looking for someone to do the musical part of the show, a genuine musician who would make people forget the performers' lack of talent and who could improvise, create a diversion if things—it was inevitable given the contents of the show—should turn nasty. A true artiste, if you will, amid the chaos and the claptrap. He was constantly telling Madame that she was a gem, a great musician; always nice and polite; that she could easily go from "classical" to "modern," from rock 'n' roll to waltz, from swing to slow, from la Bolduc to Monique Leyrac; that she was a show all by herself; that she worked away at her upright piano with obvious glee because she loved what she did, it was her passion, her life.

Fine Dumas had taken a drag on her cigarette, frowned, pursed her lips, dropped her ash with an expert flick of her index finger. When Fine Dumas is thinking something over, the room she's in fills up with the smoke from strong cigarettes that make her cough, but that she claims help her think clearly. And when she crushes her cigarette abruptly you know that she's got an idea.

And so it was one evening when Jean-le-Décollé was even more laudatory and more lyrical about Fat Sophie than usual, the boss made her decision. She mashed her cigarette in an ashtray overflowing with disgusting butts, walked with Jean-le-Décollé to the door and gave her orders almost without opening her mouth— in her, a sign of tremendous determination.

"Go and find the Duchess."

A few hours later an odd-looking trio showed up at the Auberge du Canada to witness amateur night: a huge short woman dressed all in red, with a cigarette-holder between her lips, energetic and imposing, the very image of the undisputed leader despite her size, accompanied by two transvestites with contrasting physiques, who were obviously Madame's outriders. One, the thinner of the two, was dressed in rags, grey, brown, black, thrown together any old way and worn with no concern for aesthetics or taste, a kind of long-legged bird of prey with piercing, frightening eyes; the other, fat and pink, was dressed like the perfect secretary down to the smallest detail—the cute little beret on the side of the head, the comfortable flat-heeled shoes, holding a notebook as if to take dictation, leaning towards the boss to drink in each of her words and then set them down with a view to the moral enrichment and the handing down of lofty ideals to posterity.

They took ringside seats, ordered champagne, were told that it wasn't available and had to content themselves with plain old Singapore Slings which they didn't touch in any event because they were undrinkable here, in this mecca of room-temperature beer and rye straight up.

They didn't watch a single act all evening. Their eyes were glued on the gigantic silhouette of the pianist, a mass of flesh at once flabby and solid and endowed with incredible energy, who was making an upright piano touch an emotional chord, the instrument seemingly part of her, treating it roughly but lovingly. An amazing musician, an inspired artiste, she also paid attention to the stunning belches and depressing wrong notes that shrieked out of the mike in the middle of the stage, delivered by untalented individuals whose only thoughts were of the short-lived intoxication their performance might bring them if they made it to the end. She didn't accompany them, she guided them. Without condescension. Without judging. Because she wanted them to earn their free beer.

Even from the back, in the shadows, she had talent.

In the middle of an indescribable rendition of the classic "C'est en revenant de Rigaud" executed by a one-legged veteran of the last war dripping medals, Fine Dumas got to her feet, pushed aside her chair, crossed the ringside and climbed onto the stage. She strode briskly past the one-legged vet, who consequently stopped singing, and went to stand next to Fat Sophie. On her feet, she was exactly the same height as the seated pianist. She put her hand on the pianist's right shoulder. And everyone in the Auberge du Canada that night heard her proposal. She said it loud and clear, "Two hundred a week. Clear. Under the table. Cigarettes provided."

Fat Sophie seemed to hesitate for a moment and Madame added, "Beer too."

The pianist got up without even finishing her chord and followed Fine Dumas who didn't bother stopping at the table where Jean-le-Décollé and the Duchess were waiting, stunned by her boldness even though they knew her well.

There'd been three when they arrived, four when they left.

And today, the Boudoir is unthinkable without Fat Sophie, her kindness, her good humour, her talent.

As for the Auberge du Canada, I've heard that the amateur nights were cancelled after the pianist left and that the establishment is slowly collapsing amid the sour smell of undigested hops.

As the distance between Place Jacques-Cartier and the Boudoir is very short, it takes me less than fifteen minutes to cross it every night. I walk from Place Jacques-Cartier up to La Gauchetière Street, then west to St. Lawrence, and I just have to turn right and I'm at my workplace. That's not the right expression because "workplace" suggests offices or a factory, a place where the labour is arduous, demanding and often tedious, whereas most of the time the Boudoir is sheer fun and I don't feel that I'm slaving away to earn my daily bread.

True, the hours are long, the environment can be rough despite its superficiality and sometimes even dangerous when clients have too much to drink and go berserk. The fact of being constantly in an environment where sexuality, and unorthodox sexuality at that, is of the greatest importance though I never take part in it, can be hard to explain if I think about it too much—I live in it but not on it, I witness but I don't participate. It's as if I were living in a world to which I don't have access because I am only the custodian, the maître d'. But it's never boring and the hard work, the real kind, at the end of which is the precious dollar, isn't done by me—I'm just the one who keeps the books and presents the menu. The dollars come to me without my having to expend much energy, so I consider myself lucky and I'm grateful for my privileged role as a simple purveyor of pleasures.

There are times of course when I wonder how I would react if some day I had to take part in what goes on in the rose room or the mirror room, spreading my short legs to earn my pittance, feigning pleasure with short little gasps or great desperate cries as the girls of the Boudoir do with so much talent, but I never think about it for very long. On sex and its trials and tribulations I have views and feelings that I've never been able to sort out because my own experience is still very limited and my interest not all that great. My experiences to date have not been, shall we say, conclusive—far from it—and my interest in sex, after a few attempts and some tentative groping is, for the time being, dampened. I write "for the time being" because I hope that it's temporary, that I'm not frigid or asexual as I sometimes thought when I was in my teens, because of a physique that I haven't come to terms with and refuse to impose on anyone else. Fear of seeing rejection, mockery in my partner's eyes? To some degree, yes, I can't hide it, I'm not an idiot, but it seems to me that if I really wanted to have sex, my rickety legs and my stubby arms wouldn't stop me, especially in the world I live in, where a physical difference can prove to be more an advantage than a handicap. The problem isn't finding a partner—it's me, it's the fact that even though I'm surrounded by the crudest forms of sex you can imagine, I don't have the urge (and who knows, maybe that's the reason). So I content myself with being the third party without asking myself too many questions and I put my heart in my work, concentrating on the enthralling world I live in—the Main, that grab-bag of suffering humanity, microcosm of sentiments high and low, of grandeur and pettiness, of heroism and cowardice that fascinates me like an anthropologist her field, a surgeon his specialty.

The Main has changed a lot in the past year. The Morality Squad so dear to the heart of Mayor Jean Drapeau has come calling, with its stream of undeniable injustices, its blatant bad faith and its despicable hypocrisy, content to cloud the issue, to shake the cage without offering anything new. The Main has been given a facelift, quick and incompetent and worst of all poorly conceived; they applied too much paint and powder without bothering to clean it up first, and the semblance of cleanliness that's prevailed there since April only hides the dire poverty of the girls on the street who, after all, can't stop working for six months and who often end up in jail for no reason. We praise Montreal for being the second largest

French city in the world and all we have to offer strangers after 10 p.m. is Muriel Millard on the Expo site, and an ever-so-slightly underground nightlife unworthy of a major city. Montreal looks like somebody's old auntie who usually lives in her kitchen and insists on entertaining company in the living room, which she doesn't really know and where she never feels at home. A provincial city that likes to think of itself as a capital: welcome to the Vienna State Opera—that's culture—but forget about the Main, it has to be kept under wraps, its very existence denied.

I hope that the other fringe elements, the other undesirables, the whores in the west end for instance, in Verdun or Saint-Henri, or the ones who haunt the lobbies of the downtown luxury hotels, have been able, as had Fine Dumas with the Boudoir, to carve out a niche for themselves during this six-month period of intolerance and dyed-in-the-wool respectability. And I hope that all over Montreal there exist hotbeds of resistance similar to ours, survival cells that offer visitors to Expo something other than the impeccable behaviour of a frustrated old maid who's serving afternoon tea for the first time and doesn't know when you're supposed to add the milk. I know that the Boudoir is unique because of its specialty, but I trust the other workers of the night, I trust their imaginations, their determination. And above all their survival instinct.

Surely Fine Dumas isn't the only madam in town who has connections. Who knows, maybe Mayor Drapeau has several pairs of hands around his balls!

When Mae East and I turned the corner of La Gauchetière and St. Lawrence that night, we spotted Fat Sophie pacing in front of the Boudoir. Every night you can see her ambling along the Main, half an hour before she starts work. Smoking a cigarette, hands behind her back, bending forward a little, you might think she was an angry woman waiting for her husband at the tavern door. If you asked what she was doing there she would tell you in her hoarse smoker's voice that she was getting the kinks out of her legs before she enclosed them below the keyboard for the rest of the night. Yet her legs aren't inactive: while her chubby, expert hands roam the keyboard, you can see her feet beating time, tapping the floor, giving the pedals a tough workout, moving from left to right, unable to stay in place, transported by the music too, galvanized by the rhythm.

Frowning, she watched us come up the Main.

"One of you looks like you've lost your best friend. And the both of you look stunned!"

It was true that Mae East hadn't stopped fuming since we'd left Doctor Martin's office and was looking for a way to pass on the bad news at the Boudoir that wouldn't incur Madame's wrath. I'd tried to persuade her to take the bull by the horns and speak to the boss directly, to throw herself at her feet and beg for mercy, as they say in cheap novels, but she was too afraid of the reaction and was looking for a way to let her know indirectly and not too abruptly. I told her she was being silly, that Fine Dumas would be less angry if she was direct and candid, but it was no use. Mae said she was too terrified to confront the boss.

Sophie dropped her cigarette onto the sidewalk and stepped on it, making an ugly little sound like an insect being crushed.

"What the hell, let's go!"

She turned to us, then opened the door.

"I'll tell you one thing, Madame's like a bear with a headache tonight! Bad time to ask for a raise!"

Panic-stricken, we exchanged a questioning look.

Sophie was holding open the brushed aluminium door on which the name of the establishment appeared in round, feminine letters all intertwined like a complicated piece of embroidery. Fine Dumas had insisted that the aluminium be dyed pale pink, in order, as she put it, to announce our true colours at the outset. But the result was not pleasing and the way into the Boudoir looked more like the entrance to a pretentious restaurant than the threshold of a fancy brothel. Madame had promised herself to replace it all with a simple glass door but she hasn't done anything yet, she's too preoccupied by the Boudoir's unanticipated success and too busy counting her money. One night when there was a crowd she even said, "To hell with the front door, they only see it for two seconds!" And that was the last we heard of it.

Sophie held out her arm and blocked Mae East's way. And when Fat Sophie blocks your way it's like being behind a wall of flesh that is both soft and powerful—alive at any rate, because it moves and shakes, independently, so it seems, of the rest of her body.

"Cat got your tongue, you two? Something I don't know and ought to?"

Mae East pushed aside her arm as if she were opening a second door.

"How about us, is there something we don't know and ought to before we step into the lion's cage?"

We were in what Madame pompously calls the reception area, which is actually just the end of the bar where she sits. Madame had said, "We don't need a cloakroom, we don't even know if we'll be around next winter!"

Fat Sophie coughed into her hand before she spoke.

"Greluche hasn't turned up yet, we've looked all over and can't find her and there's nobody here to work the floor."

Empty as it is a few minutes before opening, when Madame has yet to call on the assistance of the electricity fairy, the Boudoir looks to me like an abandoned movie theatre—still flashy but lifeless, drab. It lacks light, life, sounds. In that kind of gloom, gilt is depressing: like mirrors without reflections. When nothing shines in this music box made for soft, flattering light, for lies elevated to the ranks of great art, when the magic of pretence has not yet started to operate and the back of the picture is too visible, an icy anxiety settles into the pit of your stomach, makes you want to leave that dead place and take refuge where you might find a little human warmth. Deception is obvious all at once, shameless mercantilism comes to the surface and it's like being inside a broken slot machine. And since Madame turns on the air-conditioning when she arrives around six o'clock, the premises are soon too icy and, to me, it smells like the back of a refrigerator as well as cigarette butts from the night before: a cheap rip-off. Half an hour before the doors are opened, the Boudoir is a cold-storage room.

Sometimes Fat Sophie will play some happy tunes before we open—her way, she says, of bringing a little ambience to the grave. Though she pounds away on her instrument and the notes ring out to the four corners of the Boudoir, no real life can be felt until, with an imperial gesture, Fine Dumas—the fairy holding aloft her magic wand, the witch raising her arm to work a miracle—has brought down the lever on the fuse box to which, need I add, she has the only key. The miracle will happen in a fraction of a second, everything will be back where it belongs, the mirrors will come to life, the gilt will emerge from the shadows, the bar's fake marble and its genuine polished wood will gleam, the Boudoir will once again become a warm, deceitful cocoon where everything is possible if you don't look too closely, and the noxious charm of the forbidden can start spreading its poison again.

This time though, despite the morbid atmosphere of the Boudoir fifteen minutes before opening, there was a kind of life, activity made up of shrill cries and boisterous comings and goings, like a frenetic dance over which you've lost control and that no one can bring to an end. A fat woman, short and massive, an enormous shifting spot of periwinkle blue, was the epicentre of the mad jig that she seemed to be both leading and suffering in spite of herself: Fine Dumas herself in all her splendour. She was yelling as if there'd just been an attack on her life, she shifted tables by lifting them as if they were feather pillows, she bit on her cigarette-holder, which was pointing towards the ceiling in a sign of protest. Mimi-de-Montmartre followed her, arms extended. You'd have thought she was pursuing a dangerous animal that had broken out of its cage. Meanwhile, the girls were pacing the floor and letting out protests or encouraging words. Half-dressed, some still in their city clothes, their makeup barely started, more male but not yet female they cried out, squealed, cursed, but still it was Madame's voice that dominated everything, that played the theme of the musical phrase while the others were merely accompaniment. A falsely grandiose scene from an opera. You'd have sworn that a tragedy had just descended on the Boudoir, endangering its existence and our survival when, if Sophie was right, it was nothing more than the absence of a waitress.

I turned towards Sophie.

"All that because Greluche isn't here?"

The pianist rolled her eyes.

"It's true that it's totally out of proportion. There must be something else going on."

Flamboyant in her outrage, puffed up like a hen whose chick has been taken away, Madame had arrived at the pause, the summing-up, the conclusion. The affected hint of an English accent that she puts on to talk to people she's impressed by or who dare to resist her, was heightened, underlined, more fake than ever.

"How many times have I told you? How many times have I repeated it to you? A thousand? Two thousand? That I would not tolerate anyone being late! Never! No one! That the Boodwar opens at eight o'clock and I want every one of you here an hour before that! Correct? But oh no! It's do whatever you feel like! It's come whenever you're in the mood! It's do whatever you want! Who's going to serve the clients when they start arriving if Greluche isn't here? Will you tell me? Me? In my long gown? With my cigarette-holder? The boss who can't afford a half-decent staff?"

She was well aware that she was losing her hold over her audience, that she was repeating herself, that her diatribe was starting to drag on, that the girls weren't protesting too much. She decided then to change tactics and opted for wounded dignity, the pain of having been deceived when, as she claimed, she'd been about to give us some very important news.

"When I think! When I think that I came here all excited over what I had to tell you! When I think that I've been planning it for weeks, that I've been looking forward so much to surprising you that I had trouble holding it in, I was so keyed up! All for a heartless bunch of …! Pearls before swine! I feel like calling the whole thing off! Like wiping out the whole organization! Be good to your employees, spoil them, treat them like friends, and what do they do? Eh? What do they do? They shit on your front steps!"

And that's when we got it. All of us. Because we knew her so well. The whole thing, the scene, the cries, the offended manner, was just a subterfuge, an excuse, a way to draw attention to an unimportant detail in order to give us some good news, to make us, no, *force* us to be grateful in advance. If Greluche had been on time, Fine Dumas would have found something else to be up in arms about, she would have jumped on any reason, logical or not, to assemble us and insult us before giving us the gift she'd planned. A gift that she wanted us to pay for before she gave it.

Alas for her, the punchline she'd whipped up so well, the grand finale, blew up in her face before she got to it.

The front door opened just as Madame was about to unveil her secret and Greluche stepped inside, holding a huge hotdog from the Montreal Pool Room, dripping with mustard, ketchup and fried onions. Grease was sliding down her arms, dripping off her elbows. She looked at us as if we'd all come out of a box of Cracker Jack.

"I got here too early. Nobody here, not even Madame. So I went and gabbed with Thérèse at Ben Ash, then I was hungry so I got myself a hotdog steamé. Sorry, Madame, I promise I'll chew LifeSavers so I won't smell of stale grease."

During the heavy silence that followed, Mae East leaned over to me, which because of her height meant that she was bent double.

"What should I do, Céline, I can't very well talk to Madame after that!"

I patted her hand.

"We'll think of something."

We were all expecting the storm to intensify. Jean-le-Décollé and Greta-la-Vieille had even started to withdraw in the direction of the men's room to protect themselves from what would come next, but strangely enough Fine Dumas stood motionless and dumbstruck for a long moment, as if she'd been paralyzed in mid-crisis, drained of inspiration or whatever had fed her anger, though she was never short of colourful language.

She looked at Greluche who was hurrying to finish her hotdog that kept getting more limp, taking bigger bites, you could tell that Madame felt like murdering her, stabbing her in the back or the belly with a dagger, skinning her alive and then eviscerating her in front of everybody, especially because she was innocent of the crime she'd been accused of; but she just stood there, with one plump hand on a table and the other grasping her cigarette-holder from which no smoke now rose. Her own lifesize statue—meaning very short—having pride of place in the middle of her territory.

I sensed that I had to do something, that for some reason it was up to me to save the situation, or we were liable to spend the rest of the night in a menacing silence and the atmosphere in the brothel would be irreparably ruined.

I went up to Madame and faced her. She didn't deign to look at me and I thought to myself, This conversation is going to be even harder than I'd imagined.

"Mae East and I were also late, Madame. Excuse us. I had to see Doctor Martin and I didn't think of calling to tell you and besides, I asked Mae East to come with me. But we never thought that it would take so long ... There were a lot of people, the doctor took his time, you know what those visits are like ... "

I had roused her curiosity. I, the hostess of the Boudoir, her maître d' whose only contact with the clients was to offer the menu and take their money, I'd had to see Doctor Martin, the hookers' doctor, dispenser of penicillin shots to relieve diseases caused by sex? She frowned, raising her right eyebrow, the only one that moves and bent towards me a little, abandoning Greluche and her last bite of hotdog.

"Why were you at Doctor Martin's? Have you started doing clients without telling me?"

I snapped back, "Doctor Martin doesn't just treat VD, you know, and he had a life before he started looking after us!"

I'd managed to create a diversion, to forestall at least for the moment the storm that was brewing, but I'd have to think fast if I wanted to gain more time, turn Madame's interest to something besides the show she was putting on for us and no doubt found fascinating.

One lie attracts another. I launched into a ridiculous and totally unbelievable story: I'd twisted my ankle that afternoon, I'd thought that it was serious, that I'd broken something, so I'd asked Mae East to go to the doctor's with me. While I spoke I was thinking that I'd have to fake a slight limp different from my permanent one, to express pain that I didn't feel, tell her in two or three days that it was better and then, later, that it was over. Without thinking, I'd launched into a lie that would have to last for days. But it was too late to go back and I went on embroidering, hoping to be convincing.

Meanwhile, the girls had returned backstage one by one to get ready for opening, especially Mae East who would be well-advised to watch her step and who owed me one. Greluche had gone to wash her hands of any trace of hotdog and to chew LifeSavers. Mimi-de-Montmartre was slicing her lemons behind the bar as if everything were normal. Fat Sophie was playing softly, eyes vacant but ears wide open. As for Madame, she was obviously annoyed by my story, which was too long and convoluted for something so trivial and was looking impatiently around her. Life was gradually getting back to normal. The crisis was over.

But I thought I'd read in Fine Dumas's expression that she had begun to suspect that I'd put one over on her, that I'd kept her busy to divert her anger, that she'd just allowed herself to be manipulated like an amateur—she, the long-time past mistress of the complicated plot, the carefully woven little scheme, the confused intrigue that went nowhere.

She looked around the now nearly deserted Boudoir, then came back to me, wearing the spoiled-little-girl pout that never augurs anything good.

"That's right, everybody go away! Before I've even finished talking. I had more to say ... I've got some big news for you ... But too bad, you'll never know."

Draped in dignity, she took refuge in her place at the end of the bar. She screwed a cigarette into the wood and mother-of-pearl implement which she sometimes calls, pretentiously, the natural extension of her arm because it never leaves her, launched her first cloud of smoke towards the ceiling where the ridiculous mirror ball that I hate so much because it makes me dizzy wasn't spinning yet. She looked at herself in the mirror between two bottles of Scotch to check for any damage to her oh-so-elaborate makeup that might have been caused by the scene that had just unfolded. Then she put on the impenetrable expression that signalled a bad day.

Was she going to force that cold shower on us all night, sulk until closing time, greet clients indifferently, half-heartedly, grudgingly, pretend to be indisposed and then blame us for a low take, unsatisfied clients and everybody's mediocre performance? Intimidation through silence? When Fine Dumas puts on that insolent look, everyone feels helpless, even me, though I pride myself on being the only one who can stand up to her.

And why had I stood up to her? Why had I got involved in it? Why do I always feel obliged to get mixed up in what doesn't concern me when someone in my circle is in a fix? Is it really because I want to help? Had I really got Greluche and Mae East and the rest of them out of a difficult situation, or had I once again just shown off to make the others like me, accept me, love me? Céline, our saviour, who always feels she's been entrusted with a mission, who defends the afflicted, our Messiah, oh yes, how we love our Céline, we can always count on her ... Does that sum up what I've turned into? Brought up to make people forget me, now I do anything to make them notice me and like me. A little girl ready to do whatever's needed to attract attention to her insignificant self? A twenty-two-year old Shirley Temple?

I would like to say no, it all stems from natural goodness, true devotion, but if I dig a little deeper, if I study my intentions, if I put myself in the position of the Céline who dared to tell Fine Dumas a far-fetched story, what will I find? What I would like to see—a pure desire to do good that starts up by itself when a problem arises? Or Shirley Temple, the little trained monkey that will do anything to please?

No, I wanted harmony restored. And all I could think of was to get involved in the action, *to take on part of the problem*, yes, that's it, to take on part of the problem myself. A little five-foot-tall lightning rod who thinks she can divert the lightning. Not to do good, no, just to bring back harmony. I didn't want to draw attention to myself, all I wanted was for perfect stability to come back.

So I'm not as good as I might have hoped, but neither was I as manipulative as I feared, and that's reassuring.

After a few seconds, Fine Dumas deigned to take a look in my direction.

"Go put on your outfit, the show's going to start soon and my hostess looks like something the cat dragged in!"

No reproach.

Once again she isn't mad at me. She hadn't seen through me as I'd feared at first, nor was she rebuking me for carrying on about my ankle at the very moment when she was about to announce her news. I'd been granted immunity. I'd managed to pull the wool over her eyes, once again manipulation had worked.

Just before I turned towards the door that leads to my territory, Madame pointed her cigarette-holder at Greluche who, making herself as small as possible, was lighting the coloured candles that adorned each table.

"You're going to pay for that hotdog—a lot!"

Injustice again, and bad faith, to make someone else pay for her own mistake. She'd been angry for no good reason and refused to admit it.

I could have hit her.

This time though, I decided not to intervene.

Fine Dumas got down from her stool, headed for the electrical panel behind the bar and, with a regal gesture, brought down the lever that would set off the miracle of diffuse lighting that flatters and lies and has so much to do with the success of her establishment.

I found Mae East collapsed on the round red velvet sofa. In my place. Next to my stack of menus. Jean-le-Décollé was holding one of her hands, Greta-la-Vieille the other, while Babalu was smoothing her hair the way they do in movies with a feverish child.

"What will become of me? I'm finished! Washed up! I know she's going to kick me out! Did you see the state she's in already? Just imagine when she finds out about me!"

A voice came to us from deep in one of the rooms. It was Greta-la-Jeune, who the night before had been given the thankless task of opening that night's show and hadn't had much time to get ready.

"We'll think of something! Céline will come up with something."

Here we go, I thought to myself, once again I'm the Messiah. Oh yes, we know that Céline always finds something to say or do at difficult moments. We can rely on her. Especially when it's about sweet-talking Madame. A lie like the one a few minutes ago or an artfully concocted half-truth, and that's that. I've become the one who deflects tricky problems, who manages the crises, major or minor, that are always poisoning the atmosphere at the Boudoir, the one who has been a buffer between Fine Dumas and her employees since the club opened.

When all's said and done, I think I would have made a terrific union rep.

All heads turn towards me.

I offer a vague grimace.

"At least give me time to think about it! I'm not a machine for solving problems!"

This time I had to climb, and rather awkwardly, onto what we all call "the red button," because someone had moved the little footstool that usually allows me to save face every night. Because of a small carefully placed stool that acts as a stepping stone, I can play at being a *grande dame* and assume a superior expression without looking ridiculous. Shift it a few inches though, hide it just once, and the Boudoir would collapse under the laughter and jeers of the clients who have already, and often, felt like laughing when they go backstage because they've just accomplished something here they didn't think they were capable of and that made them nervous. Not only are they going to have sex with a man disguised as a woman, they're greeted by a midget decked out like a Christmas tree! Is there anything more weird, more "world's fair" more "summer when anything goes"? So just imagine if that mini-hostess can't hold on to a minimum of decorum and has to get down from her throne like a three-year-old from its high chair!

Slowly I touched up my lipstick while they wiped Mae East's nose and patted her hand and rubbed her back. In vain, because the poor thing seemed inconsolable. People say that penicillin is a downer and now we had blatant proof. But what could we do with her? Obviously I couldn't let her work. To risk passing on gonorrhea to some redneck from New Jersey or a Pakistani on a spree would be criminal, but Madame must not find out that there was one girl less on the floor ...

Unless ...

The story I'd made up a few minutes earlier might be useful after all.

Amazing as it may sound, I drew up my plan in the time it took to walk back across the Boudoir. When I jumped off the red button I had only a vague idea of what I was going to tell Madame, but a few seconds later, when she was standing there in front of me, everything was ready. I suppose you could call it lying in a propitious place.

She was glued to her seat as she is every night around a quarter to eight. Even if the early hours are often super-quiet and it's hard to imagine that the Boudoir will ever come alive, she feels that she has to be at her post. She can spend hours there, motionless on her stool, dragging absentmindedly on her cigarette, watching Fat Sophie bang away on her instrument. When the time seems to us in the back of the shop to be dragging and we come to the bar area for a gab or a drink or to think up a show in our own way, she'll sometimes tap the edge of the bar with her cigarette-holder.

"Ladies! Ladies, calm down, please! Clients could arrive any time now!"

But never does she leave her spot. She witnesses everything from the end of her bar—rows, battles, spontaneous parties, stags, over-indulging—smiling if someone congratulates her on such an unusual establishment and on how much fun can be had there, otherwise impassive and cold. One look at her and you know that she's the boss and that she won't budge and people leave her in peace so she can get off on her success.

Actually, she only moves when big international stars visit the Boudoir. They're not as rare as you might suppose. They hear about us and want a closeup view of this centre of resistance thrust into the self-righteous and mercantile world decked out as a song of universal love and brotherhood that the Montreal world's fair is supposed to be. The bride's underwear, if you will.

Maurice Chevalier, who is putting on his show *Flying Colours* somewhere in town, stuck his nose inside a while ago and Madame nearly had a heart attack. The great Maurice Chevalier in her house! Ex-boyfriend of Mistinguett! Star of so many films that she'd seen at the Bijou or the Saint-Denis with her girlfriends from Betty Bird's house! Sing "Valentine," Monsieur Chevalier, sing "Valentine" for us! She tottered on her high heels, she stammered, Mimi-de-Montmartre brought her a slice of lemon because her mouth was dry and she couldn't produce saliva. He, a good sport, laid on the *Madames* and *My dears* whenever he opened his mouth, which entitled him, of course, to an evening on the house—champagne, champagne, champagne—watching one of the worst shows in the prestigious and pretentious World's Fair. Towards the end of the night he even came to check out my domain. He said, the shameless sycophant, that you'd find nothing better in Paris but left without sampling the goods. What I wanted to yell at him was, "Better? I'm pretty sure there's *nothing* like it in Paris but you're too proud to admit it!"

Carol Channing breezed in too, after a performance of *Hello, Dolly* at the Expo-Theatre. But she thought she was at a review by female impersonators and left in a hurry, disappointed, when she realized that no one was going to impersonate her and that the quality of the show was, to say the least, questionable. Personally, I'd never heard of her, but the Duchess of Langeais and Jean-le-Décollé nearly blew a fuse when they found out she was there. This time it was the Duchess who went to tell Madame that a big Broadway star was there and that she should be treated accordingly. The boss took a lot of persuading before she brought out the champagne because she didn't know who Carol Channing was either, but she finally gave in when she heard the title *Hello, Dolly* which everybody knew, especially Louis Armstrong's version.

After the big Broadway star had gone, the Duchess went on stage and performed "Diamonds Are a Girl's Best Friend," which gave us a good laugh. We asked why she hadn't sung it for Carol Channing whose signature song it apparently was, and she replied that one day someone had told her she was nothing but a salon comic and that she'd decided she would never try to go on stage professionally. To which Babalu said, "You don't think our stage is professional, Duchess?" and the Duchess had snapped, "What goes on here, sweetheart, isn't even amateur!"

When I was nearly at her stool I decided not to let myself be taken in by Fine Dumas's fractious look and I jumped in without a second thought.

"You're going to be even more pissed-off Madame, I'm warning you, maybe you'll hate me forever, but I have to ask you anyway … "

She frowned, removing the cigarette-holder from her mouth.

"If you're about to ask me for a favour, Céline dear, the answer is no. And admit that it takes a hell of a nerve to ask a favour after what just happened."

I answered without bothering to catch my breath, "I'm not asking for a favour, I just want to present you with a fait accompli. It won't make you happy, but that's how it is and neither one of us can do a thing."

She leaned over slightly in my direction.

"So! Another tragedy, is that it!"

"That's right. A tragedy. But don't worry about it, it can all be worked out with a little good will."

"I hope so! Because I'm in no mood to put up with one more aggravation tonight! Understand?"

This time though I took the trouble to breathe before I presented my lie.

"Sorry to tell you but I need an assistant for a couple of days … On account of my foot … "

"An assistant! Where do you think you're going to find an assistant?"

"I've already found her."

"Good Lord! That was fast!"

I let it all out in one breath, not knowing how my sentence was going to end when I started, I talked about three things at once while watching for Madame's reaction to every word, hoping to avoid a crisis or a whole dish of insults that would just be a waste of time because my mind was made up—I had no choice, Mae East must not work—and I wasn't going to give an inch, whether she liked it or not.

"I had to think fast, you see … Since I can't walk much, you saw me come in just now, it hurts a lot and I'm limping more than usual, you should see my foot, it's all blue, I decided on my own I admit, before I spoke to you, to ask Mae East to be my assistant until it's better. But I swear that you won't even notice."

"Mae East! But Mae East is too busy to be your assistant! And what does it mean anyway, to be your assistant?"

I knew I was saved because she'd asked me a question instead of being dogmatic as she'd been in the first part of her reply. Something told me—maybe she'd observed me while I was walking up to her and maybe I'd played the role of the walking wounded better than I'd thought—that she realized I needed help, for that night anyway, and she shilly-shallied just so as not to agree too quickly that I was right, and to show once again who was the boss of the Boudoir.

"It means carrying the menu for me, Madame, and showing the clients to the rooms ... As for me I'll just stay in my place on the red button, advise the clients, handle the money ... As you know I wouldn't let anyone else take the money from the clients."

She took a long drag on her cigarette-holder.

"We-e-e-ll. That means one less girl on the floor, it ... "

"It's Tuesday, Madame, we may not be all that busy ... If it does get too busy I'll let her do some tricks ... "

"And do you swear that I won't even notice ... "

"Yes, I swear! The other girls all agree. They'll take on a heavier load as a favour to me. And if Mae East gets bored, someone else will replace her ... And if it gets clogged upstairs, I'll make sure the clients drink to pass the time!"

People claim that the Boudoir makes as much from booze as from the girls, so that was an excellent argument.

"It's what I always do in any case, as you know ... "

She was frowning and looking me right in the eye. I was laying it on a bit thick.

"You don't have to boast, Céline, I'm well aware of your virtues, there was a reason why I chose you! I know your failings too and I know that you've got a way of presenting the facts that isn't always kosher, so I'm going to say just one thing: if I ever find out that you're hiding something from me, you could find yourself out on the street or waiting on tables at the Sélect like you were when I found you! I let things go because you're a good worker but don't go too far, you might live to regret it!"

I thanked her without pushing it, I swore that the night would pass without a hitch, that she'd have no complaints about what we took in and I hobbled away just a little more than usual.

Fat Sophie was playing "One of These Days," the old Sophie Tucker hit, laying on a little honky-tonk that got me right in my soul. Greluche and Mimi-de-Montmartre hummed the words while they worked, Mimi busy with her lemons, Greluche dusting off the menus on the tables.

Mae East was waiting backstage for me, wringing her hands.

"You don't owe me one, you owe me two!"

She had to get down on her knees to throw her arms around me.

"I promise I'll get better fast! Faster than fast!"

The girls wanted me to report on my conversation with Madame, but all I wanted was a good stiff Scotch even though it was early. It was only a quarter after eight, the first clients had just arrived and Greta-la-Jeune, the poor man's Marilyn Monroe, was getting ready to go on stage.

How the Boudoir Operates

It's simple.

Certain clients are well aware of what they'll find here. They don't need preliminaries or instructions or the alibi of alcohol. They walk through the bar without stopping, often as proud as Artaban (heads held high, talking loudly and making their selections quite openly), sometimes bent under the weight of guilt or remorse because they think of themselves as outcasts. Those, the reluctant ones, don't look me in the eye when I offer them the menu, they whisper to me, look over their shoulders for spies or informers, follow the girls with a hangdog expression and hunch over to pay. The rest—and they're the majority—are neophytes who come there for the simple reason that it's fashionable, one of the Expo musts, or out of pure bravado. Rich students on vacation for instance: boys from good families who're used to wasting money they don't have to earn, turn up in hordes and make an unbelievable commotion. And all these debutantes need to get drunk before they can climb upstairs—to give themselves courage because they're straight and only come to the Boudoir so they can boast about it—or so they claim. You have to try it once in your life, now's the time, let's go for it, it won't do any harm and who knows, maybe we'll discover some fantasy we didn't know we had. (But no one, ever, will be able to make us acknowledge it. We're real men after all, we like real women, life is full of new experiences and just this once won't do any harm!)

The first person they see when they leave the bar is a midget whom they'll often inspect, frowning and wondering if this is a woman or a particularly successful transvestite. When I sense that they're reassured by my candid smile and my disarming kindness—I always talk in generalities before I move onto serious matters—I present the menu, explaining that unlike certain other houses, we don't put the girls on parade and that they have to make their choice on paper; that I'll tell them myself if the girl they choose is available; and if she's not, how long they'll have to wait if they persist in their choice. Ninety percent of them go on to make the usual jokes about how much the Boudoir looks like a restaurant or saying that they feel as if they're ordering something from a catalogue, but never know what they'll get in the mail! Or else they talk to me about the daily special, the chef's suggestion, the house dessert. I pretend that it's amusing, that I'm hearing their stupid jokes for the first time; it relaxes them and I offer them a final drink which I serve myself, some sickly sweet liqueur that makes them not want seconds, indeed makes them want to forget it as soon as they take a sip, an invention by Mimi-de-Montmartre which she calls "*Sirop d'Arabe*" or, in English, "Mabel's Syrup."

The six girls we can offer them are far from being beauties—except maybe Babalu when she takes the trouble—and the photos in the catalogue are neither artistic nor flattering. But to my amazement, in the beginning at any rate, when I wasn't used to it yet, it seemed not to make any difference. If the clients are startled, it's from amusement. I suppose that they think it's all part of the trip, as long as they're slumming they might as well go all the way, accept the clichés, play along for the time it takes to get it off with an object of lust who is *truly* different from what they know, from what they're used to, from what they usually experience. Beauty doesn't enter into it, and ugliness doesn't matter in the least.

If they're in a group, as is often the case, they make a big fuss over what happened once it's over, as if to trivialize it, to bury it under a pile of joking remarks, of raunchy comebacks, no doubt to erase from it anything serious. They'd come there to have fun, they've had their fun, they won't start again because it's not their cup of tea, but they're glad they tried it once and, why not, maybe they'll even boast about it to amaze their pals, to impress anyone who dares accuse them of lacking fantasy or tolerance. And they go back to their countries with an image of Montreal very different from the one that the Expo organizers intended.

Repeat visitors are rare though. As I've already written, the exorbitant prices keep the ladies' clients from coming back, condemning the Boudoir to upscale successes because of our prices. Madame thought quite rightly that well-heeled visitors to Expo would be prepared to pay a fortune to strut their stuff at our place. They just do it once, which makes us view the future with a certain apprehension. The girls may say, "We'll go back to the street, that's all!" but I'm pretty sure that none of them really wants to and that the prospect of ending up at ten below in the winter to feed Maurice and his henchmen turns their stomachs. But the boss—and we have to trust her—has started talking about a possible post-Expo plan, an infallible one that would let us continue to ply our trade year-round without going back to the street or, in my case, the Sélect. But could the Boudoir survive with cut prices? And would Maurice allow Fine Dumas to go on making money right under his nose? And Mayor Drapeau? He won't last forever, he'll end up dead like everybody else. But then again, I don't suppose that any mayor is immune to a big fat bribe.

As for the women who come to our establishment, they hardly ever come to consume. A few, yes, and they emerge from the rooms swaggering like men, proud of their victory over themselves, surprised at their own boldness, though they haven't changed the sex of their partner because they've just had sex with a man. Most of them though are there as observers, to push the men into slightly more risqué adventures, to encourage them and in some cases hold their hands while they're whooping it up. But their tips aren't generous. Like at the restaurant.

But if Madame had hoped to attract wealthy foreign homosexuals passing through town she'd made a mistake: it was obvious that they preferred genuinely sleazy joints or Mount Royal by night, which is said to have always been the favourite meeting place. In any case, genuine homosexuals are reputed to have good taste and the show that we put on is undoubtedly not worthy of them. And if they pay for sex, it's for sex with a real James Dean, not a false Marilyn Monroe! One or two show up every night but they realize soon enough that they're in the minority and leave the Boudoir after one quick drink.

My job, though, involves more than simply offering the menu and showing clients to the rooms. As a good manager I have to know at every moment who is with whom and for how long, who is free, who is busy, both on stage and in the rooms, and word my sales pitch accordingly, extol the virtues of one when she's not "performing," make the client who becomes too insistent wait, confuse the issue by saying whatever comes into my head to keep him there ... The worst is when all the girls are in rooms—let's say Saturday after midnight—and a line forms in the corridor to the men's room because my salon is overrun with impatient and overly playful males. At those times I'm no longer the manager, I become the evening's hostess, dispenser of games and pleasures, a veritable holder of a *salon*, responsible not only for comings and goings, for payments in due form—cash on the barrel head because we only accept cash—but also for conversations, performances if there are any, in a word for the whole range of festivities. I am hostess *and* actress. Sure, it's exhausting, but when I feel as if I have all these fine folks under control, when laughter erupts and criticisms are rare, when people are enjoying themselves while they wait to move on to serious matters, it can be quite heartening or at any rate gratifying for me.

At such times I sometimes climb onto the red button so that people can see me clearly from all sides, I lean against the cone-shaped back and tend to my business while behaving as if nothing else was going on. It impresses people and once again, it pays to be casual: they are more respectful if I'm the same height as them, more polite, they don't feel so superior and I have them in the palm of my hand when I strike poses similar to Madame's, without the cigarette-holder of course. The brothel hostess who's knee-high to a grasshopper suddenly takes on a vital importance: since her head sticks out above the jubilant crowd, others can sense that she sees everything, knows everything, records everything. With regal gestures she pockets the money that's held out to her and they say that all the same, despite its faded and outmoded aspects, this establishment has a certain class.

As early as opening night, Madame made a long speech to explain to us that since the Boudoir does not exist in any official manner, no sign of its passage on earth must remain and that consequently what circulates there is old-fashioned cash, Canadian preferably, though American is not to be sneezed at. No Diners Club cards are accepted, or travellers' cheques. Clients are notified of that by a placard at the entrance, in five languages if you please, and I myself see to it that they're reminded before they leave with a girl.

When a client vacates a room, I am there on his path again, smiling and with hand outstretched, polite but firm, and he complies without arguing, red-faced with shame or pride, fulfilled or let down, serious as a pope or shaking with laughter he has trouble hiding. I count the bills, slip them into a big five-pound Lowney's chocolate box that I use as a cash register—it's discreet, people just think I have a sweet tooth—and I forget them until the end of the evening after I've consigned them to what I call my "festivities ledger," an enormous account book, austere and serious-looking, in which I note all the tricks every evening, who did what, how much is owed to each girl, how much we'd made so far, so I can give Madame a very precise report if she asks for one. I separate the evening's results into three very distinct categories: mediocre, good, excellent. At the end of the mediocre ones, Madame is furious and leaves the Boudoir without saying good night to anyone; when they're good, she merely heaves a long sigh while holding out her hand; but when I give her the takings from an excellent night's work, her eyes light up with greed, she puffs up with pride as she slips the wad of bills into her bag—and into her bra if they are too voluminous—and doesn't leave the Boudoir until she has offered a round of drinks. And on the very rare nights that are truly exceptional, Madame favours me with a huge smile.

"We put in a good night's work, my dear!"

And gives me a lovely fat bonus.

The woman who leaves the Boudoir then, biting on her cigarette-holder, is up to her eyes in bills of every colour.

Where does that money go? Into what mattress? Under what bed? Into what safe at the back of what closet? Who takes it: Maurice? The police? The mayor? And in what proportions? I prefer not to know, to be content with my salary—which is more than respectable, by the way, and is also paid out in cash—and rest easy. What I don't know doesn't hurt me and I'm quite sure even protects me from possible problems.

When we leave the Boudoir at dawn, a lot of money has circulated, a lot of laughter too, and alcohol and bodily fluids. Some men dressed up as women have sung—badly—before screwing to earn their living—divinely, if I'm to believe their reputation, while others have paid dearly for the pleasure of whooping it up in a foreign land. A fat little woman, always dressed in the same colour head-to-toe, an ambulating monochrome, all red or all green or all yellow, has got significantly richer and goes home humming an old French floozy's song; another woman, tiny and hobbling, has managed to get through one more day without giving in to her natural penchant for self-criticism and fatalism.

Need I point out that when I came back that evening from my brief visit to Madame, I was welcomed as a heroine?

Mae East stood up and lifted me in her arms to waltz me around, one of the things I hate most of all in this world. I'm not a child to be dragged around like a rag doll! I may be the size and have the look of one, but I'm not a toy!

Fat Sophie had just started the first measures of "Heure exquise," the great hit, for some reason, of Greta-la-Jeune, who puts on the voice of Yvonne Printemps to perform it even though she's dressed like Marilyn Monroe in *The Seven Year Itch*. Marilyn Monroe singing operetta, badly—you can't believe it till you've witnessed it!

I kicked my legs and punched Mae East on the shoulders; indeed, I must have looked like a spoilt little brat who's making a fuss because she hasn't got what she wanted.

"If you don't put me down this minute I'll tell Madame what's really wrong with you and you can deal with her yourself."

She left me standing on the velvet sofa, red with humiliation and short of breath. The other girls had slipped out to the rooms; they must have sensed that danger was imminent and made their getaway.

"You know how much I hate it when you lift me up like that! I'm twenty-two years old, not two!"

She apologized profusely, swore by all that's holy that she'd never do it again.

"It's just that I'm so happy! You've saved my life once again! I'll never forget it. Do you want me to give you a cut on what I make next week when I'm better? I'd be glad to—honest—what you did for me is priceless!"

I brushed my clothes as if I'd spent ten minutes being dragged through the dust.

"Never mind the cut, let's go and change. All I want from you right now is to spare us Michèle Richard at 9 a.m.! All right ... Greta-la-Jeune has started to sing, the first client's going to turn up and we aren't even in costume yet. You heard what I told Madame: for the next few days it's you who'll hand out the menus and show the clients to the rooms, but I'll do the talking! I'm still the hostess and you're the assistant, you listen to me and don't say a word and you don't take *any* initiative, got it? Not one!"

Mae East promised to do everything I asked and we went to get dressed, she as a giant Brigitte Bardot, me as a hostess in a whorehouse who's seen it all before because she's been there, done that and nothing can surprise her—which is far from being true where I'm concerned. We were going to be the last ones to get dressed when we should have been ready before everyone else.

Though the Boudoir doesn't offer a parade of the girls available, it's hard to keep the ladies in the rooms at the start of the evening when the rush of clients hasn't started yet, when the atmosphere is sluggish and they could use something to pass the time. Before— and this is the real danger—lapsing into drink. Sometimes I let them come and chat with me while awaiting the first prospect. They're quickly distracted, get lost in pointless conversations and gratuitously vitriolic remarks and drag their feet when it's time to get down to work. Not because they're lazy, they aren't, but they hate to leave a story unfinished or a piece of gossip not neatly sewn up, and they'll stay in the salon even after I've told them three or four times to leave. Then I feel obliged to punish them by keeping them in their rooms, like children.

"Heure exquise" was hardly finished, the girls had come back to the salon and were waiting for Mae East and me to see how things were going to proceed. I found them gathered around the red button, ready for action and also for a pithy remark: they hadn't had time yet to carry on about Mae East's malady and it wouldn't take long for their tongues to loosen …

Babalu was quite pretty in her lemon yellow silk pants and her transparent apple green bra. She'd covered herself with jewels and jingled non-stop, a genuine little Tinker Bell. Jean-le-Décollé looked scary, as usual, in clothes more worthy of a gypsy in a Théophile Gautier novel than the pride of a chic Paris brothel—and he would be among the most popular, as usual. Greta-la-Vieille was repeating her vaudeville star number with feathers in her ass and a tiara on her head. We'd all seen it a thousand times but never tired of it because she was hilarious. As for Nicole Odeon, she'd opted for a western look and had on a fairly sexy Indian outfit that would excite the Europeans, especially the French who came here more interested in seeing Indians than their little cousins from America.

The evening started out as one of the most depressing since the Boudoir opened. As surprised as we'd been the day before, Monday, to see so many people come in when we were getting ready for a quiet night of chitchat over a drink in a nearly empty house, so we were this early evening which seemed so long, when we had such a need for action, laughter, movement to wipe out the negative atmosphere that had been hovering over us since the deplorable incident with Greluche and her goddamn hotdog.

On the stage, act followed act amid general indifference. The very few people there were too shy to react—they watched one another drink their drinks and wondered what they were doing there. Especially an old Japanese man who'd no doubt been promised heaven on earth but found himself here in an empty dump devoid of any interest. Downtown Tokyo wouldn't ring out with praises of the Boudoir the next week! Greluche and Mimi-de-Montmartre had tried to explain, with signs if necessary, that it was too early, that things got going later, after midnight, but doubt could be seen on faces and potential clients left without dropping into my place. My girls, at loose ends, had joined me in the salon—

I couldn't keep them prisoner after all—and were doing their nails or touching up their makeup while they talked in low voices, though it's not in their nature to do so.

Meanwhile, still ensconced at the end of her bar like a periwinkle-coloured, baleful stone, Fine Dumas was seething. You could almost hear her raging inside her head, hurling insults at us, execrating us: we were the cause of all her woes. Once again, I was sure of it, she was blaming others to explain what was going wrong in her life. If she had given us the good news earlier, she probably would have cancelled it with a sweep of her hand to punish us, though after all it wasn't our fault if no one turned up at the Boudoir on this Tuesday, July 25, 1967! I'm convinced that she even counted the money she should have been earning as time went by.

Leaving the stage, Jean-le-Décollé, who had just murdered with great confidence the Luis Mariano hit "Les filles de Cadix," because he hasn't the faintest idea about what a note of music should be, told us that unless something happened, Fine Dumas was going to set fire to the place!

"Believe me! I kept an eye on her while I was singing ... She was looking around as if she wanted to rip the paint off the walls!"

Nicole Odeon heaved a long sigh.

"Anybody who had to listen to you sing 'Les filles de Cadix' would want to rip the paint off the walls, dear!"

Jean-le-Décollé took it calmly. He's used to Nicole's jabs, the two of them are always insulting each other, presumably for fun, in the apartment on Place Jacques-Cartier. He's also used to snapping back.

He straightened his carefully dishevelled wig which bore some resemblance to number five steel wool and glanced vaguely in the direction of our roommate.

"Better to make somebody want to rip off paint than to kill themselves!"

Nicole was quicker to fly off the handle than he was and her hackles shot up.

"What do you mean, make people want to kill themselves? Eh? Who are you talking about? I'm not the old bag, Jean-le-Décollé! I don't make clients shriek in horror when they see me naked! The walls are thin, you can hear everything!"

It could go on forever and I wasn't in the mood, so I put an immediate end to the conflict by sending everybody to their rooms. Then I discreetly called Jean-le-Décollé back.

I could hear Gretà-la-Vieille, breathless and quavering, droning "Paris, reine du monde," and for once I felt sorry for the poor clients. When we have a full house, Greta-la-Vieille can be an entertaining, wheezing Mistinguett you can make fun of at leisure because that's what she's there for, but in the deserted Boudoir, alone on stage and singing "T'auras pas ta pomme, ta pomme, ta pomme, t'auras pas ta pomme" because there's no one to reply to her, the show is just too grotesque and your heart breaks at the pathetic lack of talent.

Jean-le-Décollé and I stuck our heads into the glass bead doorway that separates the performing space from the men's room, the one with the pink flamingos and the dubious sunset. Jean was nervously playing with the coloured beads, rubbing them together with an unpleasant squeaking sound, his hand level with the sun as if he wanted to extinguish it.

"We have to do something, this is ridiculous!"

Fine Dumas was obviously about to explode. Her anger had shot up several degrees since I'd left her less than fifteen minutes earlier. Her skin, red with anger, presented an unflattering contrast with her periwinkle blue gown. She was practically glowing like a lantern at the end of her bar. And strangest of all at this hour of the night, there was a double martini in front of her on the marble which she claimed was genuine. The boss doesn't often drink and when she lets herself go it's not a pretty sight. I've seen nights that ended very badly because Madame had decided to drown some problem or other in martinis, which take away any inhibitions, any varnish, and make her nearly as crazy as Thérèse, the waitress at Ben Ash whom Greluche had gone to gossip with earlier and who becomes a monster when she drinks. In fact she confided to me once that that's what holds her back: she didn't want to turn into a legend like Thérèse, a pariah who can't work in the bars on the Main any more because no one wants her and who ended up, to her great shame, as a mere waitress in a smoked meat joint—when once she'd reigned over the Coconut Inn and the Zanzi Bar. I didn't know that Madame had been a drinker and I'd realized then how she had acquired her restraint and her admirable self-control. But as restraint and self-control were about to forsake her, the situation had to be avoided at all costs.

I left the bead curtain and went to my salon to which the other girls had come back, worried about what was going to happen.

I climbed onto the red button, using the footstool.

"I can't offer to talk to her, I just did that—twice!"

Jean-le-Décollé sat next to me on the battered red velvet and pinched off a bit of horsehair that was sticking out of some slashes in the upholstery. It was yellow and stiff and it smelled of dust. It had known generations of backsides of whores of every sort, in the red light district or the west end of the city, it had absorbed countless thrusts of varying sincerity and from now on it was useless in my territory, where it was merely decorative, slowly giving up the ghost as it disintegrated into dust.

Jean-le-Décollé crumbled these remnants from the glory days onto the fake Turkish carpet that was also Madame's pride.

"There's just one person that can cheer her up at times like this."

The Duchess of Langeais.

The Duchess is a unique phenomenon on the Main. A shoe salesman at Giroux et Deslauriers at the corner of Mont-Royal and Fabre by day, he is transformed at night (at least he thinks he is) into a gorgeous creature before whom all men swoon, though his none too pleasing physique—five feet ten, two hundred and fifty pounds, redhead's complexion—just makes him look vaguely like a big Sophie Tucker or an obese Juliette Petrie. The Duchess has been hanging out with the local girls for years without ever actually plying the trade herself, for the fun of it as she puts it; she brushes up against the unlawful without touching it, and people tolerate her for one simple reason: she is very funny; if she weren't, Maurice's hitmen would have long since wiped her off the face of the earth. She entertains the girls when they're tired, runs their errands, makes irresistible puns, passes on the most incredible gossip, instigates really bad tricks that will fuel conversations for weeks and, most of all, she's been able to win the confidence of Fine Dumas, who protects her and pampers her like an effeminate and oversensitive little brother who's too weak to defend himself on his own against the vicissitudes of life, though he's probably three times as strong.

Along with Fine Dumas and Jean-le-Décollé, the Duchess is also one of a trio that's much respected, much feared in the neighbourhood, a triumvirate known as "the trio from hell" or "the three fat faces," even though Jean-le-Décollé is as thin as a rail, and the trio has been calling the shots on the Main for some years. The three of them have developed an information network that's quite broad and powerful and in which the Duchess is the mobile element, because she's the only one of them who moves around freely, the other two being prisoners every night of the Boudoir's demands.

Madame has adopted her, she adores her, and the Duchess is the only one who can speak to her when things go terribly wrong. She is our final resort, our last hope.

"Have you got her phone number?"

Jean-le-Décollé opened the mock crocodile purse that's always with him.

"I usually know it by heart but I'm too agitated."

"Does she still live in the same place?"

"Yes, on Dorion below Sherbrooke. She's been there for years. Since the end of the war I think ... Ah, here it is!"

"Do you think she'll be able to come right away?"

"If she's at home she'll come running!"

"On Tuesday night? Doesn't she work tomorrow?"

"I'll tell her to stay in men's clothes ... We haven't got time to wait for her to turn herself into a Hollywood star; it would take her all night and we need her now."

Jean-le-Décollé hurled himself at the telephone that sat on a small end table from which it's impossible—Madame has seen to it—to make a long-distance call. It's all right with the boss for people to make calls from her brothel, even the clients, but she refuses to accept astronomical phone bills. She's quite right.

Jean-le-Décollé's face lit up.

"Hello? Édouard? Are you finished eating, you big pig? We need you at the Boudoir! Make it quick!"

Legends of the Boudoir

II—The Queen's Visit

At the beginning of Expo, a few days before Queen Elizabeth II arrived in Montreal, the tenants in the apartment on Place Jacques-Cartier each received a strange invitation. Mock chic, printed on cream-coloured imitation vellum, the lettering had loops and swirls and embellishments—it made you think of a toy store at Christmas time and the wording was enigmatic:

> In place of the official reception given by the City of Montreal,
> Her Majesty Elizabeth II, Queen of Canada,
> invites you to a grand ball
> in the sumptuous dwelling (the Boudoir Palace)
> of Lady Fine Dumas, knight of the Order of the Snapping Garter
> and former purveyor of pleasures of all sorts
> to Prince Philip.

There followed the date, that of the grand ball put on for the Queen by the City of Montreal, the time (*on the stroke of midnight, the hour when carriages turn back into pumpkins and young beauties into old hags*) and the address (*Saint-Laurent Boulevard, Montreal's epicentre of good taste and elegance*).

At the very bottom was a rather surprising postscript: *If you don't have a thing to wear, don't wear a thing!*

As Fine Dumas hadn't planned any reception for that evening we guessed right away who the invitation was from. Jean-le-Décollé, though, couldn't get over the fact that he hadn't been told about it.

"Not only did she not ask Madame's permission, she didn't even tell me, her best friend!"

She, of course, was the Duchess, who'd taken the liberty and who had the nerve to plan a party at Fine Dumas's place without asking her permission or even advising her in advance!

But advised she was, because she was holding the invitation when we got to the Boudoir that night. Looking excited. So excited she couldn't stand still. Pink with pleasure.

"What a great idea! The publicity! It will bring a crowd. We can make a fortune with that party if we do it right! You have to hand it to the Duchess—who else would think up such a thing? I assume she's behind it?"

If one of us had come up with the idea, the boss would probably have shut that person up after three words, claiming it was too complicated, too expensive for what it might bring in, that it would take too much energy, that she had better things to do than plan grand balls to celebrate Queen Elizabeth's visit and so forth. The suggestion would have gone straight to the wastebasket and that would have been that. However, coming from the Duchess, her favourite fatty, as Jean-le-Décollé often called her when jealousy drove him over the edge, all of a sudden it became interesting.

The struggle between the Duchess and Jean-le-Décollé for Madame's attention and favours is legendary on the Main and any proof of victory by one or the other is always a source of chitchat and gossip for the girls of the Boudoir who've been following the story with great interest from the beginning. This anticipated triumph of the Duchess was gossiped about in the area all you might want. It was seen as definitive. It was far more than a point that the Duchess was going to score: it was to be, undeniably, her crowning achievement.

Jean-le-Décollé was manic the whole time the Duchess was planning her party; he refused to speak to her and there was even talk of a definitive split. Fine Dumas seemed to be amused at the chill between the two (divide and rule, it's as old as the hills). She set one against the other, told Jean-le-Décollé one day that she was starting to question the need for such celebrations that were liable to be disappointing, then heaped congratulations on the Duchess, saying how grateful she'd be if the ball was as successful as she hoped. Those few weeks were known on the Main as *the reign of the Duchess*.

Which was short.

Because as you may have guessed, the Queen's visit to the Boudoir was a long way from the anticipated triumph.

When word got around that a grand ball was being planned at the Boudoir on the occasion of Queen Elizabeth's visit to Montreal, surprisingly, instead of taking it lightly, the whole district became passionately interested, most likely because of the Queen herself, who was hated by some and worshipped by others. Some claimed that the Duchess was planning to poke fun at the monarch, others swore that the ball, though grotesque, would be a tribute to Elizabeth II. If you asked the person at the centre of it all, she would reply, with her nose in the air and a smile on her lips, "Ask her, she'll be there herself in person!"

Madame did her best to publicize the event but it was hard, the Boudoir being a place you pass through, which doesn't have regulars, and spreading the word that a funnier version of Queen Elizabeth was going to visit us was especially complicated because the clients, mainly foreigners who understood no French or just a little English, couldn't care less about a phoney Duchess of Langeais, which is understandable—she's a local star, I would even say a star of our neighbourhood, even a specialist in Elizabeth II—the real one. If we'd announced the arrival of Brigitte Bardot it would have been something else—though our own Brigitte, Babalu, is not the most popular of our gorgeous girls (I've mentioned before that our hideous horrors are the ones most in demand)—the Queen of England however didn't interest them at all and they gawked when Madame offered one of the many invitations she'd had printed at tremendous expense, or so she claimed. In any event they'd all be back in Moscow, Cairo, Valparaíso or Pittsburgh on the night when the Queen came to call.

For all these reasons, I tried to talk the Duchess out of it; but she wouldn't budge. She said she was doing it for her own enjoyment, that the Boudoir was the ideal place, that she didn't give a damn if there was an audience or not, that we were going to have some fun even if nobody but the people she'd invited (who were numerous all the same) turned up for her little party.

You couldn't talk to Madame either. She was still toying with the idea of an event that would bring in lots of money from drinks and not-so-young bodies, though Jean-le-Décollé and I tried to warn her. When I told her for instance that she was liable to end up with no one but people she knew, who couldn't afford to visit the Boudoir, she replied that on the night in question, she'd find a way to make them cough up.

And so the days before the party passed in an atmosphere of excitement mixed with anxiety.

Half an hour before the Queen was due to arrive, the Boudoir was as empty as on any Monday—three Japanese, an Arab, who wasn't even an Emir, and a few noisy Swedes—and Madame was chain smoking. As for me, I was already trying to find a way to pick up the pieces, to restore harmony, while Jean-le-Décollé snickered, savouring his victory in advance.

At two minutes to midnight, just as Nicole Odeon was withdrawing to a bedroom with a Japanese man dripping cameras, Madame swept into my den, something she doesn't do often.

"What if it's a trick?"

I was stuffing into my Lowney's chocolate box the money that Greta-la-Jeune had just made with the Arab she'd said was nice before, brutal during and contemptuous after. I looked up, startled, as if the boss had caught me red-handed.

"What?"

"The party! What if all of a sudden it's a joke, a trick the Duchess has played on us, damn her! What if all of a sudden there isn't any party? And the Duchess did it all just to get us worked up!"

I set the box under the red sofa, pushing it in with my foot.

"Come on! The Duchess wouldn't do that to you, Madame! She's a friend!"

"I hope so. Because she wouldn't be my friend for long! Or a Duchess, for that matter. If you've ever seen the colour of real blue blood … "

She turned and went into the bar where Mae East was singing an old hit of Michèle Richard's, "Lipstick on Your Collar," that no one but her wanted to remember. I ventured a glance between the beads of the curtain that separates our two kingdoms. Hardly anyone. A few clients were laughing at Nicole, another was glancing furtively towards the brothel. When he spotted me he gave me a wink, intended to be sensual, that was merely pathetic.

Madame had gone back to her seat at the end of the bar and kept turning towards the front door. It was too cold in the Boudoir, there was no atmosphere, no one would have imagined there was a party in the works.

If Queen Elizabeth didn't show up in the next few minutes, I was predicting a grim tragedy: a very ugly settling of accounts; a bloodbath; an unending quarrel from which the Main would never recover; the fall of the Duchess, her permanent banishment from the district. I was picturing as well the lethargy that would take hold of the district, the boredom I would feel in the absence of the only truly funny person who could embellish our nights that were sometimes so long because they were so predictable.

At least the Duchess is unpredictable!

Around half-past midnight—the Duchess would have said after a reasonable delay—a hullabaloo could be heard at the front door, a kind of muffled rumble like a brass band in the distance. From my red sofa I didn't hear a thing but Jean-le-Décollé, who was getting ready to go on stage, cried out, "What are those drums all about? Don't tell me she's finally here! And with her own brass band!"

We had all abandoned our positions, all but Greta-la-Vieille who was working hard, as she told us later, on a big Swede who was a gorgeous hunk but lacked motivation.

Even Madame got down from her precious stool to check out what was happening on the street. She did it warily, as if it didn't concern her, but her face showed relief as well as curiosity. Fat Sophie, the waitress and the barmaid came next, so that the Boudoir was abandoned for a few minutes. The clients who were there went outside with us, thinking perhaps that they were going to attend one of the many daily parties put on by the City of Montreal that were usually as exciting as a long rainy day.

A procession of four or five old cars—more or less decrepit but rubbed down with care and decorated with flowers and ribbons—was approaching the Boudoir with calculated slowness. A hesitant horn could be heard now and then, a hand waved, too enthusiastically, at the window of the fourth car to salute the rare passers-by: the onlookers were content to bend down and try to see to whom the long white glove, no longer very clean, which seemed to be calling on them for help, belonged. When they got the picture, they responded to the waves; too late, the car had gone by. It looked a little like a poor person's wedding. The music of the brass band, wheezy and croaking, was coming from the first vehicle that seemed to have too many people packed inside it. No real brass band, no real majorettes. Queen Elizabeth was being heralded by a recording!

The procession came to a halt in front of the Boudoir, the music stopped right in the middle of a phrase. Heads had turned, a few individuals were making their way towards the cars, but you couldn't call it a crowd yet. And it certainly wasn't ecstatic. People were silent, frowning, wondering what this was all about. They seemed not to want to take part or to play along, maybe because they hadn't yet grasped the absurdity of the event and the role that the participants would have liked them to play.

Car doors opened and some very strange creatures emerged.

They were all between fifty and sixty, most were big if not downright obese, and their costumes—flung together pretty well any old way, stolen from forgotten corners of some old ladies' closets, out of bits of anything patched up anyhow—were grotesque but, surprisingly, did a perfect job of creating caricature and mockery. You could recognize the silhouettes of forgotten aunties, distant cousins spotted at funerals and first communions, neighbours you'd have laughed at as a child. You could practically put a name to every one of these individuals.

The oddest and possibly the oldest was dressed like a majorette—a majorette ravaged by life, crippled with arthritis, with flabby skin and sparse hair, but with belligerent pompons on her boots and a sprightly baton. This was the one who was making the most noise, shouting the loudest—and who seemed to be having the most fun.

Each car ejected onto the sidewalk its overflow of these unlikely beings, noisy and laughing amid widespread indifference. They overdid it, piling it on thick and fast, what they most wanted was to talk themselves into thinking they were enjoying themselves and wanted everybody else to be at their party too. But it was obvious that no one wanted to: people craned their necks, shrugged their shoulders, stifled laughs but didn't applaud, didn't shout *Bravo*, had no desire to fall in line behind this ridiculous farandole because they hadn't been prepared.

All at once, the majorette rushed to the door of the fourth car and opened it while attempting pirouettes, each one more ludicrous than the last.

And there was Queen Elizabeth.

The first thing you noticed was a flying saucer trimmed with burnt orange point d'esprit and topped by a bow made of corset-pink pongee. Bent over at first, as if she was about to crash to the sidewalk, she straightened up as if at the last moment someone inside had found the right joystick to save her from disaster. This Elizabeth II was obese, squeezed into a sheath dress with too many flowers the same colour as the hat, the face plastered with so much rice powder that it seemed not to have features: it was perfectly smooth and white, with no texture or character. Only the lips, painted a red that suggested more slut than sovereign, sliced in two—like a fresh wound that had yet to heal—this face covered with too much powder to be human. A few centuries earlier people would have thought that she had the pox. The eyes were bright though, and the smile terribly intelligent. This Elizabeth II was far more brilliant than the original, less uptight too, and as was obvious at first glance—a lot more amusing. You couldn't read the English kind of humour—chilly and deadpan—on this powdered face; this humour was the kind of maximum fun, wild and abandoned and out of control, of the worst nights at the Boudoir, where nothing is respected and everything is allowed. She went on waving her glove of a dubious white, handing out well-aimed kisses here and there—all to men, every one handsome—and when she spoke it was with a phoney English accent that was not unlike the one Fine Dumas would put on for foreign clients.

"My deayah subjects, how enchahnted I am to be heayah with you!"

Gradually, the crowd intensified, onlookers were more numerous and less discreet—word must have travelled on the Main that the time had come, the Duchess was finally here—and some enthusiastic shouts mixed with insults, though not all that many, could now be heard outside the Boudoir. People were finally playing along, acclaiming the Queen of Canada—or booing her, happily and cheerfully depending on one's political sympathies. There were even a few *Vive le Québec libre's* and the odd modest *Le Québec aux Québécois!* Elizabeth II turned towards Fine Dumas, who didn't hide her pleasure at seeing the monarch there at last, and told her in a snooty accent taken straight from the Victorian era, "Lady Dewmass, allow me to present my Royal Family."

Then from the cars emerged creatures more and more weird, whom to our amazement we easily identified at first glance, their shapes were so recognizable.

First of all, a Queen Mum, pissed to the eyeballs, hat askew, stockings ripped, dress also flowered, of course, and stuck in her crack as if she'd just got off the toilet and hadn't pulled it down properly, holding an empty glass of gin and a half-full bottle that jutted out of her transparent canary-yellow plastic purse. (It was La Vaillancourt whose first name I've never known, great crony of the Duchess, her principal partner in crime for ages—like her, too fat, but in a different way, all flab while the Duchess is nothing but fat, nerves and muscles, and nearly as entertaining as her friend. She's a ticket-taker at a movie theatre in the west end of town and she brags that she's seen Edwige Feuillère tumble down her stairs more than three hundred times at the end of Cocteau's film *L'Aigle à deux têtes*.) She sprawled on the sidewalk, lost her hat—a cake made of garish fake flowers and real exotic fruit—pulled herself up with difficulty and stepped inside the Boudoir without a word of greeting to the owner. She was at home wherever she went and made sure that fact was known.

The Queen thought she had to apologize for her.

"I do hope that you'll excusez mummy. Le gin does keep her young, but it has killed off a good many of her neurons ... I cannot deny though, the deah thing drinks like a poisson and we're obliged to scoop her off her sitting room floor every night."

Then a strange Princess Margaret Rose made her appearance, a swirl of peacock blue, all tulle and gestures, surmounted by a hat that looked like a cement pedestal on which had been placed a whole brood of white owls. She was staggering even more than the Queen Mum. But this Royal Family member was more jolly, more sociable too, to the point of lavishing, along with appropriate greetings, somes caresses. Very precise ones, too, on the handsomest male specimens she could find. This Princess Margaret Rose was there to party and nobody was going to stop her, not even her sister, the Queen, who pretended to be ashamed of her, hiding her face behind her not very clean gloves. Eventually she, the neglected sister, the outcast, strode into the bar on the arm of a French sailor who didn't seem to know what was happening. (I'd recognized Rolande Saint-Germain—real name Roland, of course—another friend of the Duchess who, if I remember correctly, works in the costume department at Radio-Canada. At any rate, her own was a success!)

To take people's minds off the state of her mother and sister, Elizabeth II decided to make a little speech to her subjects who'd gathered on Saint-Laurent to welcome her. She turned towards them, holding her purse next to her body like an old woman who's afraid that her money will be stolen.

"Excusay my mother et my soeur, c'est le jet lag... We've actually just arrivé and we haven't had le temps to freshen up our armpits... Race to la limousine, race into Montréal, race to the Boodwar... But if vous voulez to be entertained, come avec us, we've preparé some chahming vaudeville numéros and I'm here pour vous dire, you're going to have a hot time ce soir! No *Vive le Québec libre*, here it's *Vive la Queen and her Famille Royale!* And fuck the separatists who I hear are a bunch of ignorant youths who stink to high heaven and jamais take a bath!"

And then, to boos from the crowd, she turned around, grabbed Fine Dumas by the arm, and pulled her inside her own bar.

I was going to follow when a car door opened and out stepped a handsome hunk as stiff as a board, dressed in grey, looking dull and moody, who didn't seem to realize where he was. As soon as he'd extricated himself from the limo, he looked around vaguely, probably to locate his wife, then shrugged and crossed his hands behind his back, bending forward a little. The prince consort with all his lack of personality. As no one was applauding him because there was nothing to applaud, he turned to me, bending down as if he were picking a flower.

"Tell me, child, where d'you suppose my wife is?"

It was Samarcette, real name Serge Morrissette, ex-boyfriend of the Duchess, who had unscrupulously broken her heart a few years earlier but was still attached to her because, as he said, he couldn't get along without her wit, which was so unique it could never be found anywhere else.

I adore Samarcette, he's one of the only people I allow to go too far. And to call me a child in front of a crowd like that. He knows it, and I could see a triumphant little glimmer in his eyes, which are so beautiful. I contented myself with pinching his cheek, hard, and scowling before I took his arm to lead him into the Boudoir. Playing Prince Philip, he bent double to lower himself to my height. People laughed, I was humiliated, I was annoyed with him.

"You didn't really have to call me *child*, Samarcette."

"Yes I did. When you're performing, Céline, you have to realize it's not what you feel inside that's important, what's important is that people laugh."

"I wasn't performing."

He stopped dead in front of the bar where Fine Dumas had gone back to her seat like a queen to her throne and put his hand on my shoulder.

"Ever since you've been working here, Céline, you've been performing."

Abruptly, I pushed his hand away.

"Think that if you want, but just remember, don't ever call me little girl in front of the girls in the Boudoir or you'll be sorry—and you'll stay sorry."

If the atmosphere in the Boudoir was going to be festive, it needed more people. The girls had left the brothel and were walking around the bar, laughing with the Duchess and her friends, Fat Sophie was doing her best to add some atmosphere by pounding away at her upright piano songs with a rhythm that nobody was listening to, Greluche was serving complicated drinks prepared by Mimi-de-Montmartre, but it was just us, there was no one to laugh at the clowning by the fake Royal Family and its entourage. Worse, there was no one to spend the precious dollars that kept the establishment going.

The Duchess made her way straight to the boss, who'd just lit a cigarette, a French one, the smelly kind, which she reserves for grand occasions because according to her, they smell exotic.

"Where is everybody?"

Madame took a long drag on her cigarette-holder.

"How many invitations did you send?"

"Umm ... I don't know ... around twenty-five ... I thought you'd handle the rest ... "

"It was your party, Duchess. And besides, you never said it was all your doing ... "

"Wasn't it obvious?"

"It was obvious but not official."

"So you didn't do any publicity?"

"Everybody on the Main knows about it."

"But the Main can't afford to come here. You should've publicized it elsewhere—at Expo, or the west end of town."

Fine Dumas gave her friend one of those glacial looks she alone could bestow, that freeze you to the spot.

"Ouch! If you really want to know, I tried. But my clients don't all come from England and they're more interested in Marilyn Monroe or Sophia Loren than in Queen Elizabeth! If you'd organized a party with a theme, I don't know, one that had something to do with Hollywood—Rita Hayworth, Betty Grable, Mamie van Doren—maybe I could have brought in people, but the Queen of England, honestly! If you'd come to see me, if you'd asked me, maybe I could have done something, but you never said a word to me. As far as I'm concerned, Duchess, it's a private party! And your Royal Family needs to spend, and spend plenty, or you'll be doing your act on the sidewalk!"

So much bad faith infuriated the Duchess.

"That's right! Do what you always do! Accuse me of causing the flop!"

Madame merely shrugged.

"That's what happens when you want to do everything on your own ... You want to be a clown? In front of your girlfriends, as usual? Well, be my guest ... "

The Duchess looked around her, appearing desperate.

"At least you could, I don't know, cut prices tonight! We could go out on the sidewalk and tell the people outside the Boudoir that the price is down, just for tonight … "

This time Fine Dumas straightened up as if she'd been slapped.

"Cut my prices! For a bunch of nobodies straight off the sidewalk! Never! I'd rather die like a dead fish with bulging eyes and gaping mouth!"

Immediately, the Duchess turned her back while she pulled up her less and less white gloves. She crammed her purse under her left arm like a reticule and said for everyone to hear, "Samarcette! Rolande! Vaillancourt! The party's over! We're leaving!"

She started off in their direction like a goose-farmer trying to gather up her flock.

"Come on, come on! Move it! We're out of here! We know when we aren't wanted and Madame doesn't want us … "

The boss stayed rooted to the spot, eyes wide, cigarette-holder clenched between her teeth.

Protests rose up from pretty well everywhere. The Duchess's girlfriends refused to have got dressed up for nothing, the girls from the Boudoir said they finally had something new to sink their teeth into—though they realized they weren't going to get rich off that particular gang—even Fat Sophie gave us her own display of discontent by folding her arms over her vast bosom, though she's usually rather placid in the face of our frequent conflicts. No more music to conceal criticisms and acerbic remarks. The few clients present were following it all with great interest, hoping, I suppose, for a real battle.

But Madame didn't say a word, merely watched the Duchess get ready to leave. I'd been about to suggest that she do something—submit, in fact—but I didn't dare. Then I changed my mind and went to sit at the table with Jean-le-Décollé, who seemed to be panicking at the prospect of an imminent disaster. A battle of wills had just begun and only the two protagonists could do anything. Above all, no one else must butt in. But it was well known that both were tremendously proud and we all knew that each would rather die than give in.

The Duchess fanned the flames by pretending to brush some non-existent dust off La Vaillancourt's dress, "Try to do *that one* a favour and you'll see, it's got a heart of stone and the gratitude of a sewer rat. It would sooner eat your garbage than admit it needed help!"

La Vaillancourt answered her very quietly, "Don't provoke her, Duchess! We can't just get up and go, you told the limos to come back after 3 a.m."

"We don't need limos."

"What will we do without them?"

"We'll walk."

"Forget it! I'm not walking halfway across town dressed up like the Queen Mum!"

"We'll go up the Main in a procession, we'll be a sight to behold!"

"A procession! There's just ten of us! Eleven with the majorette. Eleven people isn't a procession."

"When eleven flaming queens like us start up the Main, believe me there'll soon be a procession following behind! We'll put the majorette in front, she'll lead the way. And we'll have a little talk with my niece, Thérèse, at Ben Ash, you never know, maybe she'll treat us to a smoked meat ... "

Then she raised her voice so that Madame would hear, "This place is as dead as last week's fish. And cold as the South Pole! Though there's probably more atmosphere down there. At the South Pole at least they've got penguins in tuxes. Even a toy penguin would liven up our parties.

The boss struck the marble bar just once, hard enough to startle everyone. She must have scratched the surface but she didn't seem to care.

"Okay! That's enough! You aren't leaving, Édouard, I'm kicking you out! Now move it! Go on, clear the floor, I don't want to see your face in the Boodwar ever again!"

The Duchess raised her head and straightened up as if she'd just been struck in the heart. The character Elizabeth II quickly came back to the surface and it was a genuine monarch who made her way at a regal pace to the door of the Boudoir, trailed by her quartet of outriders and her pathetic court.

"Kindly inform the person in charge of this filthy place that Elizabeth Windsor, Queen of England and Canada, is accustomed to grand palaces, not brothels from the days of her great-great-grandmother Victoria. This place is so foul I wouldn't let my corgis do a poo in the corner!"

And exit, singing *Rule Britannia*!

We were all expecting a hideous outburst from Fine Dumas—shouts, insults, jerky and uncontrolled movements like a dislocated puppet's, condemnations too, harsh and final decrees hurled at the Duchess and her gang, voice resonant, finger pointed—but instead, a long silence settled into the Boudoir after they'd left. Fat Sophie played a slow waltz that Madame was particularly fond of, "Heure exquise" from *The Merry Widow*; Mimi-de-Montmartre had gone back to her lemons—by then she must have cut enough for the week; Greluche made her way through the tables to serve the very few clients who must have been hoping for one brief moment that something was finally going to happen; the girls, let down as well, had left one after another for their workplace, deserted now for lack of clients. As for me, I was torn between my urge to talk to Madame (to defuse her, in fact, because to me she was like a time bomb ready to explode at any moment) and the duty that was waiting for me backstage: the red button, the pouffe, the menu. I finally told myself yet again that I should mind my own business; it wasn't up to me to fix everything all the time; I motioned to Greluche that I was going home.

Just as I passed the bead curtain, I heard the voice of Fine Dumas, a small voice like a tiny little girl's, hardly more than a breath, the lament of a child who realizes that she's just done something very bad and doesn't know how to fix it. A most surprising remark coming from her, who never admits she's been wrong, who even takes the path of bad faith and injustice rather than give in to other people's arguments.

"As far as that's concerned ... Poor Duchess. It was all my fault."

Surprisingly, nothing more was ever heard about the incident on the Main. Not officially, anyway. Everyone of course had their own version of the facts, of their meaning, of how it could influence the relationships among the members of the trio from hell, but none of the three ever brought it up again, not even Jean-le-Décollé, though he could have had fun with the Duchess's faux pas, used it to further his reputation, beg for Madame's favour, and to supplant his opponent once and for all. Did they know that they were more powerful as three than each in his own corner? That their dependence on one another was more important than a squabble that could only end badly and strain their relations forever? And did they choose peace to avoid a war that would weaken them all? They decided by common consent—there were probably some phone calls I didn't hear about—that the Queen's visit hadn't happened and during the early days, if it was mentioned in front of them they looked away, especially Madame, as if something very important was going on somewhere else, and we quickly got the message.

And so the story is in the process of becoming—because of the three protagonists' denial and because you can invent whatever you want since nothing happened—one of the strangest and most multifaceted legends of the Main: some maintain, while knowing that everyone knows it's not true, that there had been bloodshed, that the Duchess had spent the night in the hospital, that Fine Dumas had had one of her worst attacks of hysteria, that Jean-le-Décollé, that godly man, had been forced to separate the boss and the false Queen lest they kill one another. Others swear to anyone who'll listen that the members of the triumvirate have been at daggers drawn since that evening; that the air is filled with the meanest, the crudest insults whenever they're together; that they speak to each other very formally as if they're barely acquainted; that their association is dying a natural death; that the atmosphere in the Boudoir will never recover.

I tried to talk with my roommate about it, once. He just looked at me, shaking his head.

"Some things deserve to stay in the shadows, Céline. As if they were asleep. Do you know what they're called? Hidden ammunition. We don't know when they'll be useful, but we know that they're there, ready to be used when we need them."

"Do you think that one of the three of you will use them some day?"

"I don't think so, I'm sure. And not just one! Each one of us—now listen carefully, you'll be able to tell me I was right—I'm convinced that each one of the three of us will find a moment or a way to bring that evening back to life in order to harm either the other two or just one ... It's inevitable and it's only fair. Meanwhile none of it exists. You can spread the word or not, it won't change a thing."

I didn't spread the word. It was pointless. And it's true that nothing would have changed. When the Main needs a good story on which to base nebulous theories, when perverted gossip and malicious suppositions start making the rounds, when the cruel fairy or her sister, the slanderous witch, descends among us, there's no room for common sense or simple decency: everything is allowed and we allow ourselves everything. Willingly and generously.

When the Duchess arrived, three-quarters of an hour after Jean-le-Décollé's call, the Boudoir was slightly better stocked: a few American sailors in their gorgeous white uniforms—"Seafood! Seafood!" Mimi-de-Montmartre had shouted—were drinking gin and tonic while they watched Mae East blare out that *non, rien de rien, non, elle ne regrette rien*, this time the giant was Édith Piaf—and a group of Finnish tourists, who'd never seen a drag queen because they don't exist in their country, were gawking at what was going on in the bar. The women couldn't get over it and the men wanted more. We wouldn't be making money off the Finns, that we knew, but they added to the atmosphere.

Though I hadn't seen her arrive, I knew that the Duchess was there because I heard the boss cry out at the end of the rather skimpy applause that rose up when Édith Piaf left the stage.

"What are you doing here on a regular Tuesday, Édouard? Don't you have to be selling shoes tomorrow at dawn?"

Madame calls the Duchess by his first name when she's mad or when something's going wrong. The Duchess knows that as well as we do, and she walks on eggs.

As the rooms weren't occupied—the girls were dying to meet the American sailors and the shy Finns, but none of them had yet decided to look around the back of the shop, though they were casting sidelong glances in the direction of the men's room and nudging one another—I slipped into the little corridor that leads to the bar and, once again glanced furtively between the glass bead curtains. It was the third time that evening, and I admit that I was starting to feel ridiculous.

Babalu climbed onto the stage, blowing kisses from her fingertips to the spectators, and was greeted by a burst of applause, the first of the evening. The only thing that contributed to her slightest resemblance to Brigitte Bardot was the little kerchief knotted under her chin, but the good-natured audience had decided to play along and behaved as if the resemblance were striking.

Everyone knows that Brigitte Bardot can't sing, so impersonating her isn't a problem, even for the worst impersonator. Especially because, as I've said before, at our club the show isn't all that important. So Babalu did the best she could, in a falsetto voice. Standing in profile, she arched her back, launched into *La Marseillaise* in a French accent as phoney as Fine Dumas's, and everyone was happy. I thought to myself that the sailors might make their choices soon—and who knows, maybe some big blond Finn, too, egged on by his wife—and I was about to withdraw to my den, telling myself that in any event I wouldn't hear a word of what was said between Madame and the Duchess, when I saw the Duchess lay her hand on the boss's arm. Fine Dumas doesn't like being touched, she stiffens whenever a hand comes near her, pushes away any kisses that she doesn't instigate herself and steps back at any hint of a caress. This time though she allowed her friend's hand to cover hers and didn't move, she even went so far as to bow her head, like a penitent or someone struck by adversity whose suffering has become unbearable.

I didn't hear anything they said of, course, but their body language was eloquent and from the fluttering of Madame's hands, from the tension in the Duchess's neck and the way she moved her hips while she talked, as if to accentuate her words, I could guess at how the conversation unfolded, its development, the boss's reticence, the Duchess's attempt to be more convincing, the attacks and counter-attacks and then, a few minutes later—after endless arguing, yelling, heads shaken in every direction—the long-hoped-for surrender. Which came very quickly, in fact, as if all at once Madame had collapsed, bowing to the Duchess's arguments out of pure fatigue or laziness, because any more resistance would be too demanding for a woman so devastated.

All at once she threw her head back and erupted in one of those loud peals of laughter that heralded some good news or ultimate decree that make the Main tremble. Once again the Duchess had been able to make Madame laugh!

The Duchess's shoulders relaxed all at once, she loosened up, brought her hand to her brow. I imagined the sweat, the sigh of relief, the heart that began to beat again.

I realized that Jean-le-Décollé was beside me. Had he witnessed this latest victory by the Duchess? A victory for which he was responsible because he was the one who'd called to her for help. I didn't know when he'd got there, what he'd seen, what he, like me, had been able to make out of the conversation that had just taken place. When I turned towards him he merely shrugged, with a hint of the little smile of defeat that escapes us at such moments and that says so much about our own state of mind.

"At least we're going to have peace. And maybe our present."

Jean-le-Décollé, standing with his hands on his hips, his voice more shrill than usual—though he makes a point of using a virile tone, especially when he's dressed as a woman—seemed to be on the verge of hysteria.

"Would you mind telling me what you say when you talk to her to make her melt like that?"

The Duchess pulled herself up on the red button where she'd come to join me. She shook her head to arrange locks of hair that weren't there because she hadn't taken the time to put on a woman's wig, wiggled her arm in a gesture vaguely reminiscent of Bette Davis when she's about to make some bitchy remark, and produced a throaty laugh that turned into a heavy smoker's cough. Then she straightened the little black hairpiece she wears every day as a man, thinking that it fools people, though in fact you'd swear that someone had poured a whole bottle of India ink on her head or that she's used a big brush to paint a wig on her skull.

"You know, Ti-Jean, some secrets have to stay secret. Family recipes that mustn't leave the family."

"Are you telling me that it's a family matter?"

"Yes, we're very persuasive in my family ... It's a gift."

"The only one you've got ... "

"Maybe, but it's precious. Look at my niece, Thérèse; she's been banished from the Main I don't know how many times ... But she always bounces back."

"One of these days she's going to bounce into a brick wall and she won't get up. And you can't say we'll be sorry ... "

The Duchess got up, visibly upset.

"Why did you say that? Did you hear something?"

The Duchess is very touchy on the subject of her niece, Thérèse, whom the Main has been rejecting continually for years now but who always finds a way to come back, fresh as a daisy, arrogant, inexplicably forgiven for gaffes that other girls have paid for if not with their lives then at least with their local careers. She's said to have a highly-placed protector too, and that she and Maurice-la-Piasse are childhood friends, that they've been lovers, it's even insinuated in certain circles that she started dating Harelip, Maurice's sister, just to stay in the good graces of the king of the Main. And that once again it had worked, because for some months now Thérèse has been back screwing things up at Ben Ash, which may never recover, for that matter, because clients have started to stay away. Because of her.

"Never mind Thérèse tonight, Duchess, we've got more important things to do ... "

Ecstatic at the results—he'd been able to throw the Duchess off balance—Jean-le-Décollé turned his back on us and went off to one of the many unoccupied rooms.

The Duchess turned towards me.

"Did you hear anything, Céline?"

I smoothed my green gown and looked at my toes. Word had in fact been making the rounds for a few days now that Thérèse was really in for it, that this time Maurice had had it and that Harelip couldn't do a thing: the guillotine wasn't far off. I had to change the subject, it wasn't up to me to talk about such things with the Duchess.

In my waitress days I used to like Thérèse, who often came to the Sélect for a cigarette and a coffee, but I knew why people couldn't stand her. Sober, she was the most fantastic girl in the world, hard-working, funny, quick-witted, and with a sense of repartee nearly as well-developed as her uncle Édouard's. But when she'd had one too many, she turned into a bloodthirsty monster and nothing and no one found favour in her eyes. And she screws up time and again, each more serious than the one before, becomes totally unscrupulous and sneers at everyone, sure that she'll win every time.

So I was trying to change the subject when I noticed the shoes that the Duchess was wearing. Usually she wears very high stilettos that give her a rolling gait because of her corpulence, but that night she had on little beige canvas *babouches*, oriental slippers that clashed a little with her powder-blue chinos and blood-red shirt. When you looked at her from head to toe she got paler and paler: the raven's-wing black of the hairpiece, the red shirt, the blue pants, the beige slippers. A strange effect. It may have been a reaction to the famous monochrome of Fine Dumas who never wears more than one colour at a time and who had admitted to me one day that she wanted people to know that she was all of a piece. The Duchess, then, was obviously made up of a number of pieces superimposed. I jumped on her beige canvas footwear to take the Duchess's mind off the misadventures of Thérèse.

"Where did you buy your *babouches*, Duchess?"

She sat down beside me, stretching her legs to give me a good look at her feet.

"Is that what they are? I thought *babouches* were pointed, like Aladdin's in *The Thousand and One Nights*. Nice, aren't they? Reminds me of Indrig Bergman. Did you know that Indrig Bergman always wears flats in her films because she's taller than her co-stars? They say that in Hollywood, they're all little guys that wouldn't come up to my shoulders ... What's his name, you know who I mean, oh right, Alan Ladd? They say he's practically a ... "

She stopped just before uttering the word *midget* and turned red as a lobster that's just been plunged into boiling water. I pretended I hadn't noticed, not out of the goodness of my heart but because I'm used to people making that kind of gaffe in front of me. But it was the first time for the Duchess and I didn't hold it against her.

Greta-la-Vieille, who was passing by and had heard our conversation, stopped in front of us.

"It isn't *Indrig* Bergman, Duchess, it's *Ingrid*."

"Oh come on! If anybody here knows Hollywood it's me! If I say In**drig** Bergman it's because it's In**drig** Bergman! I-N-**D**-R-I-**G**, In**drig**! Really! As if I didn't know what I was talking about! Go scare people on stage, you, instead of correcting others!"

"Check the ads in the paper … "

"Do you believe everything you read in the paper? Poor little girl! Most of the time they don't know what they're writing."

So it was settled: once again the Duchess was right and the rest of the world was wrong. We knew it was pointless to keep arguing. It runs in the family, I imagine, that certainty that you're always right, that you always have the solution to everything, that you never doubt a thing. I envy those people, those champions of certainty—I who always torment myself with endless doubts and questions and never arrive at a final conclusion.

Greta-la-Vieille, a good girl, merely shrugged and sighed, exasperated.

"Well, at least I can go on stage!"

The Duchess acted as if she hadn't heard, but I knew that the remark had hit home.

Ever since Madame Petrie told her at the Théâtre National twenty years ago that she didn't have the talent to go on stage, that she was nothing but a salon comic, that she was only fooling herself if she thought that she'd ever be able to earn her living doing something except selling shoes, the Duchess has had a genuine phobia about going on stage. Stand her at centre stage with a mike and a spotlight and she freezes like Bambi in the headlights. She loses all composure, mumbles, mutters, can't make a single joke. And if she tries to sing, she's worse, forgetting the words or mixing them up and, worst of all, unable to follow the rhythm. All this to say that she seems to go out of her way to prove that Madame Petrie was right, even though she would love to prove that the old vaudeville actress was wrong.

If someone explained to Juliette Petrie the damage she'd done to the Duchess, she wouldn't believe it. I don't even know if she still remembers the poor awkward individual who had confided in her one desperate night, and whom she'd crushed like an insect without even realizing it.

But drop the Duchess into a party well-supplied with good looking men, provide her—generously—with strong drink, especially rye, her family's poison, sit her on a straight-back chair or a comfy armchair with lots of people around her, she doesn't shy away, she comes to life, moves around, becomes the soul of the party, its essence. She talks to everyone, tells stories—invented, no doubt, because they're so ridiculous—about her travels around the globe, in particular her quick trip to Paris in 1947—and the guests eat them up. She'll impersonate all the American and French stars from the thirties and forties, from Ginger Rogers to Annette Poivre, from Rosalind Russell to Gaby Morlay, not to mention Sazu Pitts and her favourite, Edwige Feuillère, as *La Duchesse de Langeais*—of course, that's where she took her name—but also in *L'Aigle à deux têtes*, because of the staircase scene at the end. (Sometimes she claims, like her friend, La Vaillancourt, that it's Edwige herself who tumbles down the stairs; other times she says that it's Jean Marais, depending on the needs of the moment, I suppose.) She sings "Mon p'tit tra-la-la" without worrying about whether or not her voice sounds like Suzy Delair's and she dances "It's Too Darn Hot," doing a perfect imitation of Ann Miller's tics. A fat male tap dancer is a sight to behold! She adds life where boredom rules, makes people sing who've been voiceless before—she even makes elephants dance.

And that was what, true to form, she did that night.

When she went back to the bar section of the Boudoir—I followed her because I sensed that something spectacular was going to happen and I didn't want to miss a minute of it—it was still gloomy, even though Madame's mood had changed. The seafoods and the Finns couldn't make up their minds to cross over to my domain, but luckily for the cash box, they were drinking like fish. Fat Sophie was exhausted from thumping away at her upright piano. The *artistes* were tired of working their little hearts out for nothing. You suddenly had the impression that it wasn't a brothel, but any cheap transvestite bar in any town in any country. (Except Finland, of course, where, as I mentioned before, drag queens don't exist. But the Finnish tourists had already had their fill of laughing at our two fake Brigitte Bardots and our Marilyn Monroe impersonators and appeared to be on the verge of leaving.)

The Duchess quickly got the situation in hand.

Once again she straightened her black toupee, with a wink in the direction of Fine Dumas who was smoking at the end of her bar, trying to blow smoke rings as if nothing in particular was going on while she counted the dollars that weren't flying into her cash box, and made her way straight to the American sailors' table. They opened their eyes wide when they spied the fat individual, half-man, half-woman, who was landing in their midst as if they'd raised pigs together back in Kansas or North Dakota.

To sneak a peek at what was going to happen, I stayed close to Madame who, to my amazement, didn't reproach me for not being at my post.

The Duchess pulled out a chair, took a seat, legs folded like those of a woman of the world who forgets that it's not done, and says, to no one in particular, "Hello boys, my name is Cyd Charisse, what's yours? And which one of you is Gene Kelly?"

There was a brief silence before the great burst of laughter, but that brief silence was very long! I watched Madame, who was biting her cigarette-holder, prepared to do anything to save her bar if a battle broke out: intervene, threaten, flatter shamelessly and, if necessary, go so far as to call the police, even if she knew that it would cost a lot in booze and bribes.

The sailors exchanged a look, surprised at the Duchess's nerve, then decided that she was funny—after all, they knew perfectly well what kind of establishment this was—and they burst out laughing, slapping their thighs and nudging one another. Right away, the tension dropped, glasses were slammed onto the fake marble table, the Duchess threw her head back like a real courtesan who has achieved her goal and I heard, very distinctly, Madame heave a sigh of relief.

Rather than repeat her impersonation of the Queen of England, though—they were American and had no interest in Elizabeth II—the Duchess launched into an act that I'd never seen, perhaps improvised on the spot, perhaps fine-tuned in her bed during long sleepless nights, but brilliant, a kind of brief rundown of all the impersonations she can do in English, going from one celebrity to another without even catching her breath, giving no one else a chance to get a word in, hilarious, her English all at once melodious and almost learned, as if she'd been born far south of the Canadian border. She bent double on her chair to imitate Joan Crawford spotting the rat in her soup plate; straightened up, radiant, as Gloria Swanson coming down the stairs of her Beverley Hills mansion, wild-eyed and stiff-shouldered to say, "I'm ready for my close-up, Mister De Mille"; pursed her lips to coo like Mae West, "When I'm good, I'm good; but when I'm bad, I'm better!"

The Finns had gone over to the Americans' table, two Japanese were taking pictures, the few women present laughed even harder than the men, there was pandemonium—success at last, joy.

But they had to be persuaded to take the plunge, to do more than cast longing glances towards the brothel, to push aside the bead curtain and taste the perverse delights of Greta-la-Vieille, Greta-la-Jeune, Nicole Odeon, Babalu and even of Jean-le-Décollé, whose beaming face—the lure of gain erases rivalries—I'd spotted behind Fat Sophie's piano. As for Mae East, poor dear, she was going to wither on the vine because of her shameful disease.

Then a busload of French tourists turned up at the Boudoir. And things were put off once again.

As soon as she saw them come in, whining—"I can't *bear* those American buses with the air as cold as a *glacière*. And the driver! That accent! Why don't they speak proper French?"—noisy—too sure of themselves—"They won't put one over on me, no *monsieur*—after all, my dear, I've seen transvestites in Paris and there certainly won't be anything like that here!"—the Duchess practically threw herself at them, shouting, "Dessert time, girls! French pastries!" They didn't have time to notice what was happening to them when a fat and oddly dressed gentleman wearing an astonishing toupee as black as a crow took charge of them as if they were the guests of honour at a fancy banquet in the Élysée Palace and she their private maître d'. Need I add that the Duchess had changed her accent in no time and it was now Edwige Feuillère herself, but obese and dressed as a man, who was speaking to them? The Duchess is the only person I know who can talk faster than a Frenchman, more loudly and more arrogantly.

Without giving them time to protest, they were seated at four tables for eight and the same number of bottles of champagne had been ordered. The Duchess didn't listen to what they were saying; on the contrary she kept cutting them off, proffering more and more naughty winks and double entendres, calling the women *Germaine* and the men *Fernand*, she fluttered from table to table, distributing friendly pats and kisses to balding foreheads—in a word, she had wrapped them around her little finger in less than five minutes. Thinking that she was French—from the provinces though and they couldn't quite place her accent—and that she'd been hired just for them, they couldn't afford to be insolent and let her lead them by the nose and put them in their place, also feeling obliged to laugh at jokes as old as the hills and to drink champagne that their budgets hadn't foreseen. When everyone was comfortably seated, the bottles uncorked and the toast proposed to friendship between the French and their Québécois cousins, all at once and to their amazement, she resumed her crudest Montreal accent and delivered one of the finest speeches of her entire smooth-talking career.

"Everybody nice and comfy now? Germaine? Fernand? Bon, okay, I got one thing to say to you guys: you aren't here to criticize, you aren't here to claim you can't understand us, you aren't here to gawk and bitch that everything's lousy and lame: you're here to have fun so let yourselves go and fun you'll have! It's our specialty here at the Boudoir! Our specialties are quite a mixed bag and *very* interesting. So hang loose, relax the nerve that the fun travels down, flirt with the American sailors and those big hunky Finns, visit our famous back of the shop that I'm sure you've heard about or you wouldn't be here, drink, sing, dance, the bill will be steep but worth it! Just like Paris! My name is Alexandrine de Navarreins, Duchess of Langeais, I'm as vulgar as twelve but as funny as fifteen, I'll be looking after you tonight and if you trust me, you'll have the time of your lives! So loosen the tie, drop the jacket, undo the corset—the show is about to begin! I warn you though—it's cheap, the artistes work hard and they have no talent but that's *on purpose*! Okay? On purpose! So don't be snotty! Brigitte Bardot looks like she stepped out of a garbage can, Mae East has put on fifty pounds, Marilyn Monroe is anemic—but that's why they're funny! So laugh! And don't tell me you've seen drag queens like them before, because you haven't! They're ugly *on purpose*, and they're at your service afterwards. At your service, Fernand. Yours too, Germaine, if you want! And let me tell you, the talent they lack on stage they've got plenty of backstage!"

No one dared say a word during her long diatribe. They looked at her wide-eyed, a spark of fear in their pupils, impressed.

Then she pointed to the ceiling and gave one last warning.

"And I don't want to hear anybody say they couldn't understand what I just said!"

She leaned over towards a middle-aged woman, who was corpulent, even massive.

"Did you understand all that, Germaine?"

The lady opted to laugh and to agree.

"Say it, say you understand everything!"

The Germaine in question complied and I must admit, she did it with a certain grace.

"Of course I understood! I have a cousin who comes from La Perche!"

The Duchess pinched her cheek kindly.

"We must be related then, my ancestor was a four-footed Percheron! Enjoy the show, Germaine!"

She then turned towards the Americans whom she'd abandoned in such a cavalier fashion and told them, posing suggestively, "The show's about to begin, boys! But I'm at your disposal, whenever you need me! I do everything! Twice!"

She took a seat halfway between the Americans and the French, raised her arms and cried out to Sophie, "It's all yours, Sophie dear! Let the party begin!"

The rest of the night was a genuine triumph. There was tremendous applause for unspeakable things—impersonations that didn't come off, pathetically mediocre songs, sketches with no rhythm and no ending because the artistes didn't know how to conclude them, but all delivered with such sincerity, such good humour and so good-naturedly it was irresistible. Those who didn't speak French pretended that they could, and the French forgot to criticize the accent. The party, whipped up by a riotous, out-of-control Duchess, was happening in the house as much as on stage. The Duchess was all over the place: encouraging Germaine and Fernand to sing "Little Red Riding Hood" with Mae East who'd forgotten about her VD for all of fifteen minutes to deliver, quite precisely in honour of the French, her version of what she remembered of the recordings by Jacques Élian and his orchestra that her mother had adored in the 1940s; she sang "Singin' in the Rain" at the Americans' table, climbing up the Boudoir's central beam as if it were Gene Kelly's streetlamp; she grabbed lemon slices from Mimi-de-Montmartre to produce saliva; she urged Greluche to speed up her service so the clients would drink more speedily; she brought beer to Fat Sophie, who'd earned it; she patted Fine Dumas's knee when she walked past her; she murmured things in the ears of the Finns while pointing to the glass bead curtain that went to the men's room and, in particular, in back of it.

When the men began to seriously glance in the direction of my domain, I went back to my post, limping in case Madame was watching. I'd never before seen the Boudoir so lively or the boss so happy. The take was going to exceed our hopes and maybe, finally, she'd give us that present!

All thanks to the Duchess!

I took the five-pound Lowney's chocolate box out of its hiding place under the sofa, sat it on the worn velvet beside me and covered it with my hand before I summoned Mae East who was coming off stage, exhausted but smiling. And relaxed for the first time all day.

"Do you know what to do, Mae?"

"Sure! I watch you every night. I greet the clients … "

"No, never mind the greeting … I'll look after that."

"But you told Madame … "

"Never mind what I told Madame … I'll look after the greeting myself if you don't mind too much, I'm used to the sales pitch, I know how to talk to them, I've been doing it for months. What you're going to do is hand out the menus, show them to the rooms when they've finished looking at them … and bring them back when they've done their business."

I drummed on the cover of the cardboard box.

"I think I'm going to boost the rates tonight, they're having too much fun."

The first client appeared. One of the Finns, braver than the others but still red with embarrassment. Mae East rushed at him, simpering as she offered him the menu. Like most of the men who come to my part of the house, he seemed surprised at first, but quickly realized that he'd have to make his choice on paper, that the goods on offer were the same as those he'd just seen on stage and he began, somewhat nervously, to read the selection.

"You gave him the menu in English, at least? So he'll understand the specialties?"

"Sure, I'm not stupid! He has to understand that we may be ugly but we know what we're doing."

Soon others joined him, then even more. The Americans, a few Japanese and even a Quebec TV star whom we were all surprised to see there, and for whom Jean-le-Décollé was pleased to do whatever he asked. Or more. The French were the last ones to make up their minds. Maybe they thought that such a visit would be an attack on their legendary virility ... After all, those women were men, right? Once they were good and drunk though, and encouraged by Germaine who perhaps didn't mind humiliating her man a little, they came to the red sofa, leafed through the menu, sometimes wincing, but in the end they all followed Mae East to the rooms. Not only was it men they were going to see, they weren't beautiful women, so none of it mattered either to Germaine, who after all couldn't show jealousy, or to Fernand, who after all was only there as an experiment ...

The rooms were soon congested. Especially with one girl short. And Mae East, God knows, is a hard worker! And devoted!

There was a lot of traffic back and forth in the brothel, a line formed down the length of the corridor that went from my quarters to the men's room, there was singing, clinking glasses and drinking to the friendship between our peoples; they emerged from the rooms lighter, gleeful, only rarely ashamed. Some, the ones we call grouchy because they get mad at us over their recent misdemeanour and want to make us pay for it, we're wary of: they're often slow at paying and always cheap about tipping. But there weren't many of them that night, the atmosphere wasn't one for criticism and self-analysis, but for serious fun and oceans of alcohol.

One Frenchman even came out of Babalu's room howling, "That was the blowjob of a lifetime! You ought to give lessons to my wife!"

The party was at its peak, the rooms occupied, the Boudoir jubilant, the Duchess more hysterical than ever—I could hear her in my quarters, mooing "Frou frou" or "Some of These Days" in her stentorian voice—when Fine Dumas appeared in the brothel. With her sweaty furrowed brow and the crow's feet around her eyes, she didn't know that she was giving a preview of the old woman she would soon be.

"Céline! Céline! The place is going to burst if this keeps up!"

I was tidying the inside of my chocolate box, which was overflowing with money, arranging the bills in order: fives, tens, twenties, a few hundreds; the house doesn't accept ones and twos;

nothing here costs less than five dollars. And as I've already mentioned, everyone pays cash.

I gave the boss a big grin.

"I think it's going to be one of the biggest nights since we opened, Madame! For a Tuesday, it's practically unheard-of!"

She sat down next to me, fanning herself with her hand.

"We're out of staff. You'll have to put Mae East back on the floor."

Just then Mae held out to me a hundred-dollar bill that one of the Americans had given her. She froze in mid-move.

"But Madame, Céline can't walk … "

The boss went on fanning herself but with one of the menus turned to the page that sang the praises of Greta-la-Vieille.

"Oh, yes she can! She came and watched the show with the rest of us just now! And she wasn't limping that badly."

I gestured to Mae East to leave and closed the box brusquely.

"It's true I can walk, Madame, even though it's painful, but I can't haul myself up and down and back and forth like I usually do. I'd be afraid of aggravating my sprained ankle."

Fine Dumas placed her hand on my right knee, an absolutely amazing gesture from her.

"Do it for me, Céline. Try to move as little as possible but put Mae East back on the floor. Things have to move faster, this is ridiculous, we aren't providing service any more! If it goes on like this we won't be able to accommodate everybody. One girl in six missing is a lot! Try to run everything from here, move as little as possible, I know you can do it!"

She stood up like a young girl who's just been invited to dance—all at once she wasn't tired any more—and made her way to the door, going around the male clients and the two female clients, the first of the evening, who were awaiting their turn. She turned around just before she went out.

"Right now, Céline! No arguments!"

Then she disappeared, leaving behind her a spicy aroma, a mixture of sweat and the Chanel No. 5 that had gone sour on her skin again.

Mae East and I exchanged a look, stunned.

After all, I couldn't let Mae East pass on her gonorrhea to the Expo tourists, even if the ancestors of the French had spread smallpox, flu and measles to the first inhabitants of my country! I had to come up with a solution and fast. It was Nicole Odeon who suggested one without realizing it. She was on her way to the stage to do her part of the show between rounds. Exasperated at being disturbed while earning her livelihood, she tossed off as she walked past me, "How are you doing? I can't take any more! All I can say is, I'd like to hide in one of the rooms."

Immediately I called Mae East over. She was pale and nervously wringing her hands.

"I can't do that, Céline, it makes no sense! I'd give a dose to half the Expo visitors! The penicillin the doctor gave me hasn't even kicked in yet. My crotch is on fire, my throat's dry, my legs are like rubber bands! We'd have complaints by tomorrow morning. We'd be shut down by tomorrow night. And I can't rely on safes because, after all, I'm the visitee as much as the visitor … "

I offered a menu to a Frenchwoman who was clucking like a turkey that's just been fed. She opened it, skimmed it, laughing.

"I quite simply cannot believe that I'm doing this! I want the same … umm … the same … umm … the same person as my husband … The very thin one … you know … the one who sang 'Les parapluies de Cherbourg' a while ago … Apparently she does blowjobs that would turn the finest Paris pros green with envy … Do you think she'd give me some pointers? She has a peculiar name … Baba Cool?"

"Babalu is busy, but if you want to wait, Madame … "

I signalled to Mae East to sit beside me while the client walked away, blushing.

"Listen to me and don't argue, we haven't got time ... You're going to disappear for the rest of the night ... There's just a few hours left anyway ... "

"Disappear? How can I disappear?"

"I said no arguments! Madame has to think that you're working ... The best way is to hide in some corner till the Boudoir closes ... Nothing to it!"

"But all the rooms are occupied, Céline ... "

"Go and read magazines in the toilet then, I don't care, but disappear! If Madame comes back she has to think you're working on a tourist. I'll fix things with the other girls, I'll make false declarations in my ledger, I'll say that you did seven or eight clients in the time you had left ... and when it's your turn to sing, I'll let you know ... "

She looked at me with the wide eyes of Bambi looking at her mother's corpse.

"You're sure it will work?"

"Have you got any other ideas?"

"What about tomorrow?"

"Never mind tomorrow! Think about right now! And right now, you're going to disappear before Madame comes back."

She took a panicky look at the waiting room of the brothel.

"You won't find a hiding place here, Mae ... I know, go have a smoke in the shed ... "

"I don't smoke ... "

"Mae, you're getting on my nerves!"

"The shed's full of spiders!"

"What would you prefer, Mae—spiders in the shed or bruises on your face?"

I was exasperated and I confess that at that moment I think I could have hit her—I, who've never hit anyone in my life. She finally understood and walked away without another word.

The next day Greta-la-Jeune told me that several times she'd heard her howling in the shed.

A few hours later, an overjoyed Fine Dumas was counting the evening's take without even checking the ledger.

"You'll see, Madame, all the entries are there … "

"I trust you, Céline, I know you wouldn't steal a penny … It would cost you too much if you got caught … "

Mae East had come back from the shed, swearing like a trooper and as grimy as a chimney sweep, but for the time being she was silent as she watched the boss stacking bills on the worn fabric of the red sofa. Madame had assembled us in my salon as soon as the Boudoir was closed so that—and this time it was true—she announced the good news that she'd promised earlier that evening. She made us wait a little more though, picking up a wad of hundred-dollar bills to fan herself, laughing as she shook the chocolate box: an impatient little girl trying to guess how much money is in her piggy bank.

We were all exhausted and we wanted her to come out with it and get it over with. Fat Sophie was knocking back one last beer in a corner while Mimi-de-Montmartre was removing the numerous coats of Cutex from her fingernails. The smell of nail polish remover was so strong it brought tears to my eyes. Greluche, with her arms folded, was smoking one of her stinky cigarettes. As for me, I was waiting patiently for Madame to tell me to carefully close all the doors and windows before I left. As for the girls, they looked at one another, frowning. All that interested them right now was a hot bath, PJs and bed—empty. Not some present from Fine Dumas!

The Duchess was still there, saying that she would take the next morning off.

"Mademoiselle Desrosiers, my boss, is very understanding … If I party too hard on a weeknight, I just have to call her when the store opens ... I'll do that around ten and tell her I'll be in after lunch. As long as the owners don't know ... Anyway, on Wednesdays the ladies try but don't buy ... Everybody knows that no one buys shoes on Wednesday!"

Madame finished stuffing the bills into the big canvas bag that looked like nothing much and held the take every night. If the little pickpockets on the Main only knew! But they would never dare get anywhere near the fearsome Fine Dumas, the best-protected, most respected women in all of Montreal's red light district.

"I have the great pleasure of announcing that tonight was our biggest night that wasn't a weekend ... "

Faint applause. This wasn't news, we'd all suspected it. After all, we were the ones who'd done all the work!

She took out a small bundle of bills that she'd been sitting on.

"We got off to a bad start tonight at the Boodwar, but luckily, the end was a lot better ... So I've decided that to beg forgiveness for my temper tantrum and to reward you for all your good work, I'm giving you a little bonus ... It may not be much, but it's from the heart ... "

To each of us, even the Duchess, she held out a twenty-dollar bill that for some inexplicable reason she'd folded in four before dropping it into our hands. A mama with her children? A woman who's sent her neighbour on an errand? A rich lady giving alms?

"As you see, I'm not such a bitch when I'm happy ... "

Greluche coughed into her fist.

"And you, Greluche, I owe you an apology. I yelled at you for no reason and I hope you'll forgive me."

An apology from Fine Dumas! Had the sky fallen? Was this the start of a new era? We all exchanged a look, wondering just what this was all about. Was she going to tell us next that she had cancer, that she'd be away for some months having chemo, that the Boudoir would have to get along without her for a while? Now *that* would be a present!

She straightened her spine the way she does when she has something important to tell us, and we were all ears. Here it comes. At last. Soon the cat would be let out of the bag. Ordinarily we'd have been wary, expecting something stupid and dull whose importance she'd have exaggerated, whereas now, after the bonus and the apologies, anything seemed possible ... Maybe we were going to get a real present!

"To make a long story short ... I know it's late and you want to go to bed. Me too, don't worry ... Listen ... In ten days time, on August 3 to be precise, I'll turn sixty, and instead of treating it like a tragedy I've decided to celebrate it ... No, no, no, don't say it, I know I don't look sixty, but what can I say, I am!"

I didn't dare point out to Madame that no one had said anything. Because at past 4 a.m., even in the flattering rosy-coloured light of my waiting room, she certainly did look sixty, despite the saucy little girl's expression she was trying to assume, to elicit compliments.

"And to celebrate it, I've arranged a big surprise! We're all going to celebrate my sixtieth birthday ... because I'm closing the Boudoir for twenty-four hours and on August 3 I'm taking the whole gang to visit Expo! A full day off to walk around Île Notre-Dame and La Ronde!"

Thunderous applause. None of us had seen anything of the World's Fair because, as Fine Dumas had told us in April when we opened for business, we worked every night until the small hours of the morning, especially on weekends, and during the day we were too tired to walk around in the sunlight surrounded by tourists and the smell of French fries.

Quivering with pleasure at giving us the news, Madame went on, "Since there'll be eleven of us I've rented a small bus that will pick us up here on the stroke of noon and take us directly to La Ronde. At the end of the afternoon, after we visit La Ronde and, if we want, some of the theme pavilions on Île Notre-Dame, we're going to see *Katimavik*, the show with Dominique Michel and

Denyse Filiatrault at Place des Nations! They say it's really good. And that night, we'll have dinner, my treat, in a fine restaurant … And also, I saw in the paper that August 3 is Jamaica Day at Expo, so we'll be celebrating my sixtieth birthday to a calypso band, eating pineapple shish kebabs!"

Even though we all knew that Madame doesn't like displays of emotion, some of us, including me, nonetheless took the liberty of embracing her, and she didn't even protest! The prospect of a day off to visit Expo brought energy back to our bodies which five minutes earlier had none, and all of a sudden the thought of going to bed seemed ridiculous, in spite of the huge evening we'd just finished. We even overdid the thanks a little, remembering the guilt trip that Madame had started to lay on us earlier, her need to make us pay for the present before she gave it to us. If the only price to pay was a few compliments on how good she looked despite her age and thanks for her excessive generosity, we were up for it! And I would throw myself at Madame's feet and grope her knee to tell her that she's the prettiest, the nicest … She puffed up with pride, simpered like a happy child, feigned humility, handed out friendly little pats and even a few kisses, but half-heartedly, as a good self-respecting boss who doesn't want to get too familiar with the help.

So we decided to have one last drink.

To the health of Fine Dumas.

Who'd have thought it a few hours earlier?

Madame had asked the Duchess and me to stay on the red sofa with her while the others scattered through the Boudoir. We were sipping one last beer, our eyes half-closed. The others had stretched out their legs on the carpet, I'd rested mine on the now empty Lowney's chocolate box.

Now and then I looked inquiringly at the Duchess who returned my gaze, frowning. If Madame had asked us to stay with her it meant that she had something in mind ... Jean-le-Décollé, jealous again, poor thing, had of course tried to join us, but Madame had brushed him away with the back of her hand and he'd left, hanging his head in shame. Was this the end of the triumvirate? The beginning of another one? And why?

Having finished her beer, Fine Dumas let out a little belch that made the Duchess and me smile. She really was letting herself go! She yawned a little, rubbed her eyes, started to get up, changed her mind, then looked in the Duchess's direction as if she'd only then thought about something when it was obvious that she'd been getting ready to do it for some time. We'd known her long enough—especially the Duchess—not to be taken in by her not-so-subtle feints and tricks—those of a four-year-old.

"I've got something to offer you, Duchess."

It's funny, I knew right away what would come next. Because of the night that was ending, of course, but also because it was in the order of things, in a direct line with what we'd just gone through. In the end the Duchess's reaction was what surprised me most.

"I was watching you tonight ... You'd make a perfect hostess, Duchess ... That's why I asked Céline to stay here with us. I want her to hear what I'm going to offer you."

The Duchess had understood too because she turned scarlet all at once, as if someone had dropped a bottle of iodine on her head.

"I'd like you to be Céline's counterpart, but in the bar. I don't know why I never realized that the bar needs a hostess ... I suppose I thought it was enough that I was there ... When someone important shows up, remember Maurice Chevalier, Guilda, the other one, what was her name, apparently she's famous ... "

"Carol Channing ... "

"Yeah, her, remains to be seen if she's famous ... Anyway, if someone important shows up, I act as hostess but I don't think that's enough... Watching you work tonight, Duchess dear, I thought to myself you'd be perfect."

"You want me to come and work here ... "

"That's right."

"To leave my profession ... "

"That's not a profession, Duchess, it's a job ... "

"You mean every night I do what I did tonight?"

"Right."

"For how long?"

"What do you mean, how long?"

"What happens after Expo?"

Madame, visibly shaken, brought her hand to her fake pearl necklace of the same periwinkle blue as her dress.

"I don't understand ... "

"Oh, yes you do ... When Expo's over do you think the Boudoir will stay open?"

"I certainly do! The Boodwar is here to stay!"

"Come off it! You know perfectly well that what keeps the Boudoir alive is the rich tourists! When there aren't any more rich tourists in Montreal, when Montreal goes back to being the little provincial town it's always been, what will you do? Cut your prices for the nobodies on the Main? I know you too well to think that! No, no, no, when Expo's over the Boudoir will shut down, you'll be left high and dry, the girls will go back to the street, Céline will go back to the Sélect or some other restaurant that wants her, and as for me I'll end up back at square one, jobless and over fifty!"

Like every person who has ever cultivated bad faith, Fine Dumas reacted by changing the subject. Instead of responding to the Duchess's arguments, she went on the attack.

"If you want to be a loser, Duchess, tell me right now and I'll take back my offer! I don't want to find myself with a baby who shits his pants and wets his bed, who can drop me whenever he feels like it because he's not in the mood to work! I'm offering you a way out, a way to escape your meaningless little life once and for all, I'm offering you a place in the big leagues, where every night you can do what you love most—make people laugh; so answer yes or answer no, but forget about the future! We don't live for the future, Duchess, we live to have fun, right here, right now!"

She leaned across and murmured in her ear, loud enough though that I could hear, "That trip to Mexico you've always dreamed about ... Acapulco ... the Pacific ... Sunsets ... Exotic drinks ... Dusky Mexican men ... You could afford that finally, with the money you'll make before Expo is over ... "

The Duchess didn't allow herself to get flustered. I too was surprised that she didn't leap at the opportunity as I myself had done a few months earlier, thinking, To hell with the future, let's take advantage of what's happening now ... Especially after the constructive conversation I'd had with her on the eve of my departure from the Sélect, which I may talk about later ...

I earn a lot at the Boudoir, I can put some money aside and the rest doesn't interest me ... I do like everyone who works here, which is most likely the same as everyone who works at Expo: I put aside the rest of my activities to take advantage of the chance I have to make some money ...

The Duchess brought the conversation to an end with one statement.

"I'm fifty-five years old, Joséphine, Céline is twenty-two."

The boss straightened up on the red sofa, then slipped her feet into the shoes that she'd pulled off when she was given her beer.

"Is that a final no? You're going to let a chance like this pass by? You're a bigger idiot than I thought, Duchess … "

Madame had started to move away with as much dignity as possible when the Duchess seemed to change her mind. She reached out her arm to touch Fine Dumas's hip. The boss must have been expecting it because she came to a standstill just in front of me. I was still seated, my little legs stretched out on the cracked, red sofa, holding my beer. She winked at me. A triumphant little smile was already appearing on her face. The Duchess couldn't see it of course. And once again Fine Dumas was sure that she was going to win. How does she manage to manipulate us all the time, to win when we least expect it, to emerge victorious from the big arguments and the little ones, the big conflicts and the little ones? It's true that her two specialties, manipulation and guilt, are hard to fight, but she has found a way to raise them to the status of high art and she uses them like a virtuoso: two musical instruments at which she's become a seasoned expert, playing them like no one else in the world, fearlessly and shamelessly.

The Duchess cleared her throat before she spoke.

"There's one thing I can do, Joséphine … Yes, sure, I enjoyed what I did tonight, I'd love to be able to do it again … If I were younger I'd jump the fence like Céline did last year … but you mustn't ask too much of me … You know me, all talk and no action … But listen … I'm touched by your offer, I'm very tempted … I can give you my weekends if you want … I stopped working Saturdays a few years ago, I could give you my Friday and Saturday nights—anyway, they're the busiest ones at the Boudoir … "

Fine Dumas smoothed her skirt as if to get rid of some wrinkles, without giving the Duchess any indication that she'd been listening. I thought to myself, That's it, the Duchess is going to be begging the boss to give her work … Which is pretty well what happened. Fine Dumas knew that the Duchess had trouble with silence and that if she didn't say anything, the other person would want to break it, out of sheer panic, and therefore would be in a weakened position, on the defensive. So she didn't answer and the Duchess felt that she had to go on, even if it was just to put an end to the silence that was weighing on all three of us.

"Do it full-time, I couldn't. First of all, it's exhausting, and then I'd run out of inspiration ... But I know I could do it twice a week, as a favour to you ... I've been doing it every weekend with my friends for twenty-five years, in any case. Listen ... If you want ... If you want, I'll be there Friday night, dressed to kill, a real crowd-pleaser ... And I'll make them spit all the money in their pockets! Tonight was nothing compared with what I can do, Joséphine! Just watch me!"

Then Fine Dumas turned to her with a big smile.

"Okay. Welcome aboard, Duchess! The Boodwar will be waiting for you and so will I, next Friday night ... "

A handshake, a pat on the shoulder and the pact was sealed. There'd been no mention of salary or pay, but the Duchess knew that she'd be treated well. The boss may have flaws but she isn't cheap with her staff, and especially not with her friends.

The incident was closed. Fine Dumas took from her purse the long gloves, way too hot for the season, that she always puts on with calculated slowness, ostentatiously, as a woman of the world who couldn't care less about the temperature or what people might say. Those gloves represent for her the height of chic, authority and good taste, and she would wear them deep into the jungle or at the summit of the Himalayas.

"Okay, fine, that's all well and good but now we need some sleep! Good night girls ... Céline, don't forget to turn off all the lights ... "

But the Duchess hadn't finished. She coughed into her fist and cleared her throat again before she spoke.

"Can I ask you something, Joséphine?"

The boss frowned as she wedged her purse under her left arm.

"A favour? Already?"

"No, not a favour. Not really … "

"Come on, out with it, we'll see … "

"I'd like to go to your party with the rest of you next week … After all, I'll be part of your staff starting Friday … "

Madame came out with the wonderful rippling laugh she usually saves for the richest clients when she wants them to cough up everything they possess.

"If you hadn't agreed to come and work for me, Duchess, would you have asked anyway?"

"Sure. I wouldn't miss it for all the gold in the world."

She patted the Duchess's cheek before she turned her back and made her way, imperiously, to the exit.

"You know perfectly well you were invited anyway."

Jean-le-Décollé was waiting for us at the bar.

To say that he was a pitiful sight would be an understatement: he was devastated. It was the first time, or so I imagined, that Fine Dumas and the Duchess had got together without him, and he must have thought that he'd just been excluded forever from the triumvirate he'd formed with them for so many years and that I— the newcomer who'd been able through scheming and trickery to depose him in their esteem—had replaced him. *All About Eve* adapted to the world of Montreal whores. He knows me better than that, but driven by his paranoia he must have felt he'd been brushed aside and was seeing himself all alone in his corner like a rat banished forever from his rodent community, with no family and no sense of belonging—a rejection he'd already experienced from another kind of community.

He glared at me while the three of us made our way to the bar. I even had a fleeting vision of a faded and ruined transvestite driven mad by jealousy, taking a weapon from his purse to batter a poor defenceless midget to death—some exotic, jagged knife with a curved handle, the kind you see in action films set in India or North Africa, that look as if they would cause more damage, or at any rate more pain if you're to judge by the actors' contortions, than ordinary blades ... But I realized that was ridiculous and made a friendly gesture as I stopped beside him. I even put my hand on his knee, which was level with my chin.

Fine Dumas had seen it all, of course, and didn't hide her satisfaction at being once again in control of a situation. It would be up to her to inform Jean-le-Décollé, to show who was the boss and who would remain the boss.

"The Duchess will be working weekends at the Boodwar, Jean. She'll be Céline's counterpart but in the bar. That's why I wanted to talk to the two of them in private. They'll be doing the same job, the Duchess in the bar and Céline in the house. It's a thought that came to me out of the blue tonight when I was watching her do her act, and I wonder why I hadn't thought of it before. She'll be a good hostess … "

Jean-le-Décollé seemed relieved right away and he gave me the gift of a frozen smile. But he hadn't said everything that he had to say.

"Then who's going to run errands all over the Main for you, Joséphine? You were glad to have her in easy reach precisely because she could go anywhere, anytime … If she's a hostess she'll be shut up in here with the rest of us … "

The boss tugged at her gloves though they couldn't go any higher—they already covered her elbows and the flabby flesh of her upper arms, which was too generous for her liking.

"Never mind that, Jean. The Duchess will be within even easier reach because she'll be on the spot … I won't make as many phone calls, that's all. And when the Boodwar is empty I'll find ways to keep the Duchess busy, trust me. Anyway, my mind's made up … Our trio will meet here every weekend and we'll have a good time, you'll see … "

Jean-le-Décollé opted for silence, though he didn't look very convinced. And by gripping my shoulder, he let me know that he was sorry about what had gone through his mind during our conversation. He knew that he didn't have to explain himself, that I had sensed his concern and understood his distress.

As for the Duchess, she was already awash in her dreams. She was undoubtedly strolling along an Acapulco beach, scantily dressed, surrounded by men, each one hairier and more virile than the others, a three-coloured drink in her hand, something called Margarita or Pink Lady or some other name that evokes pastel colours and superimposed layers of sweet spirits. The water of the

Pacific was nearly boiling even though it was January, the sunsets killed you at point-blank range, they were so beautiful, and the night smelled of flowers whose existence you would never have imagined. The Duchess had been bending our ears with Acapulco for years, maybe now she'd finally be able to make her dream come true at the end of Expo, the end of the Grand Illusion, when we'd all be unemployed…

Mae East and Nicole Odeon were waiting for us on Saint-Laurent, impatient and nervous. They wanted to know everything. They learned everything, and were happy for the Duchess and the Boudoir. The Duchess asked our permission to come to the apartment with us because she didn't feel like going to bed after such a night. We even offered her the living room sofa to sleep on, which she accepted quickly and enthusiastically.

Five odd-looking silhouettes then set out at dawn towards Place Jacques-Cartier: a jolly, talkative fat man who was describing in great detail some incredible but heavenly night in a place that was incredible because it was too heavenly; three exhausted drag queens who were tottering on their high heels while pretending to listen to his rambling, at the same time hoping he'd shut up; and a midget who was dragging her heels a little.

While I was preparing a bed for the Duchess, who was too hyper and drunk to be sent home, I found the papers I'd scattered on the living room table when I left the apartment. I'd been right that morning—you might as well say centuries ago, so much had happened since then—to think that my rebellion would be short-lived; that I would let the ups and downs of everyday life relegate it to a corner of my memory; that the two matters, regardless of their importance (General de Gaulle with his arms flung up in a *V* and the poor black people in Detroit made violent by injustice and hypocrisy) would still be there because I couldn't do anything about them, it wasn't my role; that they would assume a secondary importance behind the problems, so superficial, of the Boudoir and those who work there. I'm not powerless at the Boudoir; I can act, get things done, as I'd proved all day long. But alas! what I read in the papers will stay in the papers. No matter what I think about it. Or what I wish I could change. I can be up in arms about it, point to those I think are guilty of all the troubles on earth, I can accuse, rant and rave—I'm still unarmed and helpless. A mere concerned reader.

I sat on the edge of the sofa that I'd just opened so I could put on clean sheets. The Duchess was taking her shower. I could hear her singing an opera aria about a holy temple and the appearance of a Virgin ... With just the inflections of her voice she can turn some perfectly innocent words into a double entendre that would make a sailor blush. It's very funny too. And that summed up her life: make fun of everything, absolutely everything that presented itself to her, turn reality inside out like a glove and remake it in her own way, by embellishing or mocking it.

And what about me, about my life: how could it be summed up? Rebelling against what I read in the papers while knowing full well that I could never change anything and collecting money in cash from foreign visitors who came to relax in the arms of not-too-beautiful fake women, each one hysterical in her own way?

I hadn't been preoccupied by my own future until then, I left it—too much—in the hands of fate, telling myself that I was young, that I had time to think about it, that I didn't know yet exactly what I wanted to do and, most of all, that nothing was urgent ... But now, sitting at the end of the living-room sofa in the apartment on Place Jacques-Cartier, worry, or worse, anguish, made me feel a pang, as if an icy vice were closing over what I was doing with my life. I didn't think I was intended for some great destiny, that's not what I mean, I may have been too late to realize it, nor did I think that I was made to spend very long as hostess in a brothel on the Main. I didn't have much education, the most rudimentary schooling, my only passion to date being the books that I'd devoured since childhood and tried to imitate in some ridiculous writing that made me feel good but that I would never dare show to anyone, so certain was I that it was bad. What then? What? Go back to the Sélect? Stay at the Boudoir, letting fate, as usual, decide for me?

I caught myself smoothing *La Presse* with one hand.

Jump into a fight? Side with those who shouted "Vive le Québec libre!" The midget separatist? To try and change the world? But who would want me? Because of my physique I knew that, in any case, I would stay on the margin of the marginal beings the separatists still are? Who might after all want nothing to do with a vulgar brothel hostess in their ranks ... But neither did I want to become a passionaria if I was not convinced, just to find a meaning for my life ...

And when the Duchess came back to the living room, draped in two bath towels that made her look like a figure out of Gauguin, a fat and ruddy-faced Tahitian woman who'd polished herself too much, I realized all at once—a ton of bricks had landed without warning—that for the time being anyway, I could not imagine life without them, without my friends from the Main, the washed-up drag queens who'd taken me out of the Sélect almost by force and whom I loved with all my soul. We make mistakes out of love, everyone knows that, but we can make mistakes out of friendship too, and I thought to myself that morning that if it had been a mistake to stay at the Boudoir with these individuals who'd become so dear to me in the past year, it was a hell of a good one, and one I would never regret. Come what may. It's in God's hands. *Que sera, sera.*

The Duchess sat down on the sofa beside me.

She picked up a paper, looking at the first page.

"Did you see that? There are race riots in Detroit and what do they put on the front page? General de Gaulle! Where's their sense of history!"

Legends of the Boudoir

III—How Intelligence Comes to Man

This story isn't really part of the "Legends of the Boudoir" but as the Duchess is now working with us two nights a week, as she's officially part of the world of Fine Dumas's brothel, I have no scruples about inserting it here. It's a story of mad love, of self-esteem, of selfless friendship and trust in another person, one of the most beautiful stories I know. When Jean-le-Décollé told it to me, he had tears in his eyes.

It all happened long before the Boudoir existed, in the days when Madame still ran a respectable brothel on Sanguinet Street; when Jean-le-Décollé was a neophyte hustler, recently defrocked, who'd quickly been appointed to head the drag queens working the Main because he was smarter than the others; when the Duchess had barely started to hang out on the Main fairly regularly, having long since exhausted, or so she maintained, all there was to plunder on the Plateau Mont-Royal.

One fine day, word was going around that a new chicken had just put in an appearance on the Main; he was breathtakingly beautiful, slim, pale, with green eyes and a smile that could drive you mad; he'd arrived at the Provincial Transport bus station a few days earlier, having come from some remote small town, Sept-Îles or Dolbeau or Rimouski, on that there was no agreement because the grapevine was already confusing the issue. He claimed to be looking for work, but people who'd met him and already seen through him said that he wasn't the type to work for his living, but a parasite like so many others, more dangerous though because he was more gorgeous than most, and in particular, more determined and more ambitious. There was something devious about his gaze, as well as about his intentions. Another one. In him though there was a smouldering violence that was easily detected from the way he clenched his jaws at the least criticism, tightening his fists in his pockets at the slightest contradiction. He could still control himself, but for how long?

From the very beginning people didn't trust him and for good reason, because victims of both sexes soon began to fall: poor girls in search of a little human warmth after years of whorehouses or hostile sidewalks, who'd be found in tears at the door of the French Casino or exhausted at a bus stop; poor guys, losers who thought that they'd found the love of their life when they drowned in a pair of green eyes totally devoid of truthfulness, and ended up lonelier than ever over a lukewarm beer at the back of a smoke-filled tavern. Easy prey—practically consenting victims.

The oldest ones, those with some experience who knew not to let themselves succumb to feelings in this world that was governed by love bought for cash, did better: first they watched him in action, shrugging, sometimes amused at how naïve he was—a guy who is too good looking, who thinks he can get away with anything and is immune to everything—doing their best to comfort broken souls, to glue back together the pieces of shattered lives. They began to see him as dangerous on the day when a case-hardened drag queen committed suicide and responsibility was attributed to him. Tears, sobs—okay, fine—they're always acceptable; you have a good cry, then you blow your nose and pull yourself up; a genuine victim though, a corpse found hanging in a seedy hotel, that was unforgiveable. And so people disliked him and were planning to banish him when Maurice, the king of the Main, sensing in him a seed of pure viciousness, started to take an interest in him, entrusting him with small depraved jobs that required a cold, unscrupulous soul.

If you want to survive on the Main, you don't trespass on the territory of Maurice-la-Piasse, everybody knows that, so people merely asked him to have a word with his new protégé, to put the brakes on him. Which he did with good grace because he wanted to attach himself to the newcomer definitively and because love stories that don't work out have always bothered him.

And there were no more romantic victims of the green-eyed son-of-a-bitch as he'd been dubbed. It was not yet known if he was wreaking havoc elsewhere. But the perverse acts, the nebulous trafficking schemes and the suspicious disappearances increased and people knew right away who was responsible.

The new kid had only been there for a few months and already he was carving out a fairly significant niche for himself; in certain circles people even claimed that he was destined for a great future. But no one knew his name because he refused to tell anyone. Not even Maurice, who simply called him Kid.

And in the end it was again Maurice who, because of the Kid's small size, his stiffness, his toughness, his shit-disturbing nature, gave him the name Tooth Pick.

At the time, the Duchess and Jean-le-Décollé hadn't known each other very long. One night the Duchess came down from Mont-Royal Street as a good neighbour and, being on the outs with practically all her friends because she'd taken advantage of them way too often, and they'd finally got fed up and told her so, she was to some degree in exile and was testing the ground in a new sector to comb. Her niece, Thérèse, had been carrying on about the virtues of the Main for years, but she hadn't yet dared to take the plunge, preferring to remain a Duchess on Plateau Mont-Royal than to risk becoming a nobody on Saint-Laurent Boulevard and having to start again from scratch. There, however, abandoned by everyone, at least that's how she saw it, she had no choice but to look for a new place where she could plant her cross, as her mother, Victoire, who'd been dead for twenty years and whom she still missed, would have put it.

To look chic and to impress the Main, on the first night she'd dressed up as Germaine Giroux in *Madame Sans-Gêne*—which made her look very much like Fine Dumas, though the Duchess couldn't know that—and quite simply introduced herself to Jean-le-Décollé after sizing him up while he was working and decided that he was old enough and seemed serious enough to be the leader, or at least the person in charge of the drag queens who plied St. Lawrence Boulevard.

Assuming that she was a new recruit who imagined herself pursuing a new career, at her age—he'd seen worse and had quickly learned how to nip that kind of vocation in the bud, before it became serious and tiresome for everybody—the former teaching brother took her to the Sélect to preach to her over a good hot cup of coffee. To his amazement she was hilarious, likeable and, most of all, cultivated—compared with Babalu and the Grettas who surrounded him and often exasperated him with their absence of general knowledge and their lack of curiosity. He realized that he'd heard about her and that people said she was the funniest amateur transvestite in Montreal, that she never took anything seriously and made fun of everything. He realized quickly as well that she had no intention of joining the ranks of the hookers on the Main, that she was there strictly for pleasure, for a change, to think about something different. He needed to do that himself and was grateful to her. They spent part of the night exchanging their sad stories, their funny stories, their passions and their allergies. All of which—and this, he couldn't get over—made them seem practically like twins.

And so they got together fairly often at the Sélect, never when Jean-le-Décollé was working, sharing their sense of humour, their likes and dislikes which, again to their amazement, nearly always complemented each other. They laughed at the same characters, swooned over the same subjects, discovered that they'd read the same books at more or less the same time, seen the same shows, hated the same films, loved the same actors—and it wasn't long before Jean-le-Décollé introduced his new friend to Fine Dumas who also fell under the spell of this big baby who was so funny and always had something to say about everything and managed to provoke laughter during the darkest moments.

And thus was born the most influential triumvirate on the Main after Maurice's gang, and not for the same reasons: the trio of friends had nothing to do with money or securing power for themselves; their reasons could be summed up most of the time as silly gossip; as conflicts instigated to disarm enemies who were often imaginary or whose importance had been exaggerated; as vicious rumours in response to other vicious rumours; as character assassinations hatched with delight and just about impossible to counter—for the fun of it.

But another encounter would soon take place, this one dangerous, the kind you don't wish on your worst enemy, and it would transform the life of the Duchess and nearly kill her.

It was around then that Tooth Pick discovered the possibilities of the Montreal Swimming Club. Which as bad luck would have it was one of the Duchess's favourite hunting grounds during the summer.

Beneath the apron of the Jacques-Cartier Bridge, at the foot of the central pillar at the tip of Île Sainte-Hélène and therefore smack in the middle of the St. Lawrence River, now home to La Ronde, an island that had been created so that visitors to Expo could squeal their terrified little cries in moronic rides surrounded by the stale and sugary smell of candy floss, the city of Montreal had in the old days created a rest area pompously named the Montreal Swimming Club by those who hung out there, and it had soon become in the summer months a hideout for gentlemen of all ages, all types and all walks of life who came there for clandestine meetings and to do forbidden things in the enchanted setting of the yellowish foam of the water and the long, brown, nauseating streak of waste from the city's sewer system. Filth passed right under the noses of the brave souls who ventured into the water—though a sign stipulated

Défense de se baigner—No Swimming—and you could sometimes hear a cry of horror and someone would rush to the shore because something that was not alive and wasn't a dead fish either had just brushed against them.

Tooth Pick discovered this lucrative spot during his first summer in Montreal. He would disappear from the Main two or three afternoons a week and come back some hours later, smugly satisfied, with a smile on his lips, an arrogant look and full pockets. He'd bought himself cherry red swimming trunks that were easy to spot against the green of the grass and he decimated the ranks of those gentlemen with the regularity of a Swiss watch. They were all crazy about him and heads fell one after the other. They wanted more? Tooth Pick gave them more. At the top price, needless to say. On days when he didn't go, the Montreal Swimming Club emptied faster and sometimes didn't even fill up because you could see from the top of the Jacques-Cartier Bridge whether Tooth Pick's shiny swimsuit, filled with such promise, was skulking around or not.

The Duchess had heard about Tooth Pick of course, he'd been the focus of everyone's conversation during his first winter in Montreal but she'd never met him because, as much as possible, she avoided Maurice's circle. Already back then, the king of the Main was starting to get pissed off with Thérèse, the Duchess's niece who, when she'd been drinking, was repeatedly and shamelessly responsible for serious errors in judgment and practical jokes, and it was important to the Duchess that she neither exonerate nor condemn her to Maurice.

The encounter, which took place in the shower room of the Montreal Swimming Club, was like a lightning strike. For the Duchess, of course, because Tooth Pick had immediately sized up this fat man, so awkward in his underwear, though nothing could stop him when he was dressed. Especially as a woman. He'd recognized the Duchess right away because everybody called him by that name, even at the Montreal Swimming Club. But not the drag queen who thought, with the great naivety of those who think they've seen it all and who let their guard down without realizing it, that he'd met the love of his life. The handsome young man had said that his name was Réginald—that one name was already suspect; in Quebec hardly anyone is called Réginald!—that he'd just arrived from the country, didn't have much money, was trying to find himself, didn't know yet which way he leaned and that he was relying on the Duchess to guide him. All with gestures full of promises and enticing touches.

The Duchess however had been warned about such things, she was hardened and rather ironic before these pretentious kids who've just arrived in town and lie so badly but think they're credible for the simple reason that they're handsome, and who can wring your heart without a hint of guilt, for pleasure and through simple speculation.

If the same thing had happened to one of his acquaintances, La Vaillancourt for instance, or La Saint-Germain, the Duchess would have immediately understood, judged, dealt with the matter. She would have pulled the ear of the guilty party and kicked the ass of the victim while hurling insults at him. Did she choose to believe Réginald, as she maintains today, rolling her eyes when she tells us about the incident, or was she cut down unexpectedly by an irresistible case of love at first sight, even though she should have realized that a young god like this phoney Réginald doesn't fall in love with an old bag like her? What matters is to know that Tooth Pick exploited her without batting an eyelid, took from her in the time it takes to say it the small amount of money she'd accumulated by selling shoes for so many years, rode roughshod over her and would have let her bleed to death without even holding out a hand if Jean-le-Décollé, panicking, scandalized and almost too late, hadn't interfered when he finally realized who Réginald, the Duchess's great love, was and how dangerous he could be for her.

The Duchess of course ignored any arguments that Jean-le-Décollé put forward about Tooth Pick. Even when she found out who he was. That he'd betrayed her. And that he was no doubt laughing at her on the four corners of the Main, describing their pitiful sexual exploits and divulging to anyone who was listening the inadequacy of her attributes. She was already too deep in the troubled waters of the passion that she'd thought had finally arrived in her life—until then she'd had only one lacklustre love affair, with no real passion, with Samarcette, the dancer on roller-skates at the Théâtre National—to give in without argument to the reasoning, though it was clear, well articulated and full of common sense, of her great friend. Accepting the obvious is not one of her main virtues—to put it mildly—and she closed up like an oyster as soon as her friend tried to bring her back to reason. She preferred to accuse Jean-le-Décollé of jealousy when he was only showing friendly devotion, to dream of transforming Tooth Pick, of curing him, of making him into a saint, for she was convinced, she said, that her love could be good for him, could make him mend his ways, cut him off from his baser instincts, no doubt dreaming of finally being worthy of the great figures in literature she admired so much because they knew how to be unhappy with panache: the Duchess of Langeais, the real one, Balzac's; or Marguerite Gauthier, whose coughing killed her after she had stained handkerchiefs of the purest possible white so that the blood-red stains could be seen at the very back of the Théâtre Saint-Denis when Edwige Feuillère came to Quebec on tour.

One day when Jean-le-Décollé was on the verge of running out of patience because of the Duchess's blind bad faith and masochistic self-satisfaction, he had said to her, "You talk about the Duchess of Langeais, you talk about Marguerite Gauthier, you talk about Phaedra who falls in love with her new husband's youngest son and dies because of it ... Does that mean you're getting ready to suffer, Duchess, that you know that everything will end in disaster, that your affair with Réginald has no future, that you don't really think you can save him ... Is it him that you love or is it the idea of being in love so that you can suffer all you want?"

The only response was a slap on his left cheek, the only one that the Duchess had ever given to anyone in her whole life. And the accusation that he'd made more out of the blue than out of sincerity he would regret several weeks later when the dramatic conclusion of the story exploded.

One night when he was quietly tucking into a jumbo smoked meat at Ben Ash between clients, Jean-le-Décollé had the crazy idea of calling Thérèse to his table, thinking that she could help him pull the Duchess out of her depression. After all, it was her uncle, she knew him better than anyone in the district, she might know what to do with him …

Thérèse was once again on the verge of losing her job on the Main because at cleaning time that same morning, the floor-washer had found her drunk behind the counter. She'd spent the night in Ben Ash's stock of cheap wine after she'd insisted—someone should have paid attention—on closing the restaurant. She was a solitary drinker who preferred to disappear into her burrow to drink. She'd been sick all over the terrazzo floor and had passed out at the foot of the cash register, unable to call a cab and too proud to go up the Main in the state she was in. When Ben, the boss, had finished lambasting her—which was happening more and more often—she had disappeared for part of the day and come back to work around six as if nothing had happened, bright-eyed and bushy-tailed, sweet, amusing, even—and this took nerve—a little more flirtatious with him than usual.

And so she planted herself beside the table where Jean-le-Décollé was finishing his sandwich, licking the grease off his fingers.

"You want to talk to me?"

Jean-le-Décollé pointed to the leatherette bench that was studded with cigarette burns across from his.

"You know I'm not allowed to sit down with clients."

"I'm not coming on to you, Thérèse, really! You know who you're dealing with. I just want to ask you for a little favour..."

"That's even less reason for me to sit down... Even if I wonder what kind of favour you might ask me for... Problems with clients? You want advice for getting rid of them?"

"The day when I can't get rid of a client, young lady, it will be on account of age and there won't be a solution, not even you will be able to help me... No, it's about the Duchess... I'd like you to have a word with her."

Thérèse shrugged and started to move back.

"Don't talk to me about the Duchess! I couldn't care less about that fat slob!"

"She's your uncle, Thérèse."

"She may be my uncle, but she's never done a thing for me, I don't see why I should do anything for her if she's in trouble!"

"Ah, you knew..."

"The Main's been talking about nothing else for weeks! If my uncle hasn't got the brains to figure out that little asshole's game, don't count on me to fill him in!"

"Why not?"

"All of you, everybody, you all say I'm crazy, Jean. Have you ever taken a good look at him? Or her? I've been watching that queen for thirty-five years, I've had enough... I watched her swish around when I was little and my grandmother fussed over her too much and in thirty years she hasn't changed! In fact if you ask me she's got worse! Fatter and worse!"

"You seem pretty glad when she comes here to see you..."

"I'm glad to see just about anybody when I'm pissed... And when she comes here to see me, like you say, it's often to ask me to feed her..."

"She can pay for her own smoked meat, Thérèse, you're going too far!"

"I didn't say she couldn't pay for it, I said she begs me for her smoked meat sandwiches, it's not the same! Sure, she's generous with her chicken but listen to me, when it's time to pay a restaurant bill ... "

Leaning on the table with both hands, Thérèse looked Jean-le-Décollé right in the eye.

"As far as I'm concerned she can croak, I don't give a shit! I wouldn't lift a finger to help her."

"You don't mean that, Thérèse. You most certainly would not stand back and let her die, she's too pitiful ... "

Thérèse straightened her blue-and-white waitress's cap which had slipped to the left side of her head.

"True, I don't hope that she'll die. But it's also true that I wouldn't do anything to help her. Anyway, she wouldn't listen to me. And if she's pitiful it's because she wants to be. We're all like that in our family: when she really hits rock bottom, she'll pull herself up, you'll see. She's a survivor, like me, she's been through more shit than all the rest of us together and she's always got out ... When we finish being pitiful in our family, we move on and nothing can stop us! If you've come to see me it means you've tried everything and nothing worked. Don't you think I know that?"

"This time we're afraid she won't get out, Thérèse ... "

"Over Tooth Pick? Over a little creep like him? Let her, if she hasn't got more brains than that!"

And she headed for the next table where three clients, adrift in their smoke-filled conversation, hadn't called her.

Jean-le-Décollé started watching her surreptitiously while he took little sips of his coffee.

She had the same profile as the Duchess. Not so puffy of course. Something in the stubborn forehead, the round cheeks, the often wild eyes, the high forehead too, the way she straightened her shoulders before replying, and the famous rictus warning of nameless horrors when she'd found the right way to express something, marked indelibly her family ties with the transvestite, the same blood transporting the same vices, the same genes that carry the same madness.

Just then, as Jean-le-Décollé was about to get up from the table, in walked Hosanna, a drag queen from the Plaza Saint-Hubert, hairdresser by trade, who was already regarded as the Duchess's heir in certain circles of the city's north end. Not on the Main though, where Hosanna was less well known than the Duchess because he hadn't had the chance to make his real debut. At the Palace though, on Mont-Royal Street near the slaughterhouses on Frontenac Street, refuge of all the outcasts and all the lost souls from the Plateau and elsewhere, the Duchess sometimes went so far as to call Hosanna "my daughter," and that was all it took for people to see the hairdresser as the next in line when the time came for her to leave the scene. But that wasn't going to happen overnight as the Duchess liked to say and Hosanna had to prepare himself for a long wait ...

Although ...

Hosanna was a bundle of nerves, all angles and pointed elbows and jutting bones. She always seemed to be on the verge of collapsing, as if a gust of wind could carry her away or a heavy rainfall could melt her, but she had an unusual power of resistance that would have been the envy of other creatures of the night who seemed stronger and better built and whom she could prop up in any endurance contest you could think up. She could drink all night without batting an eyelid, she smoked four packs of cigarettes a day and no one had ever heard her cough, she spent hours in costumes that weighed almost more than she did and didn't produce a drop of sweat. She was a bitch, she was ambitious and she was laying out a path for herself with powerful, well-placed machete blows. And well-turned outbursts.

Because she adored the Duchess, her mentor, Hosanna generally did not make her a target of her sarcasm, while the Duchess, who pretended not to notice her little schemes, returned the favour.

Without asking permission, Hosanna sat down across from Jean-le-Décollé in a whirl of swishing lace and cheap perfume.

"Is that you, Jean-le-Décollé?"

Hosanna set down her coffee nonchalantly and moved her head so that her hair, which she wore shoulder-length that evening, looked a little like Madeleine Robinson's when she was upset and was preparing a pithy reply, a woman of the world to the fingertips despite her concern ... Two weird ducks across from one another, sizing each other up, the older one tired and faded, choosing calm and superiority, the younger one fresher but already damaged, impatient to be heard, very close to impertinent.

Jean-le-Décollé arched his brows before responding. Joan Crawford now. Insulted at being disturbed without being warned.

"Who wants to speak to me?"

But Hosanna didn't let herself be impressed.

"I've been looking for you for half an hour. This eight-foot-tall giant told me you'd be here ... "

"Big Paula-de-Joliette ... "

"Listen, we haven't got time to waste on introductions ... I'm Hosanna, maybe you've heard about me from the Duchess ... Anyway, I'm here on account of her and I'm in a hurry ... She phoned me this afternoon, said she wanted to see me and I went over and found her in terrible shape ... I've never seen her like that ... "

"Yeah, yeah, sure, we all know about that, she's got a great, big broken heart ... "

"Don't interrupt, I told you we haven't got much time ... Tooth Pick beat her up last night ... "

Jean-le-Décollé straightened up, fist raised ready to attack, not in the least a woman of the world.

"What? That fucking bastard! Where is he, that stinking louse, I'll give him a pasting he won't forget!"

Meanwhile, Hosanna had drained the cup of coffee sitting on the table between them. If she'd burned her mouth—Jean-le-Décollé always had his coffee after eating and very hot—she didn't let it show. But her eyes were popping as she swallowed.

"Apparently he saw red when she told him she was out of money ... She's got two shiners, she's all black and blue, she can hardly move her right arm ... She went berserk, you can't imagine ... She was talking about death, legacy, she was practically delirious ... And I had a hell of a time getting this out of her hands ... "

Hosanna set down on the star-patterned Arborite tabletop a small bottle of pills that Jean-le-Décollé recognized right away.

"Her sleeping pills ... How many did she take? Did you call the ambulance?"

"She didn't have time to take any ... But I didn't know what to do and then I thought about you ... She always says that you know how to talk to her ... "

"Where is she? At her place?"

"Yes. I ran here from Dorion Street, I didn't even think about taking a taxi ... We have to do something, trust me, I've never seen her like this! I know she can be a tragedy queen but this time it's real, I think ... I really think she wants to die!"

They hadn't seen Thérèse come back; she was leaning against their table.

"You have to go. Right now."

Jean-le-Décollé yelled at her as he got out of the fake leather plastic booth.

"Seems to me you couldn't care less about her."

Thérèse untied her apron.

"What a person says and what they think isn't always the same ... The Duchess may be unhinged but she's my uncle! You said so yourself just now ... We can't leave her like that, she might do something crazy ... Come on, move it, I'll pay for the taxi ... "

The tiny dilapidated house stood in the middle of the hill between Sherbrooke and Ontario, framed by others like it, its twins not in genuine misery, there were worse in the east end of town, but in definite poverty. They seemed to support each other, hold each other up. No balcony. The door opened onto the street. In summer, the Duchess had to put her chair on the sidewalk if she wanted to get a breath of air. After a blizzard in winter, the snow sometimes came halfway up the forest-green door and you could see poor Édouard struggling with his wooden shovel.

Hosanna had left the door ajar when he'd gone so that he wouldn't have to ring the bell when he came back.

Thérèse had looked around her when she got out of the taxi.

"I lived on this street for a while too. Not all that long ago ... Can't say it was the most wonderful time in my life ... "

Then she shook her head, shrugging her shoulders.

"As if my life had any wonderful times since the École des Saints-Anges ... "

As soon as they were through the front door they were assailed by the remains of generations of cheap perfume, bought whenever the spirit moved her, in department store basements or drugstores, always sugary and heady, an oversized bouquet of violets, roses and jasmine that sticks in your throat like the beginning of a cold. On the other hand, no kitchen smells, you'd have thought that the apartment was inhabited not by an obese person but by someone who didn't care about food. The Duchess ate in restaurants. Had for years. Things that don't cost much, that go down fast and make you fat.

They found the Duchess prostrate in her bed, facing the wall, the blankets pulled up to her ears even though the bedroom was as hot as hell.

"I called you, Hosanna, not an army! When I need the Salvation Army I'll turn Protestant!"

All three of them knelt beside the bed from which emanated the smell of a fat person who's been sick and hasn't had time to wash.

"How many are you? A dozen?"

Jean-le-Décollé couldn't help smiling. Her sense of humour was intact, all was not lost.

"We're three, Duchess. Hosanna, Thérèse and me."

Recognizing the voice of Jean-le-Décollé, the Duchess turned over in bed. She was a pathetic sight. The right side of her face had doubled in volume, her eyes were swollen and blue and a weird hissing sound came from her mouth when she talked.

"On top of everything else he split my denture, the son of a bitch! I've got a plate that rattles around in my mouth and drops onto my tongue when I talk!"

For a brief moment all four were silent. They stared at her, she avoided their gaze. Now and then she blew her nose on the wad of used Kleenex in her hand and as usual, she was the one who broke the silence.

"Yeah, yeah, I know how I look. I also know what you came here to tell me. Save your spit. You know that when you can't talk to me there's nothing to be done ... Well, today nobody can talk to me. I was asking for it? Sure I was. I deserve what I got? Sure I do."

Jean-le-Décollé slipped his hand over the Duchess's.

"Nobody deserves what you got, Duchess."

Abruptly, the Duchess pulled her hand away. There was a nasty glimmer in the one eye that she could open, a small, puffy, bloodshot slit.

"No compassion, Jean! No condescension either! No Sermon on the Mount. Please! We're too intelligent, all four of us!"

Jean-le-Décollé was on his feet in less than two seconds.

"That's where you're wrong! Sorry to put it like this, but on this thing, you were anything but intelligent, you idiot! That's what you lacked the most—intelligence! Have you looked in the mirror? Is that the face of an intelligent woman? Well, is it? Hell no! It's the face of a new whore who's too young to listen to other people's advice! It's the face of a novice who's dumb and reckless and immature, not the face of an experienced professional who's seen it all and done it all!"

The Duchess, indignant, sat up in bed.

"That's just it! *That's* what I hadn't experienced yet!"

"What? What's *that*?"

"Love, for Christ's sake! That's what you don't understand! Laugh all you want, call me every name you can think of, strike me off your list of friends, it won't change a thing! I love that guy and you'll never make me say that I don't!"

Jean-le-Décollé sat down next to her on the sagging mattress where he would never have been able to sleep because of a back problem that sent him looking for hard beds. He took back the hand that she'd withdrawn.

"There's one thing you're forgetting, Duchess. Love mustn't be stronger than pride. Never."

They looked at each other, Jean-le-Décollé and the Duchess sitting on the unmade bed, the other two kneeling in the remains of the outfit she'd worn the night before—a dress of the same yellow as a baby chick, blood red accessories, black shoes, all scattered every which way on the fuzzy pink bedside rug. They understood each other without having to speak, they could read in the eyes of the other what that statement had just triggered, something delicate and secret, love affairs never acknowledged that you manage to forget by yourself, affairs that were so ugly and made you suffer, the humiliating compromises, the disgraceful acts of cowardice, the faces once adored now hated, revered bodies that had given as much pain as joy. A few seconds later all four were crying. Without embarrassment. Over their pride so often scoffed at. Thérèse had pressed her forehead against the edge of the bed, she seemed to be praying; Hosanna was still sitting on his heels, unmoving, his face ravaged by tears and snot.

A long moment passed before someone, again the Duchess, broke the communion of shared pain that no one could have foreseen.

"I don't think I'm the only one who's lacked intelligence and pride in my life, am I?"

They blew their noses without saying a word, they wiped the tears that were running down their cheeks to their chins. Hosanna put on lipstick before saying—while he looked at himself in the mirror in his compact, "I've never resorted to pills, you know ... "

Thérèse nudged him.

"Ever try drinking? It takes longer, it's not as violent, and nobody notices but you."

The Duchess looked at her as if she were a child about to be scolded.

"You think so?"

Jean-le-Décollé took the Duchess by the shoulder and held her.

"You owe it to yourself, Duchess, you have to tell that guy to fuck off. Even if you think it's going to kill you ... It's called self-respect. Your problem is, you don't love yourself enough. You have to learn how to love yourself more than anything or anybody. More than your reputation. More than the sarcasm you'll be hearing because you've made a fool of yourself and it's normal that you'll have to pay. A lot. Get rid of that goddamn Tooth Pick like you would a rotten tooth, it will hurt but not nearly as much as if you died watching him laugh in your face ... Move your pride a little higher than the hole in your ass, Duchess ... "

Thérèse placed both hands on her uncle's knees.

"We're here to help you."

"You? *You're* here to help *me*? You always go out of your way to put me down."

"That's because you go out of your way to make us put you down, Uncle Édouard!"

"It's a family flaw."

"I know, it's my family too."

"And I don't need anybody's pity!"

Jean-le-Décollé pushed the Duchess away very gently, as if he'd just placed a huge teddy bear on a freshly changed bed.

"I'll finish my Sermon on the Mount since that's what you think it is, I'll finish it by telling you the hokiest of all the hokey things I've ever said to you: it isn't pity, Duchess, it's called friendship. And as you know very well, friendship is never very far from love."

The Duchess put back on her forehead the damp washcloth she'd just found in her sheets and which hadn't dried too much.

"What am I supposed to do? Burst into sobs like a big soft pushover and thank you for the edifying lesson you've just given me? Take my medicine like a big girl and promise I'll be more careful next time? Swear by my most sacred possession, my collection of Germaine Giroux's old wigs, that I won't let myself be taken in again, that I've finally seen the light in the depths of the dark, that I'm a person who's been resurrected after love, the miraculous survivor from Dorion Street, the miracle worker of the Montreal Swimming Club, the one who bled in the sewage of the St. Lawrence River until she finally realized the importance of pride and self-respect?"

Seeing that she was in better and better shape and happy at the return of her legendary bad faith, the other three stood up together without adding a word and got ready to leave. Jean-le-Décollé opened the bedroom window that looked onto the most pathetic garden in the city of Montreal, a jumble of weeds, burdock and old dried-up dandelions—litter for the neighbourhood alley cats and a favourite spot for their nocturnal encounters. The Duchess never set foot out there because, she said, she was afraid of the countless creatures who lived there and hated her because she wouldn't feed them.

"We'll let you sleep now."

"I won't sleep."

"Yes you will, if you take just one pill instead of twenty-five."

Most surprising of all, they thought they saw a smile take shape among the bruises on her face.

Never again was the subject of Tooth Pick brought up between them.

The Duchess never confided to anyone how much she had suffered during the few weeks when she was out of circulation, but the entire Main, as well as the Plateau Mont-Royal and a good part of the Plaza Saint-Hubert were aware of her suffering and respected it.

It was Carmen though, the country and western singer at the Coconut Inn whom people were starting to talk about very highly, who delivered the coup de grâce to Tooth Pick—she detested him because of his arrogance and his too many, too easy victims. One night when she had just finished an American country song that she'd translated herself, she had turned towards the ringside table where Tooth Pick was holding court in the company of members of the opposite sex and said, smiling angelically, "I hear there's this little stick of wood walking around the Main that's trying to pass itself off as a baseball bat. Though I've also heard that a four-year-old would be ashamed to have what he's got between his legs!"

It was too true not to be humiliating and too false not to insult him. Tooth Pick was proud of his attributes, that had wreaked so much havoc though they were neither enormous nor as puny as Carmen had claimed, and he hated Carmen's guts. He even tried to get her fired—unsuccessfully, because Maurice, who also owned the Coconut Inn, could sense Carmen's tremendous possibilities—and swore that he'd get revenge. But he never spoke to the Duchess again.

As for her, when she finally dared to set foot on the Main again she merely said, to no one in particular, standing very straight at the corner of St. Catherine and the Main, "You girls will all be glad to know that I've had an intelligence transplant!"

(I just realized as I reread what I've written that with two of the three legends of the Boudoir, the first and the third, I've written my first works of fiction. Now I know how to embellish a story that I've been told, to leave my mark on it, to make it into something that belongs just to me, that bears my mark, and I'm very proud of it—I, who till now have been satisfied with setting down on paper problems of my own, that just had to do with my own little self. Who knows, maybe some day I'll try to write a "real" novel!)

Part Two

The Tellier House

The Duchess fit into the life of the Boudoir with the greatest of ease. She became the efficient and devoted coordinator during the two weekends before Fine Dumas's birthday, but a coordinator who stayed in the house, who never went on stage and didn't use a mike. Between two acts, especially if the preceding one had been a disaster, she made clients laugh with repartee that was usually amazing. She improvised monologues in her own particular way, went from table to table encouraging Poles, Brazilians, people from the Ivory Coast, to drink, all the while praising—and not discreetly—my kingdom. Which she claimed was straight out of *The Thousand and One Nights*. She claimed to be the poor people's Scheherazade while I, she said, laughing, was the Scheherazade of the rich. Because I held the purse-strings. They knew of my existence, then, before they stepped into my domain, which made a lot of things easier.

She left it to me, though, to explain the menu.

As for Mae East, she soon recovered, but only after a second visit to Doctor Martin, since the first dose of penicillin hadn't been enough to cure her. I had to stretch out my fake sprained ankle then and exaggerate my limp for longer than I'd planned. The boss, busy with civilities in the bar and mentally counting the money she was making, was completely taken in and didn't notice a thing. Or chose not to—with her you never know.

The night when Mae East went back to work I heaved a great sigh of relief because I was fed up with playing sick in front of Madame and especially with deceiving her as a favour to a careless drag queen who was still, I feared, just as scatterbrained as before she got sick. I couldn't tell you why but condoms were not well thought of at the Boudoir, the girls hated them as much as the clients did and I go on buying them for nothing, as a matter of form, I suppose, to have a clear conscience. They lay around in the medicine chest for months till I ended up throwing them out for fear that they'd dried out and became useless.

During the ten days or so before Madame's birthday, the big question was: how would the girls from the Boudoir would go to Expo? Dressed as men or as women? As the only three members of the female sex, Fine Dumas, Fat Sophie and I followed the discussions with much pleasure, with astonishment even, when we realized how serious some of their debates were. The girls got all worked up whenever the question arose, voices were raised, touchiness severely tested: some, who wanted to dress as boys, claimed that they'd risk being laughed at if they went in drag or even, who could say, being attacked and endangering us, the real women; others, such as Babalu and Nicole, declared that they were even more effeminate and therefore more vulnerable, as males than as females. For Nicole, the mere thought of spending a whole day—and in public—without makeup and high heels was a nightmare, unimaginable. She hadn't done it for so long that the thought of it frightened her. She was at once stubborn and impassioned.

"Can't you just see me? Dressed like a lumberjack and waving my arms around? My ass squeezed into the only pair of jeans I own? Hairless. Ponytail over the shoulder? My hysterical walk? As a guy, I look like a fag; as a girl, I look more like a human being ... I got beat up at school too often to want to try and look like a guy! When I'm a girl I can defend myself, nothing scares me; but not when I'm a guy. When I'm a guy, I'm lily-livered. I think we're a lot less likely to stand out if we go as girls and that's that."

Someone else said, "We aren't going to *not* stand out!"

To which Jean-le-Décollé replied, "We aren't going to hunt for trouble either!"

Then Greta-la-Vieille in her great wisdom declared, "Anyway, we don't dress as girls, we dress as whores!"

To which, Nicole retorted, "You can't go as a guy! You're an old fag! And that's how you'll end the day too, as an old fag: with two black eyes and a puffy face!"

They couldn't reach an agreement. Madame had refused to resolve the matter as she would have done for a problem at the Boudoir, claiming that it was a holiday, and on a holiday you do what you want. The endless arguments went on, voices were often raised and on the morning of the great day we didn't know what lay ahead.

And then a small miracle occurred.

They chose to go right down the middle.

Those who'd dressed as women because that was how they were most comfortable had opted not for the often ridiculous costumes they decked themselves out in on stage at the Boudoir to make the clients laugh before they ripped them off, but for regular and nearly discreet outfits—which doesn't mean too sober or too modest: Marilyn Monroe, yes, playing a secretary; Bette Davis, yes, but in *Now Voyager*, not *What Ever Happened to Baby Jane*... Only Babalu's inevitable Brigitte Bardot overdid it a little with the fifties-style dress and crinoline, pale pink with tiny white flowers in point d'esprit; the crocheted gloves with a mother-of-pearl button at the wrist; the stupid little kerchief tied under her chin; and the white lipstick.

Surprisingly, after all the arguments, you'd have sworn that they'd conferred, so similar were their outfits! Those who'd wanted to dress as men had abdicated without making too many concessions, they wore pants, like Greta-la-Jeune, in the manner of Marlene Dietrich, let's say, when she plays a sharp businesswoman; the others triumphed in what I could call a certain discretion in their dress, without looking like vaudeville performers. My three roommates had had time to talk without my knowing, but the others? Had they tried to surprise each other while having the same idea?

As they emerged from their rooms around half-past eleven, Jean-le-Décollé, Nicole Odeon and Mae East had a good laugh at their get-ups that were meant to be discreet. There was mocking, calling each other more-than-private secretaries, pretentious housewives and—supreme insult—doctors' wives.

Mae East said, "I'm here to tell you, this doctor's wife won't end the day till she gets her pedigree examined!"

When we got to the Boudoir, where a brand new minibus was waiting for us, we found the others, each more doctor's wife than the next except, of course, Babalu, who was playing an ingénue as usual. Four were in pants: Greta-la-Jeune, Jean-le-Décollé, Mimi-de-Montmartre and Greluche.

The Duchess of Langeais, with a Germaine Giroux red wig on perfectly straight and a pearl-grey two-piece cotton suit and blood-red jewels and accessories, had declared between two bursts of laughter, "Today it's the real women who look like whores!"

Which wasn't strictly true, but close enough to attract jeers and appreciative whistles. Fat Sophie was pink with pleasure and confusion. It was probably the first time in her life that she'd been disrespected with so much affection and she was flattered. As for me, I thought I was a very sorry sight in the eggshell dress I'd found in the little girls department in the basement at Dupuis Frères: it made me look not like a prostitute, but something like a badly dressed doll. As for the boss, squeezed into the monochromatic white from head to toe that she saved for grand occasions, corseted to the eyeballs despite the heat and reeking of perfume, she played dowager one minute and retired hooker the next, and obviously enjoyed it: she was queen for the day and she intended to play her part until it was over.

Mimi-de-Montmartre looked like an effeminate barman the morning after a big night, Greluche like Greluche. But in pants.

The night before, Madame had forbidden us to wish her Happy Birthday when we left the Boudoir, even though it was way after midnight. She had also asked us to wait till we were in the minibus before doing so. And we soon saw why.

After the usual greetings, the cries of surprise at the outfits that worked and the ones that didn't, the snide remarks because it's rare for transvestites to praise without mockery; after a show of happiness at the prospect of the day that lay ahead, with extravagant whirling rides at La Ronde ("I want to be thrown up in the air! I want to be turned upside down! But not in bed!"); of fascinating visits to the theme pavilions on Île Notre-Dame ("They say the Czech Pavilion is the best. But you have to stand in line for hours ... "); in short, after a tumultuous din that contained everything but birthday wishes for Madame, as she'd insisted, she asked us all to get on the bus whose engine was already running.

"Go ahead, ladies, step right up, get on board! Hurry and you can wish me Happy Birthday in less than five minutes ... "

A crate of champagne and lumpfish caviar was waiting on the back seat of the minibus. To say that we'd given our boss a triumphant welcome would be an understatement. A few bottles were quickly uncorked, plastic flutes raised, toasts offered to the health, happiness and good fortune of the heroine of the day, who put on a look of false humility, practised in advance and delivered now with great panache. She actually went so far as to act surprised at our excitement and we went so far as to believe that she was sincere.

And when she delivered her little speech—no doubt also rehearsed, maybe even in front of a mirror—it was with eyes lowered, hand on heart and just enough red on her cheeks to suggest embarrassment and suppressed emotion. All that was missing was the muffled sob, but she didn't dare go that far because she knew, after all, whom she was addressing and where to stop.

"You all know how important you are to me ... I picked you one by one, like flowers ... And I can't deny that I didn't make any mistakes ... You're more than my employees, you're my friends. You're more than my friends, you're my sisters ... I didn't want to pass the sixty mark without all of you or on an ordinary work night … So I've decided to offer you the party of my life. We're going to have fun all day, we're going to celebrate, on me, and after that we'll get back to serious matters … "

Cries, whistles, applause. Even though we'd all sensed a clear warning under the flattering words: it's my treat today, but you have to pay me back tomorrow! It was within the logic of her character. We decided to laugh at it while exchanging knowing looks.

Mimi-de-Montmartre murmured between sips, "Believe it, she'll be squeezing the lemon tomorrow, the goddamn tight-fisted bitch!"

And Greta-la-Vieille added, "She may squeeze a lemon, but we'll squeeze something else!"

I had studied Madame while she spoke, thinking that being around drag queens had made her look like one. She wasn't, but she played at being one. Like the Duchess in her Germaine Giroux costume. Like Jean-le-Décollé, eternally decked out like a poor wretched woman. Like me, in my hostess's gown? But I'm not a transvestite, I'm in costume. Is the difference as great as I'd like it to be?

In less time than it takes to say it, a good number of bottles of champagne had disappeared and the voices in the minibus had gone up a notch. Before we'd even left.

The driver, one Monsieur Jodoin, a retired bus driver who was quite obviously thrilled to be there, had already started flirting with the girls, though we couldn't tell if he realized that they weren't really women. But the Boudoir's reputation was well established, its popularity with foreign tourists known all over Expo, so Monsieur Jodoin must have known that we were a temporary and very particular brothel. And he was taking advantage of it by playing the innocent. A little like our clients. Especially because the Duchess, as she often does when she wants to attract attention, was speaking to him in a coarse male voice that clashed with her lady-in-her-Sunday-best outfit.

"Showffer! I've got something to show you!"

Said in a worldly woman's voice, it could have been funny; in a longshoreman's voice, it was weird.

The driver laughed at the stupid remarks addressed to him and distributed winks as he waited for Madame's signal to start rolling through the streets of Montreal.

After more effusions that seemed as if they'd never end because they were redoubled, intensified by the champagne, some non-stop *Merci*s, *Madame*s and some *We're going to have some fun*s that were too enthusiastic not to contain a hidden doubt, Fine Dumas finally raised her white-gloved-to-the-elbow hand and gave Monsieur Jodoin the signal he'd been waiting for. The minibus moved off with the purring of a new motor and under the cries of eleven hysterical children who were starting their vacation.

There were more people on the sidewalk that day watching the minibus drive off than there'd been a few months earlier to witness the arrival of the Queen of England.

The atmosphere for the drive across the city, going north on St. Lawrence Boulevard, then east on Ontario and finally turning right on Papineau en route to the Jacques-Cartier Bridge, was like a party. Helped along by the champagne (not the caviar, which had been judged too salty and which no one but Madame liked anyway), facetious remarks rang out, rarely subtle but always droll. Windows were opened—despite the prohibition because the bus was air-conditioned—to salute passers-by, shout inane remarks, blow kisses. Laughs that for once were sincere—unlike most of those heard at the Boudoir—filled the minibus. Monsieur Jodoin had turned on the radio and we sang one of the summer's hits with all our hearts. Including, of course, the horrible "Ce soir je serai la plus belle pour aller danser," which the Duchess mimed, provoking mockery and whistles. A fat Michèle Richard, who'd aged badly. Everyone was enjoying the start of this brief vacation, these few hours of freedom, to the hilt; egos had been shelved, rivalries forgotten for the duration of a pleasure trip and everyone was swooning in advance over what was in store for the rest of the day in the middle of the St. Lawrence River, in the heart of the World's Fair that we'd heard so many good things about and were finally going to see.

The Duchess had said, "We'll be able to check it out, my angels, if you get my drift!"

"No, we don't."

As soon as we'd driven onto the Jacques-Cartier Bridge we had spotted ahead of us on the left some of the main attractions of La Ronde: Dolphin Lake, where every night you could see the famous "Dancing Waters;" the much-talked-about Gyrotron, a huge, threatening machine that had been terrorizing everyone for months and that the bravest vowed they would try; and a tall mast from the top of which, according to Greta-la-Vieille in any case, you could do a parachute-jump. Apparently. But she wasn't sure. Maybe she'd seen an ad for some other amusement park ... Amid the excited shouts and promises of cheap food and cheap thrills, Nicole Odeon howled, "In my family you can't cross the Jacques-Cartier Bridge without singing a call and response song! It brings bad luck if you don't."

And she launched into a song from the depths of time and a far-off countryside, a song so vulgar that it made Fine Dumas wrinkle her nose, though it wasn't the first one she'd heard, and made the Duchess shrug because she was afraid she'd have to share the limelight with someone more vulgar than herself.

But before Nicole had finished the second verse, we were already turning right to start our descent towards Île Sainte-Hélène where, among other things, there were the brand-new Metro station, the theme pavilions of the two great world powers and rivals, the United States and the Soviet Union, and the entrance to La Ronde.

I was next to Babalu, who unlike all the others was sitting quietly in her seat, gloved hands on her knees, kerchief tied under her chin, pink dress rustling around her. She hadn't drunk much, didn't join in the effusions and explosions of merriment and now and then she took a strange look out the window.

Towards the end of our brief journey, just as we were driving onto the ramp that led to the centre of Île Sainte-Hélène, I had a hunch about what might be worrying her and put my hand on her leg.

"What is it, Babalu, aren't you glad to be going to Expo?"

The question was totally senseless, idiotic even, because I knew perfectly well what her answer would be.

Now there's no denying, Babalu is a special case. I've never known anyone as controlled and predictable as she is. Babalu is a cat who does everything, every day, at the same time, who has organized her daily schedule once and for all and sticks to it obsessively, almost pathologically. In the days before the Boudoir existed the street suited her perfectly because she had her own strip of sidewalk, her hours, her clients, her hotel; the brothel suited her just as well because everything had been decided for her and as before, the only surprises—rare, often pathetic—occurred in bed, in arms that were sometimes timid, sometimes overly enterprising, from which she could free herself very easily because it was her profession, and even that was determined in advance. Babalu also had an ability that I'll never understand: to cut herself off from everything, to act dumb—or maybe she really is!—to empty her head of any intelligent thought and take refuge in something like a vegetative state, absence, indifference to what's going on around her. That is something shocking, because you tell yourself that no one has the right to not be interested in anything or anyone. I've already mentioned my three roommates' lack of curiosity. If possible, Babalu is ten times worse. Ask her a question and you'll realize that she's been gone for a good while; when she answers you're sorry you've asked. Babalu is as fragile as a piece of porcelain and just as cold and empty. Through her will alone. Which is an even bigger shame.

Very gently, she pushed my hand away and didn't look me in the eye. Then, for once, she answered my question directly.

"Usually at this time of day I'm eating, I'm eating on my balcony."

That was all. She added nothing else. Yet I could sense the tremendous anxiety that was choking her because of the change in her routine and the prospect of spending a day differently from the others.

"Relax. Let yourself go a little. Let yourself have some fun! We'll be seeing things we've never seen before!"

"Things we've never seen scare me, Céline. I don't want that! I want my balcony, I want my cat, I want the Boudoir!"

Tears sprang to her eyes and started to run down her cheeks. Tears because her schedule had been changed?

"Why did you come then? You could have stayed home."

She took off one glove, scratched the tip of her nose, wiped her tears, blew her nose with a Kleenex she'd taken from a straw bag in the same pink as her Brigitte Bardot dress.

"I thought I could do it. Today, I don't know why, I thought I'd be able to do something different ... I thought about it most of the night and I finally talked myself into it ... "

She glanced at the trees on Île Sainte-Hélène. The sun was seeping through the leaves that were already losing their green from lack of rain; yellow spots could be seen on the lawns; some vacationers were picnicking, others flirting with the slightest interesting shadow as they strolled.

"I didn't want to let Madame down. But I can see now that I won't make it. No matter how much I want to, I know I won't make it. I'm going to sit on a bench and wait for you."

"All day?"

"Don't worry about me ... I'll switch myself off. I'm used to it."

"But what will people say when they walk by you? You can't defend yourself on your own! You don't look enough like a girl to go unnoticed and as a transvestite you don't look strong enough to defend yourself! We'll never find you again, Babalu, if you stay by yourself ... In a group there's not much risk, but all alone in your own little corner, you're too vulnerable!"

She had to face facts and she let out a sigh that broke my heart. She tightened her kerchief under her chin as if that could change anything: change an accessory to bring back to normal all that's been changed.

"Stay with me if you want, I can try to protect you."

She smiled between two gasps of sheer panic.

"Thanks for your offer, but never mind ... I'll stay in the Duchess's shadow. She gets through everything ... "

"I'm small but I'm strong, you know ... "

"Ah, I'm sorry, that's not what I meant ... I know you're strong, Céline ... But I've known the Duchess longer, she's generous and when I panic I always feel safe around her. I'll concentrate on her back and imagine I'm at the Boudoir."

Monsieur Jodoin had just shouted, "*Terminus*, everybody out," the doors of the minibus opened with a sound of compressed air, the excitement was more intense despite the smell of ill-digested champagne and the air-conditioning that was now scented with the odours of a dozen transvestites who didn't know how to skimp on perfume and who'd been generous with their L'Air du Temps, their Shalimar and their Tulipe Noire. All of it dominated of course by Fine Dumas's Chanel No. 5 which had already turned sour on her skin.

A wonderful organizer, at least that was how she saw herself, the boss had planned the day down to the slightest detail, and she wanted to attack it like a lion: socio-politically. First, the two great powers, USA and USSR, which you mustn't ignore, people said, then the much-talked-about journey across the United States Pavilion on minirail, followed by a walk across Île Sainte-Hélène which we'd cover as quickly as we could: Belgium, Japan, Korea, Switzerland, Scandinavia and so on, before crossing to Île Notre-Dame for the rest of the afternoon. Following that would come the entertainment. Around five o'clock, the show by Dominique Michel and Denyse Filiatrault in the Canadian Pavilion and then, after a good supper in a restaurant she would choose, our visit to Expo would end at La Ronde, surrounded by the Dancing Waters light show, some stupid rides that make you throw up, Jamaican music because it was Jamaica Day, which we mustn't forget and, finally, the Jardin des Étoiles, to attend one of the two daily performances by Muriel Millard, which were also very highly regarded.

Fine Dumas had spread the official Expo map across her lap as soon as the driver had opened the door of his minibus and explained the schedule in long, agitated sentences with no beginning or end, inspired more by excitement than by logic. To our great despair, besides, at the thought that we'd have to race around like lunatics all day long, line up for hours at the doors of the pavilions to be subjected to pointless and most likely sleep-inducing demonstrations of the most useless subjects before we could even think about having some real fun. But the driver, who'd been frowning since her speech began, cut her off in mid-sentence.

"Excuse me, Madame Dumas, there's something I don't understand: when I got there this morning you said you wanted to take the Jacques-Cartier Bridge ... "

"Sure, that's the closest Expo entrance to us, isn't it?"

"What it is, is the entrance for people going to La Ronde ... The others take the minirail that starts on the western edge of Expo ... "

"I don't get it ... "

"What I mean is, all I can do here is drop you at the entrance to La Ronde and park my minibus somewhere along the St. Lawrence River ... But from what you say, what you want to do is go to the other end of Île Sainte-Hélène first ... You'll have to walk all the way across in the July sun if you want to start with the US and Russia. It's all the same to me, but you're going to be tired before you even start your visit!"

Unaccustomed to being contradicted, and even less to being caught out by someone she hadn't even known an hour earlier, Fine Dumas made a face like a spoiled little brat who's just been refused an expensive present. The rest of the group felt relieved though: we already had an eye on the entrance to the amusement park. Even I, who am not at all drawn to amusement parks, couldn't see myself parading all the way across Île Sainte-Hélène in my new shoes before I got to the first pavilion ... We were at La Ronde, why not start to enjoy it right away? We all waited silently for Madame to face facts.

But it was her answer to the driver, an obvious expression of her bad faith, that brought things to a head.

"For heaven's sake! Île Sainte-Hélène isn't all that big, it just takes fifteen minutes to walk across it!"

General outcry.

It came all at once. Protests, signs of discontent, moans and groans rang out in the sunshine of this beautiful early afternoon. With the door open it was starting to get very hot inside the minibus and patience was already wearing thin. The Duchess knelt on a seat facing the boss.

"We don't give a damn about theme pavilions, Joséphine! We don't want to see how they make weathervanes in lower Brittany, what we want is to get spun around in metal shakers and eat candy floss and check out the crotches and the sweat running down the bodies of the guys who operate the rides! For Christ's sake, Joséphine, we're on vacation, not at goddamn school!"

Sustained applause, encouraging words, pats on the shoulder. The Duchess allows herself to go a step further, "I know it's your birthday, your decision, but you promised us fun, not education!"

Jean-le-Décollé was kneeling beside his friend. He looked like a pile of dirty rags had landed on him by chance. His men's clothes were as threadbare as his drag outfits, so much so that you might wonder where he found them: even the clothes at the Salvation Army were newer than his.

"The Duchess is right, Joséphine. You offered us a day off, not a course on industrial development in the rest of the world ... We'll visit that afterwards, if there's time ... But meanwhile let's have some fun. Lots of fun. Dirty fun. The kind of fun that whores who haven't had a day off for so long they can't even remember the last time they left the city have!"

Greta-la-Jeune overdid it when she served up the most hackneyed of her clichés, the one she brings out for clients she can tell are impressionable to squeeze some money out of them, "I don't know if I've told you, Madame, but I've never been out of the city, this is the first time I've crossed the Jacques-Cartier Bridge! In my whole entire life!"

A well-aimed elbow from Greta-la-Vieille brought a cry of protest, "Come on, it's true!"

Greta-la-Vieille pushed her towards the back of the minibus.

"I want to talk to you, back here … "

We could hear the first words of her diatribe, "I encourage you to say unbelievably stupid things to clients, Greta, it's true, but please spare us … "

The rest got lost in Greta-la-Jeune's protests and it ended in tears. Could it possibly be true after all? That Greta-la-Jeune hadn't lied when she claimed that she'd never been outside Montreal? Poor little thing! What kind of childhood did she have? But I had no time for further reflection. Madame had got up, playing insulted as she does when she has no idea how to deal with a problem, "Okay, do whatever you want. You always do anyway. Have it your way, I'll be right behind you, carrying the cash … Go on, Fine, pay, pay, pay for the whole heartless bunch of people who don't even appreciate what you give them!"

Ah yes, good old guilt. And it works, because dejected looks were exchanged by the ungrateful individuals we were in her eyes.

But Monsieur Jodoin put an end to discussions that could have dragged on and on by shouting, "I don't know about the rest of you, but if I stay in this bus one more minute I'll be simmering in my own juice!"

As we were exiting the bus, I heard Jean-le-Décollé whisper in the boss's ear, "Relax, Joséphine, everything's fine. We're already enjoying ourselves … Don't try to control everything, this is a holiday!"

And Madame replied, "Unless somebody tries to exercise a little control it'll end in disaster, I can tell!"

The conversation went on while the girls were starting to look around, already pointing to what they thought was funny.

"Why should it end in disaster, Joséphine?"

"Because I know you!"

"What's that supposed to mean?"

"It means that you're all out of control. Look at them, the whole bunch, they're already so excited they can't stand still, ready to jump head-first into the first error in judgment that comes their way!"

"We're adults too, you know!"

"Is that so!"

"Why give us this present if you don't even trust us?"

Madame smoothed her hair, which was too red to be natural, twirling a lock around her finger.

"I'm beginning to wonder myself."

Jean-le-Décollé gave her a slap on the rear, something I'd never seen him do, and I worried about how Madame would react. She laughed!

"Lighten up, Joséphine ... Try and enjoy yourself ... It's your birthday ... "

Then Madame looked up and said to no one in particular, "Welcome to Expo, ladies!"

What amazed me most once we were out of the minibus was that hardly anyone seemed to pay any attention to us. Not completely because a group of squealing, agitated women always attracts some attention, but because the costumes on the girls from the Boudoir were so convincing, people probably thought we were tourists from a country with manly mothers, if such a thing exists. Like in those Russian films where the heroines are spindly but the other women massive and square. After all, we were in the middle of the world's fair, and all kinds of people dressed in all kinds of ways were around the entrance to La Ronde; a bunch of females with rather odd physiques wasn't going to bother anybody.

Something I'd read in the paper, one of the odd things about Expo that everyone's been talking about since April, attracted my attention right away: American families with everyone dressed exactly the same so they wouldn't get lost in the crowd. Just ahead of us on the minirail plaza were a father, a mother and five children all dressed in a red-and-white checked short-sleeved shirt, beige chinos and a blue baseball cap. Even their shoes, though not identical, were all brown. The parents were pushing the children ahead of them like sheepdogs driving a scattered flock, the children kept shouting *Daddy* or *Mommy*, squirming because they wanted something or complaining that they were tired even though it was too early in the afternoon to be exhausted. As soon as they were inside the gates of the amusement park, they ran to the candy floss stands, parents and children both, and stuck their faces into the pink cotton with grunts of satisfaction. Sugar, supreme pleasure, even at the entrance to an amusement park!

Security officers tried to control the rather unruly crowd, giving instructions to people who didn't understand a word they were saying, directing those who asked questions too complicated for them to handle to the information booths; at the gates to La Ronde the atmosphere was cheerful, made up as much of apprehension at the reputation of certain rides, the Gyrotron for instance, as of excitement or the fear of disappointment. People weren't there to complete their education as in the rest of Expo, they were there to have fun, what Jean-le-Décollé had called earlier *dirty fun*, and they were making it known: loud voices, loud laughter, refusing good-naturedly to wait in line, they pointed at balloons getting away from the hands of careless or distracted children and listened with a scowl to the cries of those already on the rides, envying but feeling sorry for them because they were so scared.

From a speaker hidden in some tree, the tiresome Expo theme song was being drilled into our ears and I knew I'd be putting up with it dozens of times before the end of the day: "Hey friend, say friend, come on over, how'd you like to see, wide open spaaaaces." And who was singing it? Michèle Richard!

While we were regrouping at the entrance turnstiles, Nicole Odeon was pointing to another family of Americans.

"Hey, we missed a good chance to get a laugh! Can't you see us all dressed the same like them? Jean would be the father, Madame the mother, and the rest of us would be the kids! What a great laugh we'd have had!"

And I committed my first joke of the day, maybe to cheer up Madame who seemed to me still tense after her conversation with Jean-le-Décollé.

"Whose doll would I have been?"

I confess it was a success. Jean-le-Décollé gave me a wink amid the general laughter. Mae East patted my shoulder. And that was when I spotted Babalu standing in the Duchess's shadow as she'd told me she would in the minibus.

So there we all were at the turnstiles, craning our necks to see how long we'd have to wait to get access to the delights of La Ronde, when Madame cried out, "Oh my God! The passports!"

The Duchess brought her hand to her heart and exclaimed in the same tone, "Oh my God! Are we changing countries?"

The boss already had her head in the white plastic purse that she was exploring with great agitation, as if she'd lost her keys or a precious lipstick.

"Of course not, you big moron! But they sell one-day passports that let you pay just once and you can circulate all over Expo … And I bought one for each of you … Ah, here they are!"

While Madame was handing them out, the Duchess turned towards the pillar of the Jacques-Cartier Bridge, which wasn't far behind us, and jerked her chin in its direction.

"That's where I first met Tooth Pick."

Her eyes were misty. In spite of what Tooth Pick had done to her, in spite of what he'd become—an unscrupulous thug, maybe even a killer—did the Duchess miss him? Or was it what he had represented for her, what she thought she would never experience again, that she missed? Because of her age? Because of her physique? Because of cynicism, the shameful disease that made her think she would never experience love again?

But she quickly regained control of herself. She squared her shoulders, heaved a long sigh and said to Babalu, who'd been watching her, wide-eyed, "If we'd been here two years ago, La Ronde wouldn't have existed. We'd be standing in the St. Lawrence River with turds floating around us!"

Good old vulgarity once again, to ease a difficult moment. The throaty laughter of ten individuals—because we did have a good laugh—as a poultice for pain that was still acute after so many years. The Duchess had followed Jean-le-Décollé's advice and placed her pride above everything, especially above the hole in her ass, but she still experienced some moments of weakness—proof after all that she was alive and able to feel emotions.

The ticket-taker (and passport-checker) gave us all a very strange look. He had time to stare at us one by one and it wasn't long before he suspected that we were something different from what our clothes might suggest. Either he was family or wished he were but didn't dare: still too young—barely out of his teens—to confront his demons. He was actually quite cute in his little short–sleeved white cotton shirt. When the last member of the group, Fat Sophie, held out her small piece of cardboard, he gave us a cheerful, "Enjoy your visit, ladies and gentlemen!"

And aimed a big smile at Babalu who practically melted before our eyes, like an amorous schoolgirl in front of a grade-nine boy she'd had her eye on for months without daring to dream that one day he'd say something to her. So, I thought to myself, she didn't want to come, now she won't want to leave … At once, we removed her from the danger by walking quickly away from the turnstiles. When she craned her neck we pushed her from behind. When he blew her a kiss, we shielded her with our bodies.

But after just a few more steps, another squabble: the bravest of us wanted to try the Gyrotron, whose menacing silhouette rose up at the end of the path on our right at once, while the others, more cautious or more fearful, opted instead for a stroll, a survey of the site before we got on the rides, a way of testing the ground instead of immediately taking the plunge. As there was no question of our separating, Madame having sworn to watch out for us as if we were a class of dangerous delinquents, we took a vote, after a heated discussion during which the terms used were unflattering and not in the least generous. It was Madame, of course, who served as referee. The intrepid won, six to five, and our group made its way, chattering—the protests were as loud as the excited cries—towards the metal monster.

Madame shook her head, "You'll get sick and that will be the end of the day!"

Jean-le-Décollé put his arm around her waist. They were an odd couple: a lanky green onion of a man dressed in shapeless rags, and a corseted, perfumed and massively fat little woman.

"Aren't you coming along, Joséphine?"

Shrugging, Madame pushed him away, "Did I vote yes? No! So I'm not!"

The Duchess followed them, laughing.

"In that outfit, Joséphine, you look like an Irishwoman we used to see on Mont-Royal Street every Sunday during the 1950s. She went to Mass at the English church on de Lorimier and afterwards, she'd walk along with her nose in the air and never say hello to anyone. The men thought she was pretty tempting. My brother Gabriel talked about her a lot and my sister-in-law, Nana, didn't like it. In the summer that woman always wore white and her hair was red like yours. If you stood beside one another, you'd look like twins—a tall one and a short one! She'd be around your age now ... I wonder if she spoke French ... We never found out ... "

The boss turned to face her. "Tell me, Duchess, did you come here to dwell on your memories and put us to sleep with your stories from the fifties? Is that what you call dirty fun? What the hell is it like when you're bored!"

The Gyrotron stood in front of us. And we could hear the terrified cries coming from it. Those who didn't want to give it a try sat on benches while the others bought their tickets and got in line. The tickets, of course, were paid for by Madame who'd been startled at the price.

"Pay that kind of money to be scared! And line up for half an hour! I'll put a Gyrotron in the Boudoir, there's money to be made!"

To which Greta-la-Vieille snapped, "You've got six Gyrotrons in the Boudoir, Madame, and you don't appreciate them!"

Mae East added, "Maybe we scare people too, but we give them as good a ride as that machine!"

Madame was visibly shaken but she gave a dubious little smile that had the good fortune to insult all the hookers present.

We, the brave ones—yes, including me—watched the unfortunates who'd just emerged from the huge machine: some were smiling, odd smiles, the kind you put on so you won't lose face. Others were green, from fear and from nausea. And everyone was staggering as if they were drunk. All at once I was not so sure that I felt like getting into it, but my ticket was bought, the line was moving fairly quickly and I didn't want them to think I was a scaredy-cat. I asked myself why I didn't leave the line and offer the ticket to a bystander, why I insisted stubbornly on doing something I didn't want to. And I realized that it wasn't just a matter of pride. It was the prospect of danger—the idea of danger, rather. (It would only be in my head, after all; the Gyrotron was just a ride and the thought of letting myself be dragged into a universe I knew nothing about and that was said to be terrifying was exciting enough and I suppose that was why it existed: to sell fake danger for a small fortune to people who would play along, knowing they were safe.)

Some of those who had just experienced it stopped near us and begged us not to get on, it was a waste of time; others said that it was fantastic and that they'd go back and do it again.

Whom to believe?

Here I have to make a confession: I've never liked rides, or anything that goes up, comes down, that turns or tosses you around. As a child, when my mother took me to Parc Lafontaine when there weren't too many people, I avoided the swings, the seesaws, the ladders—anything that moved—and took refuge in a book in the shade of an elm tree or in the sandbox that smelled of cat pee. My mother would say, "Honestly! We should have stayed on the balcony, it would have been just the same!"

That wasn't true. The balcony of our apartment meant noise, heat, the smell of car exhaust; there, under the shifting shadow of the trees in Parc Lafontaine, with my legs stretched out in a pool of sunlight, books seemed more alive to me, more easily penetrated in a way, I could slip more easily into the worlds of Berthe Bernage or Trilby, and what I noticed when I looked up was beautiful, not chaotic and, above all, restful. A little of the bucolic is always good in city children's lives, even if they don't know how to express it.

All that to say that if I agreed to line up in front of that menacing double metal mountain, whose two parts were linked by a mechanical bridge, it was really more to be with my friends than because I liked danger as I'd thought at first.

We were promised a journey in space and a drop to the centre of the earth, no less. Of course my companions—good hookers, all—claimed predictably to experience those sensations every night, several times even, but I knew they were just showing off to hide their apprehension before what awaited them, and I let them talk.

When we were standing still and the Expo visitors had time to get a closer look at us because we weren't being so careful, they didn't see us in the same way. I can't say that they guessed right away what we were—look at me, including myself in my group of transvestites!—but when they heard a voice that was too low (the Duchess, as usual) or when they saw a very unfeminine calf or an overly abrupt move, they would nudge one another, whisper in each other's ears, some even laughed. I don't know if they thought we were part of the festivities, paid by the City of Montreal like sports club mascots to clown around for the line-ups at La Ronde, but the fact is that to my great surprise, I felt no hostility coming from them, no rejection, just terrific amusement at these strange men who dared to appear in public dressed up as they were. Could it be that Expo really was sparking a certain open-mindedness in Montrealers? But how many of these people were from Montreal? If I imagined us at the corner of Peel and St. Catherine, the picture that appeared was very different: no doubt people wouldn't be as tolerant as they were here. Clowns at La Ronde, sure: drag queens on the street, in everyday life, that's another kettle of fish! Maurice's hired thugs, whose job before Expo was to protect transvestites, were well paid to know that.

Finally we stuck together to form a solid circle; we turned our backs on everyone to look inside the circle and talk among ourselves, thereby attracting less attention. At one point Fat Sophie, who had earlier admitted to her passion for rides, leaned across to me and asked, "Do you think they think that you and I are drag queens too?"

I replied in the affirmative and she came out with a wonderful loud laugh that made her whole body shake.

"And just think—a year ago I would have been insulted!"

Half an hour later we'd finally come to the smaller of the two pyramids where people got on and off the rides. There was nothing Egyptian about them, they were blood red as in "horror," it was ugly and looked more like a coffee mill than a ride in an amusement park. Some of the people coming out of it were green, as I wrote earlier, while others seemed blasé. A tall pimply-faced teenager yawned as he went past us to show what a letdown it had been. Then he cupped his hands around his mouth and announced to the people in line, "You'll be bored! They had to slow it down because it was too dangerous and now it isn't dangerous enough! It's like the escalator at Eaton's!"

A woman holding a handkerchief in front of her mouth gave him a slap upside the head.

"Don't listen to him and don't go on that ride! It's a washing machine without any water in it! I don't know what's up and what's down! I nearly threw up my whole breakfast!"

Just then a great chorus of horrified cries came to us from deep inside the Gyrotron and the pimply-faced teen shrugged.

"Don't listen to her! Those cries are pre-recorded! There was nothing like them when I was inside!"

Once again, whom to believe?

I have to confess, I was becoming curious. I would let myself go on the astral journey and then drop into the entrails of the earth. We would see …

Before we set off on our adventure, we were fastened inside a slightly sinister pod looking like a lidless coffin that could hold four persons, two on the front seat, two on the back. Given my small size, I of course ended up on the front seat with Sophie, who was all excited and didn't hide it.

"When I was little and I used to go to Belmont Park, yes, yes, yes, I was little once, don't get started on that, I rode the rollercoaster over and over … I never got sick of it, I could have spent the whole day there! My heart would sink in my chest, I felt as if I was going to die and I loved it! And the peanuts! Did you ever ride in the peanuts at Belmont Park, Céline?"

I didn't dare to tell her that I'd never been to Belmont Park, I was too afraid she'd think I belonged in a curio cabinet …

Riveted to our seats by rather forbidding metal bars, we had left the small red pyramid and with a loud clanking noise, we were on our way to the big one when, unbeknownst to him, Jean-le-Décollé, who was sitting in the back with the Duchess, issued my death warrant without knowing it.

"They say that it's totally black inside and you really feel as if you're climbing up to the stars at the speed of light … "

No one had told me that it all took place in the dark! I should have thought of it: there were no windows in the big pyramid, but I'd been too busy, as usual, looking at what was going on around me to stop and think about what awaited me inside. I'd jumped into the Gyrotron without thinking, I wanted to seem brave, when at this very moment I could have been enjoying an ice cream along with Madame and the others who'd been too smart to let themselves be talked into risking their lives in mid-air at the speed of light …

I'm afraid of the dark! I can't stand being in the dark! At night I need a nightlight and I never open a closet or even a kitchen cabinet without feeling tightness in my chest! I know I'm exaggerating a little, but it's true that I've always been afraid in the dark and that I try as much as possible to avoid it ... So I saw the opening in the big pyramid, a big mouth ready to swallow me whole, with the kind of terror I hadn't felt for a long time. I wasn't even inside the damn thing and already I was scared to death!

Close my eyes? Why bother? My body would feel the jolts and the jerks and the shaking and my imagination would do the rest. So I kept my eyes open after I'd warned my companion in adversity that it was possible I might claw her arm during the next five minutes or that I'd climb onto her like a little monkey on its coconut palm. She simply laughed, saying that there was no danger of the thing going off the rails. I admitted it wasn't *that* I was afraid of, but the dark. She laughed even harder.

"You're afraid of the dark? Stick with me kid, I scare monsters!"

In the end, I have no precise memory of the next five minutes. I see hazy images, I experience some terrible but vague sensations and nothing is very clear: all I know is that I was stirred up, spun around, shaken and buffeted; that at any moment I was liable to be ejected from the pod and end up squashed on the rails or flattened against a metal beam; that I climbed at top speed while whirling around into a black sky shot through with stars that rained down around me like a shower of spangles; that my drop into the depths of the earth, into the heart of an erupting volcano, made me produce sounds I'd never thought myself capable of making, drowned in fumes that I suspected were lethal; that the monster awaiting us at the centre of the cataclysm, a kind of giant crab with eyes of fire and huge claws I'd have laughed at in any other circumstances, it was so grotesque, nearly made me wet my pants because I wasn't expecting it and I thought it was going to chop me to pieces; and at the exit, my nails were stuck in Sophie's right arm and she didn't dare push me away out of respect for my terror that may not have been warranted, but was certainly impressive.

I was not just afraid; I was so terrorized that I didn't know where I was, who I was, or what was happening. I was in a kind of trance that was absolutely petrifying where nothing existed but pure terror. Because it was dark, yes, but also because everything was moving too fast and I had no control over my environment. I wasn't even free to break loose and drop into space! I, who always tries to stay in control, had let myself plunge into a chaos over which I had no hold and it was mainly that, I think, that destabilized me most.

While we were making our way to the small red pyramid where we would disembark, Sophie, after plucking my nails out of her arm, told me with a hint of envy in her voice, "You're really lucky to get scared like that! I had fun, but not nearly as much as you!"

I would have gladly changed places with her. My heart was still pounding in my chest like a broken-down clock, I wiped my tears with an already soggy Kleenex, I tried in vain to control the trembling in my hands. I wanted to get out of that place, to banish all recollection of it from my memory, to think about anything else, leave La Ronde and its evil spells. And our visit to Expo had barely started!

The Duchess stuck her head between us.

"I think I left my dentures in the stars just before we dropped into the volcano!"

She saw the state that I was in and that I didn't feel like laughing, so she withdrew, staring wide-eyed at Jean-le-Décollé who merely said in a hushed voice, "I hear they had to slow down the Gyrotron after a few weeks because it was too scary! Imagine what it used to be like!"

My three companions in the pod agreed that the past five minutes had been gruelling but wonderful, that the sensation was more like excitement than fear, and most exhilarating. If you believed them, they were even prepared to start again, any time. I just felt like telling them to get lost.

When we were all together on the sidewalk in front of the ride, surrounded by those who'd been smart enough to stay on the ground, I was one of the green and shaky ones who disdained the Gyrotron. I was so shattered that I couldn't even answer the questions people asked. Madame gave me a funny look.

"Are you okay, Céline?"

All I could do was say in the same tone that she'd used earlier with Jean-le-Décollé, "Do I look okay? I don't? Well I'm not!"

The Duchess, her face brick-red, was wiping her neck with a Klecnex.

"I tell you, this is one pooped Duchess! But I loved it!"

I was surprised to find Monsieur Jodoin among my companions from the Boudoir. When I jerked my chin in his direction, Madame whispered to me that he hadn't felt like spending part of the day waiting for us while he read his newspaper on the shore of the St. Lawrence; he'd visited Expo several times with other groups and could probably be useful to us. She said that with a greedy air and I guessed right away to what kind of usefulness she was alluding. It's true that Monsieur Jodoin was a good-looking man. And he seemed to find Madame to his liking, because he looked at her longingly and didn't even try to hide it. I thought to myself that he would make an interesting surprise present at the end of this party to celebrate our beloved boss's sixtieth birthday. As long as he didn't think that he was dealing with a man dressed up as a woman—you never know—and didn't end up with a very strange surprise when he didn't find the object of his desire.

Mae East, who had been twinned with Greluche in the pod ahead of ours, whom I remembered hearing scream even louder than I did as we plunged into the erupting volcano, was describing the Gyrotron to the two Gretas and Mimi-de-Montmartre very enthusiastically and concluded by slapping her forehead, "The lava went flying, there was all kinds of smoke, it was simple, I thought my gonorrhea was coming back!"

Surprisingly, we were hungry! Mind you, we hadn't had a bite since the mediocre imitation caviar that had come with the champagne in the minibus. (It turned out that those who hadn't followed us onto the ride had waited for us politely, without ice cream as I'd thought at first.) We set off to look for something other than candy floss: a hotdog stand or a little fast food stand where we could stuff our faces with yummy fat that had no food value. We headed for the Carrefour International at the other end of La Ronde, just across from the Jardin des Étoiles, where every night our beloved Muriel Millard—whom Greta-la-Vieille impersonates so badly, all sequinned costumes and feathers in her ass—sings her tremendous hit "Dans nos vieilles maisons." Monsieur Jodoin had told us that we'd find all kinds of specialties from pretty well everywhere in the world, to which the Duchess had remarked, with a teasing wink, "Like at the Boudoir?"

And it was at the very moment when we were turning right towards the Carrefour International that we realized Babalu was missing.

Madame, who was holding Monsieur Jodoin's arm, suddenly craned her neck to ask everyone, quite simply but with a hint of apprehension, "Has anyone seen Babalu?"

No sign of a candy-pink Brigitte Bardot dress.

Tragedy.

Eleven heads turned in every direction, hands brought to hearts, voices until then feminine dropped an octave. Greta-la-Vieille, without a doubt the tallest person on the whole Expo site, stood on tiptoe and cried out, "Babalu! Where the hell are you? Babalu! Babalu!"

Our very noticeable panic started to make heads turn in our direction. Strollers stopped to get a closer look, thinking maybe that this was a show put on twice every hour, twelve hours per day, in the central avenue of La Ronde, by a company of street performers. Two families of laughing Americans were pointing at us and some Japanese were taking photos.

The show really must have been entertaining: a bunch of men dressed as women running all over, crying out the title of a Cuban song, accompanied by a midget—man? woman?—doing his or her best to keep a low profile and a bus driver, cap in hand, who was gesticulating desperately as if to chase away a swarm of wasps.

All at once, Fine Dumas realized that we were attracting a little too much attention so she called her troupes to order.

"Ladies! Please! A little maturity! We look like a henhouse being visited by a pack of rabid dogs!"

It was then that Monsieur Jodoin quite candidly asked Madame, "Babalu, that's the one dressed up like Brigitte Bardot, right? The little pink dress with the cute little kerchief tied under her chin? If that's her, I ran into her on my way to join you ... She was talking with one of the guys taking tickets at the gate."

Before he'd finished his last sentence, seven hysterical false women and three real ones went running to the entrance to La Ronde, while the one who seemed to be the group leader, dressed all in white and crowned with a head of red hair, reproached him, "Couldn't you have told me before we attracted the attention of every single person at La Ronde?"

We found them deep in conversation at the turnstile. The young man's ears were the colour of Babalu's dress and she'd untied her Brigitte Bardot kerchief and was now twisting it between her fingers and simpering. As soon as she'd spotted them, Madame seemed relieved.

"At least they haven't done anything crazy yet ... "

I was wondering just what she meant by *crazy*: she owned a whorehouse and Babalu was one of her girls! But I didn't have time to ask, she was already going at them, waving her arms, "Babalu! Are you out of your mind? I told you I wanted us to stay together all day!"

Babalu put on the innocent look she wore on grand occasions, the look that makes us want to slap her because we know that she's acting in bad faith and trying to manipulate us.

"There were six on a ride, I thought there could be a seventh one here!"

Madame couldn't stop herself from slapping her on the hand, like an anxious mother who has just found her child who'd been lost in a department store and doesn't know how to show how upset she was.

"They were shut up inside two metal boxes in midair, I knew where they were, I wasn't going to lose them!"

This time Babalu's expression was crestfallen and repentant. She'd stuck her nose into her square neckline and was pretending to be fighting tears.

"I'm sorry, Madame … "

"Why didn't you tell me you wanted to come back here?"

"Because you wouldn't have let me go!"

"You couldn't know that unless you asked!"

The boss studied the ticket-taker from head to toe, making a disgusted face.

"Honestly, Babalu! He could be your child!"

Insulted, she raised her head abruptly.

"He could not!"

Babalu was undoubtedly much older than thirty or so, as she claimed, patting her eyes to make the crow's-feet disappear, and her suitor looked barely out of his teens, so Madame was right on.

"Come on, just look at him! He doesn't even shave yet!"

This time it was his turn to feel offended. His ears had gone from pink to red while he cried out in a falsetto voice, "I beg your pardon! I shaved this morning!"

Madame looked down at him.

"Was it the first time?"

Then he blew up. Which was quite funny given how slim he was. He squeezed past Babalu, went up to Madame and said insolently, "First of all, who are you? Her mother? Because if you aren't, you haven't got any business here! She's old enough to decide who she talks to, right? At her age she doesn't need a chaperone and you can't claim that she does!"

Fine Dumas didn't move a hair. She was shorter than he was and she had to raise her head to look him in the eye. She held his gaze for a long moment, then said, "I'm more than her mother, little boy, I'm her protector! And I'm not afraid of a young punk like you! Even if you offer her undying love while you're tearing a ticket for Expo! Babalu is old enough to be your mother, but she has the brains of a four-year-old and she needs to be protected against the idiotic things she's liable to do every day of her life! And that's what I do, among other things."

Unimpressed, he faced up to her with quite exemplary courage.

"I don't want to marry your Babalu!"

"I'm well aware of what you want from her ... Did she tell you how much it costs?"

Madame was going too far. Shocked, Babalu pulled back several feet and took refuge in Fat Sophie's arms. I felt as if I were watching the final scene in a nasty melodrama: the wicked stepmother was going to win against the sweet little loving couple unless someone intervened. And so as usual, I went over and tried to calm things down. The boss raised her hand in my direction without looking at me.

"Céline, stay out of this! I know what you want to do and this is not the time, believe me!"

Then she placed her index finger on the tip of the young man's nose.

"You don't know who you're dealing with because if you did, you'd go in your pants! Babalu is called *hands off*! Understand? I know you find her to your liking, I know that she finds you to her liking, but she isn't free and she won't be for a hell of a long time either! So go back and tear your tickets to pay for your university education if you don't want to see your future compromised! Because believe me, young man, I could do that!"

It was the first time I'd seen Madame so close to being truly violent and I was stunned. Of course I'd heard about her famous fits of temper that were so often unfair, about the sheer terror she caused in those whom she threatened seriously, but so far I'd never witnessed a scene like this. It was impressive and it was also terrifying: at the heart of the icy chill in the tone of voice she used with the young man, you could sense a raging fire, an inflexible will, an absence of scruples a lot more terrible even than the Gyrotron, because the danger was genuine. She was no longer the mother worried about her missing child, she was the owner of a flock of hookers who was talking business. She was the red light district, the Main, the shady world of Montreal, who would do anything to protect her work force. And he understood right away. Within a few seconds we saw him go white, then he returned to his turnstile without even glancing in Babalu's direction. He knew that he'd made the right choice, that he would avoid calamity.

Babalu left Sophie's arms and joined me.

"See what happens when my routine is upset?"

All that had, of course, cast a chill over the party. Madame sensed it and I saw her make an effort to restore the cheerful mood that had been there since morning. She waved the group away from the turnstiles with a smile that we all knew was phoney but that we'd decided to interpret as genuine, out of weakness. How were we going to survive till the end of a day that had got off to such a bad start? Silence, a rare commodity among drag queens, had fallen over us and we were now moving along like zombies.

Monsieur Jodoin was also seeing Fine Dumas differently and he stood some distance from her, out of reach, in a way.

Madame had her arm around Babalu's shoulder.

"I'm sorry, Babalu dear, but you have to understand, I was so worried! Don't do that again, stay with the rest of us ... "

The Duchess gestured towards the pointed white canvas roofs of the Carrefour International that stood out at the other end of La Ronde.

"I was hungry before, imagine how I feel now!"

We devoured huge quantities of German sausages, looking at the gorgeous old carrousel set up at the very centre of the Carrefour

International, a nineteenth-century antique imported from Belgium apparently, which was delighting children of all ages. The crowd was moving around the carrousel, holding paper plates loaded with Hawaiian or British or Czech dishes ... The food streamed with grease that stained fingers and then trickled down forearms; you had to bend double to eat, but that was part of discovering the *international gastronomy* advertised in the official Expo program and nobody minded. After all, it's as interesting to know other nations' fast food as their fancy cuisine. Even more, I imagine, where the English are concerned. Lips glistened, chins were smudged, clothes already showed fresh grease stains that might never dry and everyone was smiling contentedly. At La Ronde the subject of calories was banned from conversation.

I had chosen the cervelas from West Germany because I'd never eaten one and the other sausages, darker than the ones that we eat here and advertised as spicier, I imagined were too heavy ... Accompanied by sauerkraut, which I'd also never tried—not the fresh kind anyway—and a cold beer, it was delicious, though rather copious as a noon meal for me. The juniper berries burst when I bit into them, they burned just enough to be pleasant and the hot mustard warmed your palate very nicely.

I won't repeat here my friends' smutty remarks at the display of sausages, indecent remarks crude enough to damage their reputations. I'll just say that they gave them the names of clients ... especially the smallest ones. As for the Duchess, she seemed to have taken Babalu under her wing and, for once, she wasn't one of those making stupid cracks.

The three of us—the Duchess, Babalu and I—were sitting on a wooden bench, watching the carrousel while we finished eating. It was so delicious that I licked my fingers before wiping them on my paper napkin.

"That's what we should have got on before ... "

The Duchess collected our dirty plates and empty paper cups and reached out her arm to drop them in a garbage can at the end of our bench.

"Carrousels are for wimps, Céline ... "

"First of all, I know I'm a wimp and I'll say again that it's the most I can take of things that go in circles and shake you up ... If I'd known there was a carrousel here, I'd have gladly left you at the Gyrotron and come here to get some fresh air with the five-year-olds."

Babalu, who had tied her kerchief under her chin again, didn't seem to be following the conversation. The Duchess was growing impatient and she heaved a sigh that spoke eloquently of her growing exasperation.

"For Christ's sake, Babalu, I hope you aren't going to claim you've got a broken heart! You talked with that guy for fifteen minutes! Don't tell me you were ready to start a new life with him, he'd have bored you to death before the end of the day! He's a student, Babalu, he goes to university, what would you have talked about once the deed was done?"

Babalu merely tightened the knot in her kerchief.

"For once I did something on impulse ... I knew I shouldn't ... I told you, Céline, that I'd be better off on a bench waiting for the rest of you ... "

Meanwhile, a little farther away, Madame was trying to regain the confidence of Monsieur Jodoin with those regal airs and that rippling, nervous laugh that sounds so terrible. But the minibus driver was resisting. He seemed a little alarmed, as if he'd just found something very ugly at the bottom of a pretty box.

We'd finished eating and nothing was happening. It was barely 2 p.m. and boredom was already showing its chilly nose in our group, which was usually in such high spirits. Even Fine Dumas seemed not to know what to do about this strange day that had got off to such a good start. I was afraid that she'd resort to blackmail, as usual, that she would lapse into bad faith and blame it all on us:

her ruined birthday party, the visit to Expo endangered by her totally pointless anger that had brought nothing but discontent and displeasure.

But no.

All at once, her energy seemed to come back. She raised her shoulders, put back a lock of hair that hadn't moved and declared with little bells in her voice, "All right! Ladies, I know it's a little hard to stay alert after a heavy meal like we've just had ... And I know that you'd rather take a fifteen-minute nap than go on with our visit, but we mustn't forget that other rides are waiting for us. We've hardly seen anything of La Ronde!"

So it wasn't our fault, our heavy meal was to blame! We were content with that better-than-nothing and we gathered our energies to show a semblance of enthusiasm.

Fine Dumas was right about one thing: an amusement park is made to be seen at night. In the August sunlight, with no shade because the island had just been pulled out of the St. Lawrence, and the trees, of which there weren't many and had been planted only recently, did not create any. La Ronde was beginning to look like a forced carnival and even more, an amusement park too new to have had time to reach its cruising speed. Everything was excessively coloured, the fresh paint glistened aggressively because it was so new, the rides glistened with their chrome plating, the firing ranges and all the candy stands seemed out of place without their coloured lights and the complicity of the night; even the visitors' pleasure seemed false because shrieking with horror in the sunlight is unnatural. There was a smell of stale fat, sweat and sugar; children were crying because they were hot; mothers were getting impatient; fathers were threatening spankings or a return to the hotel. We were there to enjoy ourselves but the heat and the noise were too weighty and we soon lost interest in what was around us. After no more than an hour, I wanted to leave the place and never come back.

And I wasn't the only one.

Boredom was decimating our ranks.

Makeup was starting to run, my companions were fanning themselves as best they could with magazines they'd found here and there, cries of rapture at the sight of a ride or a boutique were becoming rare, even Madame, frustrated and on the verge of panic, was looking around for something interesting to do.

Babalu took refuge in the Duchess's shadow, the two Gretas had linked arms as if to give each other courage, Jean-le-Décollé had been looking after Madame ever since Monsieur Jodoin had started to avoid her, Mimi-de-Montmartre, Mae East, Greluche and Fat Sophie were moving together in a single compact group, as if they needed mutual support to keep going. As for me, I limped along behind all the others, cursing inwardly because I'd wanted to have fun and I hadn't!

Like La Ronde, drag queens aren't made for daylight and like it, they can easily look out of place. People were staring at us less sympathetically now, weren't being mistaken for a clown act working for Expo, we even heard the occasional nasty crack or contemptuous laugh. We'd chosen the easy entertainment of the amusement park over the rather dry educational events in the theme pavilions and we were all starting to regret it. Madame was kind enough not to say I told you so and we were overdoing the protestations of pleasure a little, in the hope that she wouldn't realize how depressed we were. But she sees everything, damn her. I sensed that she was miserable and despite the demonstration of her foul mood at the turnstiles, I felt sorry for her.

The Lac des Dauphins was just that, a lake, and without the magic of the light show, the Dancing Waters resembled the fountains at Parc Lafontaine on an anxious Sunday afternoon. You can't do a parachute jump from the top of the Spirale as Mae East had claimed in the minibus, it's just a cab in the shape of a ring that goes up a central pillar, then comes down again with exasperating slowness while nothing more exciting happens: is anything in the world more boring than a perfect view of the Jacques-Cartier Bridge? The Safari is also a waste of time during the day because you can see the mechanisms of the animals crouching in the fake tropical forest and the loudspeakers hanging in the treetops. The Jardin des Étoiles is only open at night (at least Muriel Millard could have shaken us out of our mid-afternoon torpor), but the Village with its displays of felt boots and quaint pottery—straight from the Salon des métiers d'art—being made at least drew the hostility out of our bodies and woke us up for a few minutes: my friends made some of their all-time best bitchy remarks and we had a good laugh.

Jean-le-Décollé, pointing to a black pottery plate: "Look, the Duchess's daytime wig! Do you warm it up in the oven before you screw it on your head every morning, Duchess?"

The Duchess, spying a macramé plant-hanger: "Look, Jean-le-Décollé's new winter coat! I thought you made them yourself out of rags from the St. Vincent de Paul Society! But no, you have them made to measure! In Saint-Jean-Port-Joli!"

Madame, handling a blood-red fibreglass ashtray: "Look at this, the backsides of the two of you if you don't stop bitching!"

We sampled local cheeses—Yuck!—and attempts at fermentation christened very ostentatiously *vins québécois* that tasted like cold horse piss. The Europeans erupted with cries of horror even more piercing than ours and for once they were right.

There was one moment of genuine pleasure though on this afternoon when everything was going badly: the Prague theatre's Laterna Magika which drew cries of joy, because what we saw was so glorious: the characters who seemed to emerge from the screen, the blend of film and theatre thrilled us. The Laterna Magika alone was worth the trip.

And so, before I carry on too long, let's say that the afternoon passed with exasperating sluggishness and that we got to the other end of Île Sainte-Hélène around half-past four in front of the nearly empty marina where in everybody's opinion none of the sailors was worth the trouble of turning your head to check on a round butt or a bulging thigh. Very few boats were moored there, in fact. There's nothing sadder than an empty marina; it was as if something had just ended and everyone had gone home.

Still, we pretended to be excited for Madame, who wasn't fooled and quickly put an end to our inflated exclamations. "Everybody's here for once? Good. We have to be at the Canadian Pavilion an hour before Dodo and Denyse's show if we want to get tickets ... And it starts at six-fifteen ... Does anybody know where the Canadian Pavilion is?"

Monsieur Jodoin raised a finger. "It's totally at the other end of Expo."

"The other end of Île Sainte-Hélène?"

"Uh-uh, a lot farther than that. At the other end of Île Notre-Dame ... "

"And I assume it's a long walk?"

The bus driver coughed into his fist, turning red. "Well, it's ... Yes, sure, it's a long way on foot ... I'm sorry, everybody, but I made a mistake when we got here ... I thought about it too late and you were already inside La Ronde ... "

Feeling another disaster on the way, Madame tightened one of her earrings that didn't need it.

"Okay ... Now what ... "

Monsieur Jodoin seemed more and more embarrassed. "Look, I told you at the beginning of the afternoon that to get to the pavilions on Île Sainte-Hélène you had to walk ... That wasn't true ... I made a mistake ... "

We looked at one another, frowning. Madame went up to him, fists on her hips—nonexistent, since she's built like a barrel.

"Are you saying you could have driven us there in the minibus?"

Monsieur Jodoin threw up his arms in protest.

"No, no, no ... It's actually because I drive a minibus that I didn't think about it right away, I suppose. You could have taken public transportation."

He pointed up to the little train filled with blissful, smiling tourists zipping by above our heads.

Madame stretched up on tiptoe so that her eyes would be level with the driver's.

"We could have taken that thing? And not had to walk?"

Monsieur Jodoin coughed into his fist again.

"No, not that one ... That one just goes around La Ronde. But there's another one called La Balade that circles Île Sainte-Hélène ... "

The boss was ashen-faced with rage. She had changed her plans for this festive day because of what he'd told her and now he was confessing that everything could have been the way she'd wanted.

"Is there another one too?"

"Yes ... A bigger one ... It goes along the road that crosses the island ... Mind you, it's not a suspended train, just a regular little one on tires ... Anyway, if the whole bunch of you had started walking you would have realized it and taken the train ... "

She brought her hand to her heart as if he'd stabbed her. "If it goes on like this you'll be blaming it all on us, you'll be telling us it's our fault!"

For once someone was using her own strategy to get out of a bad situation and the boss didn't see it!

It was obvious that Monsieur Jodoin didn't know what to reply. The poor man was practically shaking at the sight of Fine Dumas's threatening expression, his neck was sweating heavily and his mouth was dry. He saw the moment coming when she would threaten him as she'd threatened the ticket-taker earlier.

"No, no, Madame Dumas, that's not it at all ... Look ... There's a minirail station not far from here, next to the marina ... We'll take it to the end—the entrance to La Ronde. And then we won't need to take La Balade to cross Île Sainte-Hélène, we don't go that way ... But there's a big train that travels all around Expo ... It's called the Expo-Express ... There's a station at the entrance to La Ronde."

Fine Dumas turned her back and headed for the minirail station he'd just pointed to. "I can't follow you, Monsieur Jodoin, there are too many trains and minrails and Balades in your story ... Show us the way, we'll follow you ... "

And the flock of geese fell in behind Madame. If we'd been asked to vote at that moment we would all have chosen to go back to Montreal, open the Boudoir and spend an evening like any other, serving up relief to a regiment of tourists of all origins and colours; it would be less tiring than a visit to Expo!

Babalu was standing between the Duchess and me. She raised her head and jerked her chin in the direction of the minirail.

"I could have spent the whole day on that ... It goes around and around ... "

Before she boarded the minirail, Madame tightened her other earring that didn't need it either.

"What a goddamn idiot!"

Crossing Île Sainte-Hélène on a suspended train was the second best moment of the afternoon, after the Laterna Magika. Seen from above and crossed quickly, the amusement park looked less ugly, the visitors less ridiculous. And the cool breeze, besides dissipating the smell of greasy food, made everyone feel good. Armed with their lipsticks and compacts, the transvestites had time to put their faces on, not completely but enough to reassure them. The real women, including me, fanned ourselves with whatever came to hand and didn't bother to check the state of our faces; it was less important for us than for the others, I imagine. Monsieur Jodoin was ashamed and looking pitiful in his corner. When we got close to the Gyrotron everyone booed in unison, even those who'd claimed that they'd enjoyed it.

The minirail station was beside the entrance to La Ronde and as we got out of our convoy, we could see the poor ticket-taker who kept craning his neck. He seemed to be watching for Babalu's return, in the hope of intercepting her, I suppose. Had he already forgotten the terror that Madame had inspired in him earlier? But he hadn't thought of keeping an eye on the minirail and we snuck out of La Ronde without his seeing us. Babalu, with the boss looking daggers at her, didn't even glance his way. Had Brigitte Bardot been tamed? I would never have thought that I'd see such a thing—the submissive prostitute winning out over the demonic actress. Pity.

The Expo-Express resembled a real train. We had the impression that we were boarding it for a long journey, almost expecting to hear a whistle and to see steam coming out from under the wheels. In black and white.

Mae East said, "Have you seen *Some Like It Hot?* I always love it when you see Marilyn Monroe walking along the train with her pelvis gyrating ... "

She imitated it while the Duchess and Jean-le-Décollé did Jack Lemmon and Tony Curtis. It bore no resemblance to the scene in the film, but we had a good laugh anyway. I have to confess, I needed one.

Just as we were about to board—the line was short and we advanced quickly—Madame turned towards Monsieur Jodoin, though without looking him in the face. She does that when she has something sensitive to tell us: her head is turned towards the person she is addressing, but not her eyes.

"I've thought it over, Monsieur Jodoin ... I don't think we'll be needing your wisdom any more today ... You've guided us quite enough ... If we keep listening to you, we'll miss the good things and just see things we didn't want to see ... Wait for us in the minibus; we should be there around ten or eleven tonight if we don't party too much ... And if we do party too much, wait for us anyway."

I would have expected him to submit right away, go back to his hole with his head down like a child who's been punished—and like us, because we're afraid of her—but the boss's words had cut him to the quick, so much so that he forgot about his fear. And practically climbed in her face: "I made a mistake, Madame Dumas! One mistake! And I apologized! Everything else I told you was correct! The Gyrotron was where I said it was, the Carrefour International, the carrousel, the fast food stands ... Even the minirail station ... You would have walked all the way back across La Ronde if I hadn't told you about the minirail station next to the marina! Maybe Île Sainte-Hélène too! Even all of Expo! You're mad at me, I can understand that, but when you get off the Expo-Express on Île Notre-Dame, do you know where to go? No! And I do!"

"So we'll ask!"

"Who? Tourists who don't know any more than you do? Who'll have you going around in circles for hours? I'll get tickets for the show while you visit the Canadian Pavilion if you want ... I can be useful! I can reserve a table in a restaurant ... I can take you around the French Pavilion, I've been there at least five times, it's so great! I don't feel like spending hours waiting for you when I could help you enjoy your evening!"

"It's part of your job ... "

"True, it's part of my job ... But ... Look, I'm not saying this to flatter you, but you're clients—all you ladies are clients who're so much more interesting than I usually see! You're funny, you're different, I'm happy to show you things ... Even if you're not paying extra ... I won't even ask for a tip, just the pleasure of your company!"

We held our breath. When all's said and done we were fond of our minibus driver, we'd got used to his being there and we didn't want to lose him.

Flattery always works with Fine Dumas. Always. And Monsieur Jodoin knew how to go about it. Because of his job, most likely. Either that or he'd quickly understood whom he was dealing with and brought out the heavy artillery just for her ... (You have to admit that the line about the tip was a stroke of genius, especially when you're familiar with Madame's legendary stinginess ...) The fact remains that his little speech saved, if not his life, then at least his day, because we saw Madame's face transform as he talked ...

She tightened an earring again—it was definitely becoming an obsession!—and allowed something to appear on her mouth that could suggest something faintly resembling a smile.

"You might as well ... "

That was her only comment.

She didn't demean herself and put her compromise into words, she just didn't stop Monsieur Jodoin from boarding the Expo-Express with us.

She rested her head against a window in the compartment and told us, perhaps to show Monsieur Jodoin that she wasn't totally ignorant, "I think we'll be travelling along the Seaway ... "

Legends of the Boudoir

IV—Resurrection of the Midget

A few days before she left the Sélect a powerful doubt took hold of Céline. She no longer wanted to give up her job, her friends at the restaurant (her life that was so simple, so orderly) and risk embarking on an existence at society's margins—with outlaws, as her mother would have said—in the heart of a cruel and untrustworthy world where nothing is ever stable or conclusive. Fine Dumas was determined to open an annex to her Boudoir, but who was to say it would succeed? And even if she did, the World's Fair would only be on for six months and at the end of October, Céline would end up with some precious dollars in her pocket, granted, but at loose ends and unhappy. She knew that she was too proud to go back to the Sélect begging, disgraced and muttering apologies, so what would it be? Sell pizzas at Da Giovanni beneath mauve and yellow pictures of gondolas at Easter and jolly Santa Clauses at Christmas, or serve over-spiced pepper steaks at Géracimo's, the Sélect's main competitor? Leave a restaurant just to come back to another one across the street a few months later? No thanks.

She had been living in the apartment on Place Jacques-Cartier with her three roommates for several months so she knew how the world she was about to throw herself into operated but she wasn't sure that she belonged there. Seen from afar and occasionally, when she was a waitress on the night shift whose clientele was mainly weird creatures of the night who behaved not like ordinary mortals but like the chosen members of an obscure religion based on black humour and smirking, a world of perpetual partying, a slapdash existence in which nobody gave a damn about the rest of society or even more its laws, had attracted her because she needed a change and this one came along at exactly the right moment. And yet

Céline suddenly doubted that she was made for this endless whirlwind—she who needed harmony so badly.

She had moved in good faith and with a certain excitement into the apartment of Jean-le-Décollé, Mae East and Nicole Odeon on the night of the première of *The Trojan Women* at the Théâtre des Saltimbanques; she'd liked them right away, got along well with them and, best of all, she loved the beautiful room they'd given her, with its skylight above the bed. Still, she had quickly realized how hard their lives were, how humiliating; the injustice of what they had to put up with every day was blindingly obvious from the start, and she didn't know if she would be able to tolerate it, even if her new job as hostess in a whorehouse had nothing to do with theirs. They were going to leave the street for the warmth and security of the Boudoir—and good for them; their lives would be more bearable; would hers be too, away from the Sélect and the life that she'd chosen until then?

She supposed that this concern and these questions were normal; they were hard to live with though and she was becoming seriously afraid of the great leap that she was preparing to make without bothering to think it over. Because even that—genuine reflection, ideas that went against her plans—she erased, censored, in her determination to have made the right choice when she accepted Fine Dumas's offer: if good old doubt landed on her between customers, if she started to imagine what might happen to her after Expo, she simply thought about something else, diverted her negative thoughts and concentrated on the money that she'd make at the Boudoir and the positive side of living in the atmosphere of a perpetual party.

For a while though, she'd been having less success. Panicking at the prospect of ending up with nothing made her feel more and more anxious; she was on the verge of turning around, of choosing the uneventful life of a midget waitress relying on the kindness of the hungry and impolite strangers whom she served every day, when one night she had a visit from the Duchess.

She was finishing one last Pepsi with the night staff. They had worked hard and were exhausted and the conversation was flagging, as it often did when they couldn't make up their minds to leave and adrenalin would keep them from going to sleep. If she went to bed within the hour she would see grotesque orders dancing before her eyes—mounds of food of every kind would parade around her room, ridiculous orders would be shouted that she couldn't understand, and she probably wouldn't get to sleep till early morning, waking up early in the afternoon more tired than when she'd gone to bed.

Nick took advantage of her once again to try—half-heartedly it's true, but still—to persuade her to stay at the Sélect. He'd been reluctant to hire her two years earlier because of her physique and now he didn't want her to leave. He'd become attached to her, or so she assumed, just as she had grown attached to everyone who worked at the Sélect. She was telling him yet again not to lay it on so thick, to stop taking advantage of her hesitations, of a temporary weakness, to deliver a message as obvious as the nose on your face, when who should appear in the restaurant window but the Duchess.

Céline adored the Duchess. She was a fascinating character sprung from the overflowing imagination of a dreamer for whom a small glimmer of hope was a lifeline in an everyday life that was both tedious and meaningless. She admired the courage of this fat man named Édouard who as himself had no personality, but who became incredibly amusing, perceptive and tender when he transformed himself into a fake noblewoman. He had not only invented a life for his character, he lived it. Not always for real, of course—the tales he told contained tons of superb fabrication and wonderful acts of deceit—but he was convinced that it was all true, which was the main thing. In his mind, if he said something it became true and that was the only way he had, Céline thought, of surviving his fate—a shoe salesman with extravagant dreams. He carried his character around with him: in a way, he donned like a precious garment the woman within his body, he followed her in adventures that afterwards he couldn't remember having invented; he soared above a life that would otherwise have been unbearably tedious without his waking dreams. He was taller because he'd become taller in his own eyes and Céline thought it was fantastic. If she'd had fat Édouard's imagination when she was a child, would she, like him, have invented for herself the character of a giant through whom she would have solved all her problems? Her very own Duchess of Langeais, adapted to her needs? She hoped so. But alas, she didn't have his talent and had been a prisoner of her nightmares for a long time.

All dolled up as she would be for a serious date, a little makeup here and there, loads of black around the eyes, a hint of lipstick to fill out her rather thin lips, a tiny black wig on top of her head like a woman's new hat, the Duchess had come to sit at Céline's table while the others pretended they had something to do elsewhere in the restaurant. They all knew that when the Duchess came to the Sélect on her own it was because she had something to say to Céline, and they gladly made room for her.

Over the past months she and the Duchess had developed a conversation that was more than friendly, it was a kind of grave and significant exchange that helped them both to understand certain things and to accept others; a kind of mutual self-help club that sprang from the margins that were home to them both—Céline's dwarfism, Édouard's incurable daydreaming—and that for the young waitress at least had become indispensable. Céline could not confide in her three roommates the way she did with the Duchess because the everyday life that she lived in their company—housework to be done, dishes to be washed, whose turn it was to clean the bathroom, a constant closeness that was too big a burden, that lacked mystery—prevented any serious exchange, a little like it had been at home with her family. She had put together a new family which she loved, with whom she was happier than she ever had been before; on the other hand, she also had some of the same problems as with her real family, nearly all generated by the exasperations of everyday life, a private life lived with a number of others and the risk of getting bogged down in it.

The Duchess had taken off her soft leather gloves, stretching each finger with tremendous care. It produced a pleasant faint sound of furtive sliding and it smelled of damp animal, because it was raining.

"Nice, aren't they? I bought them at Ogilvy's on sale yesterday afternoon. I could never have afforded them otherwise, you see. It's genuine leather too, my dear, not boiled cardboard! It was once the skin of a real live animal! With real hair! That probably ate things that would turn our stomachs … "

She held them in her hands like precious objects.

"They're kid. What's kid in French? *Chevreau*? What's a *chevreau*? A little *chevreuil* like Bambi?"

She'd winked at Céline to let her know that she was kidding; Céline had honoured her with a smile.

"But I have to admit that I kind of stole them. I changed the price tag for one on a cheaper pair. You should've seen me! Joan Crawford as department-store thief! Bette Davis as vicious bandit! I'd stretched my chin, I was waving my arms, I must have had the word *thief* carved in fiery letters on my forehead! I went out of my way to get caught, I think! But the saleswoman didn't notice a thing, the idiot, all that time she was looking somewhere else! Too bad, she won't be getting a bonus for catching shoplifters!"

She was obviously proud of her petty theft.

"I was brought up never to steal. But I was also brought up thinking that men don't wear dresses!"

She erupted in a huge burst of laughter that made heads turn. Céline gestured to Janine to bring the Duchess a tea before she took the last sip of lukewarm Pepsi that was sitting in the bottom of her glass.

"Were you also brought up to beat about the bush before you get to what you really want to talk about, Duchess?"

The Duchess had taken off her spring coat which she must have bought on sale as well, because it was more chic than what she could afford.

"I haven't had time to beat about the bush, I just got here! Give me a minute to unwind my nerves! And get my breath back! And get my motor going with a strong cup of tea!"

"I was just leaving, Duchess. It's nearly time for the last bus."

"Take a taxi."

"I can't afford to."

"When you say things like that, child, you miss out on life!"

She had placed her hands on either side of the mug of tea that Janine had just brought her. She leaned across the table slightly towards Céline.

"Okay, I'll stay."

She had taken a few sips, pretended she'd scalded herself, stuck out her tongue to fan it with her hand. Was she trying to make Céline laugh before striking the decisive blow, to distract her the better to surprise her? She'd only managed to extract a vague smile from her and seemed disappointed.

"I just want to lighten up the atmosphere before I get down to the reason for my visit, but I can see that it's pointless … "

"That's right, stop being a clown and out with it! Who sent you? Madame? Is the deal off? Is the Boudoir going to be just a bar? Expo won't bring in the fortune we've been hoping for?"

"Of course not, where did you come up with that? The Boudoir is opening its annex next week, as anticipated! What a tragedy queen! My goodness, you're a bigger tragedy queen than I am! And God knows that's saying something!"

She pretended she'd been insulted or disrespected, decided to leave before ending a scene: she picked up her gloves and her raincoat, started sliding out of the leatherette booth.

"I'm sorry, I just came to do you a favour."

Impatient, Céline had been tapping her nails on the Arborite table.

"Duchess! Please! You're dying to tell me what brought you here, so go for it, shoot, quit fooling around!"

The Duchess straightened her wig, lowered her gaze in the manner of her idol, Germaine Giroux, when she's about to deliver a highly dramatic monologue that will shed light on the three long acts of various disasters we've just suffered through, then started talking, her voice lifeless, nearly timid. The Duchess, timid! This time it was Céline who wanted to get up from the table and leave her and her silliness behind, but curiosity kept her there.

"Listen … Jean-le-Décollé told me you've been looking strange for a while now … "

So that was it. The Duchess was her roommates' emissary. People in her new circle of friends were worried about the poor little midget who wasn't herself and wasn't talking about it. And they knew that the Duchess was the only person Céline was liable to confide in.

"Stopped listening already, Céline?"

"I am listening, I was just thinking that I should have known it was my roommates who'd sent you … "

"Not your roommates, just Jean-le-Décollé. He's worried about you. Really worried."

"In that case, tell him from me that if he wants a confession he can him come and get it himself! What's this all about—suddenly he's a coward? Is he scared of me, for heaven's sake? He can't talk to me? I'm really not dangerous!"

Well aware of what would come next, Céline was stalling to avoid a conversation that she needed. But not there. Not then. She was tired, she knew she was fragile, she wanted to go home, get into bed, put everything off till the next day or later or indefinitely. It was very kind of Jean-le-Décollé and the Duchess to worry about her like that, but no, she wasn't in the mood to face up to everything that night; maybe tomorrow, maybe some other time …

The Duchess had taken Céline's hands in hers and was squeezing them very hard. The clown had disappeared, what was left was only her legendary generosity, her goodness that always won out in spite of all the Duchess's efforts to be the scariest bitch on the Main.

"I know what you're going through, Céline. I went through it myself long ago and I made the wrong decision. I don't want you to make the wrong decision and that's the main reason I'm here!"

Céline looked her right in the eyes. A single sentence then emerged from her mouth, a question, but without any doubt one of the most important, the most fundamental of her life.

"Staying here would be the wrong decision?"

The Duchess did something so amazing, so beautiful, that all of Céline's resistance dropped away at once. She kissed the tips of her fingers, first one hand and then the other, like a lover who's asking the big question and is afraid of a negative response.

"The wrong decision would be not to jump at the chance you've been given."

Céline knew the answer, though, and always had: she had to leave the Sélect, that was obvious, before she sank forever into the vicious circle of habits so deeply anchored in her that she wouldn't be able to escape. She'd been given the choice, she'd accepted Fine Dumas's offer to become the hostess in her new brothel, but someone had to erase her hesitations, her concerns; that was why the Duchess was here, but would she find the words to wipe out Céline's last doubts?

"Not long ago Fine Dumas, Jean-le-Décollé and I came to persuade you to leave the Sélect and become the hostess at the Boudoir. You said yes. But now you seem to be losing your nerve and everybody's worried. Look ... I don't know how to say this ... There's a difference of more than thirty years between us, Céline. Look at me. I could be you in thirty years. Not physically of course, you could never be as ridiculous as I am ... Oh boy, this speech is getting off to a bad start ... Sorry. What I want to say is ... I didn't get the chance to leave my shoe store, nobody opened any door for me, nobody even showed me one ... All I needed was a bit of encouragement and I'd've jumped over the fence, changed everything, thrown away everything I'd lived till then and flung myself into the perilous unknown. Just one conversation like the one we're having, the advice of just one sensible person with a head on her shoulders or even a drop of craziness in the right place would've been all I needed to become the Duchess for real, with or without talent, with or without a future. I couldn't talk to my family any more than you can, my friends thought I was funny, probably they didn't want to lose me so they gave me the wrong advice, I was totally on my own and, unfortunately for me, I stayed that way. What you're going to do takes courage, the kind of courage that I didn't have, so if you don't want to look like me when the third millennium rolls around, jump! With both feet! And if it doesn't work out, if the Boudoir doesn't succeed or if it shuts down after Expo, at least you'll have tried! You will have tried! You'll still be young, everything will still be possible ... You don't know what I'd give to be in your shoes, to have one more chance to make a choice, even if it's not a final on—because at your age, nothing is final ... If I'd told myself twenty years ago that it wasn't final, that it wasn't true that I was nothing but an amateur comic, but had enough talent to go on stage, if I'd had the courage that you're going to have, Céline, they wouldn't be announcing that Muriel Millard would lead the program at Expo's Jardin des Étoiles next year; it would be the Duchess of Langeais! Guilda wouldn't have even existed! I wouldn't have allowed it! If you screw up, the Sélect will always be there. If I'd told myself that twenty years ago, even if it was kind of late in my life, I know that today there wouldn't be any shoe store in my life! Because I'd have succeeded, Céline! I'd have succeeded! I swear that I would have succeeded! And I'm here now to ask you for just one thing: avenge me!"

The Duchess was crying as though her heart would break; Céline as well.

Paper napkins were used as handkerchiefs, tears were wiped away with the backs of hands, but not another word was said. The silence that expressed their relief was welcome at the end of that long monologue, that deeply moving confession, and they let it gently stretch out between them.

After one last sip of tea, the Duchess got up from the table to put on her spring coat, pulled on her gloves again, taking care to push each finger into the kidskin, straightened her wig yet again in a final attempt to be funny, then leaned across to Céline. It looked as if she were going to kiss her on the forehead, but she stopped at the level of her ear.

"Avenge me, Céline! Succeed! Be rich! Be famous! Piss them off for me, the whole gang!"

And walked out, erect and dignified, without a word to anyone.

On the night of the opening of the brothel in the back of the Boudoir, now recognized as the exclusive territory of Céline and stocked with the most preposterous hookers ever seen in a Montreal whorehouse, when she saw her friend, who looked so impressive in her green sequined gown and her red shoes like Dorothy's in *The Wizard of Oz,* and visibly so happy to be there, the Duchess had given her a thumbs-up and shouted through the crowd, "The future belongs to the bold!"

Fine Dumas, standing nearby, assumed that the compliment was meant for her and she squeezed the Duchess's elbow.

"I know. I've always said that. Our future may be just six months long for the moment, Duchess, but I'll have you know you've never seen anything half so bold!"

(For writing this fourth "Legend of the Boudoir" I tried something new: even though I was part of the action, I told the story in the third person, as if it had all happened to someone else and I was just the narrator. It seemed to me that I could take some distance, that I'd be a little more objective about what I had to tell; I was very happy to step outside myself and watch myself move and act. Suddenly, Céline the waitress was a character among others and I was watching her from outside to see what was inside rather than the opposite. I expect that I'll repeat the experiment because I found it fascinating.)

A long line stretched outside the Canadian Pavilion where every night, a bilingual show called *Katimavik* was staged, starring anglophone comics from Toronto, all unknown to us, and some favourite Québécois actors, particularly the fabulous Dominique Michel and Denyse Filiatrault, whose adventures we'd been following on television every week for several seasons with unfailing loyalty: every Tuesday night from September to May the world stopped turning and the entire province settled down in front of their TVs to watch "Moi et l'autre," the wacky adventures of little Dominique and big Denyse, the little victim and the big troublemaker. The creatures of the Main as much as the rest of the population had become the show's devoted fans, which meant that impersonations of Dodo and Denyse were becoming more common among drag queens—the ultimate recognition for a popular star. I was even convinced that Madame wouldn't be able to open the Boudoir before half-past nine on Tuesday night starting in September ...

So seeing these two idols in person, free, became for Québécois visitors to Expo an absolute must and every day a crowd of five hundred lined up to applaud them.

The few persons we knew who'd already seen the show—Thérèse and Harelip, for instance, who'd come to tell us about their disappointing visit to Expo one Tuesday night when they had nothing better to do—had found it totally uninteresting except for Dodo and Denyse, whose appearances, though not long enough in their opinion, had them on the floor laughing. It was out of the question, then, for us to miss them and we'd walked, or rather run too fast across Île Notre-Dame to get there on time. As soon as we were off the Expo-Express, from where we'd been able to admire the

Seaway, which had been opened by the real Queen Elizabeth in 1959, Monsieur Jodoin, this time without making a mistake, had steered us through the maze, the roads, routes and canals of the island to bring us to the Canadian Pavilion whose wonderful view of Montreal with its one skyscraper had made us cry out with excitement.

We had rushed past the Jamaican Pavilion. A group of musicians, the Dragonaires, was churning out the most promising calypso beats, and pelvises were gyrating on the tiny dance floor outside the beautiful and tasteful Jamaican inn that harked back to colonial days.

Madame, out of breath, had said, "This is where we'll be eating tonight girls! Today is Jamaica day at Expo and they're going to find out at their cost that it's also Fine Dumas's day!"

Cries of joy had greeted the boss's words, especially because around twenty handsome Jamaican cadets were on duty outside the pavilion to direct traffic and let people admire their spotless uniforms and their superior physiques.

While Monsieur Jodoin went to get our tickets, we formed a line and watched what was going on around us.

Before us stood the most peculiar structure I've seen in my whole life: on top of four or five white aluminum pyramids, quite attractive actually, light and floating, was a gigantic inverted pyramid that looked more like a gargantuan funnel than a World's Fair pavilion. It was big, as high as a ten-storey building, it was imposing, but most of all it was hideous.

Greluche summed up everyone's thought when she said, "My God, it's ugly!"

Madame tapped her arm.

"It's not ugly, it's our country's pavilion!"

Greluche shrugged, rubbing her arm because Fine Dumas's taps, even the little ones, hurt.

"Could be, but why an upside-down pyramid? This isn't Egypt!"

Madame was visibly exasperated at such ignorance. Rolling her eyes, she heaved a sigh. We were all waiting for her reply because we shared Greluche's opinion and wanted to be enlightened.

"It's not an upside-down pyramid, my dear, it's an upside-down *teepee*! Or maybe an igloo, I don't quite remember … In any case, it's a *katimavik* which means a meeting place—in Eskimo! Now I remember! *Katimavik* is Eskimo! So it's an upside-down igloo!"

"But it doesn't look a bit like an igloo, Madame! It's a pyramid! Eskimos don't build pyramids! They wanted to pay tribute to the Eskimos by building an Egyptian pyramid upside down? Call me stupid if you want, but I don't get it!"

When she runs out of arguments, Madame often opts for anger. Intimidates her way to success. She turned red and pointed to the pavilion, crying, "No matter if it's a pyramid, an igloo, a teepee or a toilet bowl, it's our country's pavilion and it deserves respect! Period!"

I didn't know that Fine Dumas was a patriot or a nationalist—I'd never even heard her talk about anything bigger than the Island of Montreal, so I realized that she was saying whatever came into her mind just to have the last word. Especially on the sacred day of her sixtieth birthday.

I took Greluche by the elbow and led her out of the group.

"It's her party, Greluche, let her like the Canadian Pavilion if it makes her happy!"

"Okay, but it's so ugly it's scary! It looks like one of Guilda's hats at the end of a show. I think I saw Joséphine Baker on TV with a thing like that on her head!"

The plaza outside the Canadian Pavilion was right in the five o'clock sun; it was muggy, people were getting heated up over nothing and the tension was rising in our group. Madame was off to the side sulking because we didn't like the Canadian Pavilion, and even though we all thought it was childish, we were trying to find a way to bring her back to reason or to create a diversion.

Once again, it was the Duchess and Jean-le-Décollé who tried to save the situation. But without meaning to, they only made matters worse.

Over the two weekends the Duchess had worked at the Boudoir, she and Jean-le-Décollé had started to develop a fairly amusing act that enjoyed a certain success, even if most of the clients in the bar had never watched *Moi et l'autre* or heard of Dodo and Denyse. The Duchess, ever the good hostess, stayed in the room to seat the clients and encourage them to drink, while at the end of a song Jean-le-Décollé would heckle her, imitating the character that Denyse Filiatrault played on TV or in the shows she'd been doing with Dominique Michel all across Quebec for years—the anglophone saleslady in the dress department who spoke the most hilarious broken French, rushing a shy little customer by trying to convince her that a dress suits her when it clearly doesn't. The Duchess and Jean-le-Décollé had seen the act countless times, at the Beu qui rit or on TV or in clubs; it was one of their favourites and they practically knew it by heart. When they forgot a line they would improvise and make it even funnier.

While impatience was at its peak outside the ugly Canadian Pavilion, handkerchiefs on heads or around necks were becoming soaking wet and unusable—Babalu looked so hot under the kerchief she refused to take off that I was sure she was going to melt like candy—at the very moment when Monsieur Jodoin came back, brick red and triumphant, holding up our tickets as if he'd just won the world heavyweight boxing championship, we heard a husky voice, inflected with the weirdest English accent rise up in the middle of the rows.

"I may get a hard time to speaking the French but I should wish you to know, that dressing is a perfect feet!"

Jean-le-Décollé, with hands on hips and tapping the pavement with his right foot, was heckling the Duchess who'd put her head down like a fearful little girl being scolded by a stranger.

Nearly everyone in the queue recognized the line or the accent and turned their heads, thinking briefly that their idols had come to put on a bit of a sketch to help them wait until the show began. Jean-le-Décollé and the Duchess left the line briefly to go on with their act. The Duchess, a very fat and very tall Dominique Michel, proceeded with the next line, her voice gentle and submissive, "But it seems to me, Madame, that the dress doesn't suit me very well ... It's terribly baggy ... "

People were forming a circle around them, leaving the queue to see who these two peculiar individuals were who were decked out so bizarrely and allowing themselves to imitate Dodo and Denyse just before going to see their show.

Did they think it was another act presented by Expo to entertain the people waiting outside the Canadian Pavilion when the line-up got too long, a street clowns' performance like the one at La Ronde, a farce cooked up by comic actors to pass the time while waiting for *Katimavik* to begin? Whatever it was, it was a tremendous success: neither Jean-le-Décollé nor the Duchess were built like their models of course, but the conviction they displayed and the fact that they were really, truly funny made people forgive them for the flaws in their impersonations and the vulgarity of certain gags which they added to their parody of Dodo and Denyse.

What surprised me most though was to see that Jean-le-Décollé could be funny. This contradicted everything I knew about him: his sometimes imperturbable seriousness; his sense of the tragic; his fast and furious life which was hardly amusing; even his character—a sad, sardonic, scruffy hooker who's seen it all. His acts at the Boudoir were among the least successful and the most painful to watch: his outmoded props, his jokes as well; his shrill voice that was incapable of hitting the right note even once; his songs delivered like the chores they must have been to him. But here he was with a partner more comical than he was—and nobody's more comical than the Duchess. He accepted it and left her as much room as she wanted for improvising, like the American second bananas you hear so much about—he was transformed, he let himself go, in a sense he gave himself over to comedy and was able, perhaps without realizing it, to attain the heights of buffoonery. When their act was over, when he left the stage at the end of his song, he became again the Jean-le-Décollé we knew: too serious for the world he lived in and too often cynical. And he went back to his clients as if nothing had happened.

I had tried to talk to him about it one night when I'd slipped through the bead curtain to watch him and the Duchess do their act, but he had pushed me away gently, "What happens on stage, Céline, is forgotten as soon as I leave it."

Yet here he was proving the opposite, since there was no stage on the plaza outside the Canadian Pavilion and he seemed to remember every single detail about their act ... He was having as much fun as a child at the Duchess's silliness—she of course was piling it on for this wonderful audience—and even allowed himself to break out laughing right in the middle of a line.

The only person who didn't seem to enjoy the improvised show was the person to whom it was addressed: Madame. After all, it was to wipe away her four-year-old's sulk that Jean-le-Décollé and the Duchess had decided to behave like clowns. But she sulked even more, content to admire, very conspicuously, the river, Montreal's skyline standing out against Mount Royal, and the few white clouds passing from west to east, while the pair knocked themselves out trying to make her laugh. I wouldn't have been surprised to learn that she was ashamed of them. She was the boss, she'd given them a day off at her expense so they could celebrate her birthday—and she was ashamed of them!

I could have hit her.

The doors to the theatre opened before Jean-le-Décollé and the Duchess had finished their act and the audience for les Feux Follets, which had just ended, started leaving, visibly delighted. They were talking in particular about the finale, when Dominique Michel herself had made a surprise appearance, so amusing in a folk-dancer's costume with a hood on her head and clogs on her feet, to break into a boisterous jig with them.

"She's wild!"

"What a clown!"

"We laughed so hard ... Little Dominique trying to dance in her clogs, it was priceless!"

Some were shouting at the people in line, "You're lucky you've got tickets for *Katimavik*! You'll see Dodo and Denyse ... We only saw Dodo ... and some ridiculous folk dances from centuries ago nobody's done for years!" Interrupted in mid-movement and just before a good comeback, the two drag queens were a little frustrated because they hadn't been able to finish their sketch, as if they'd stopped existing the minute the doors were opened, and they grumbled as they got back in line.

But a certain excitement, tangible because of the nervous tension and loud because the conversations had gone up a notch, was stirring the crowd of Denyse and Dodo's fans; people took out their tickets, some even waved them as Monsieur Jodoin had done earlier, there were enthusiastic *Hurrays* as soon as a theatre door started to open and people pushed more aggressively, nearly stampeding.

Madame—who'd stopped sulking because she didn't have to be ashamed of her flock any more, and maybe too because she had finally acknowledged that the Canadian Pavilion was ugly—was back among us and the entire group from the Boudoir had closed around her like an oyster around a pearl. As much as Jean-le-Décollé and the Duchess had done to attract attention by impersonating Dodo and Denyse a few minutes before, now we all wanted to go unnoticed so we could watch the show in peace.

But discretion was not our fate, nor was disappearing into a crowd our speciality.

An elderly woman touched the Duchess's arm.

"You're quite the comic, Madame, did you know that? But you aren't a real woman, are you?"

The Duchess raised her chin and replied in her stentorian voice so that everyone could hear her, "I'm not a real man either!"

The old lady swallowed her gum and turned away.

The Duchess continued, majestically, "A lady, yes, to the fingertips, to the roots of my wig, to the depths of my very core, but a woman, no ... And not a man either ... "

Just then the doors opened and attention finally turned away from this strange group of gentlemen of a certain age who were trying to pass themselves off as young women, and who might not actually be actors ... But heads continued to turn in our direction, remarks were exchanged in low voices. The elderly lady was scratching the tip of her nose. People must have been wondering about the midget too, who was so amusing, who didn't look like a guy; about the short, fat woman dressed in one colour from head to toe who seemed to be directing the others with an iron rod; about the poor man's Brigitte Bardot who kept craning her neck as if she were waiting for someone who wasn't coming ...

We advanced fairly quickly, the ticket-takers barely bothered to check the coupons they were shown and once everyone was through the doors, we all rushed at the available seats. Babalu was nearly trampled by a whole family of bad-mannered Americans and Fat Sophie had to take out her asthma medication when she got to her seat because she'd run too much. The triumvirate took their places in the middle of a row, with Fine Dumas in the centre, her two outriders on either side of her, like bookends protecting a fragile and precious volume.

The actual show was pretty lame, at least in the opinion of the five hundred people in the Canadian Pavilion theatre that night, who howled with laughter at the acts in French, of which they felt there weren't enough, but were unmoved by the others. The two kinds of humour, the Latin and the Anglo-Saxon, didn't go well together, the actors didn't know each other well enough to work together convincingly and when they had to, it seemed strained. The acts that involved them all seemed to be forced and performed without feeling. As usual, it was the francophone actors who had to speak English because the Torontonians didn't know French. The atmosphere may be different when there are more tourists, Americans who understand and prize the kind of over-the-top humour that English Canadians like, at least I hope so for the poor actors' sakes; the performance I saw must have been hard on them. When Paul Berval, our very own "Beu qui rit," our laughing Ox, came on or when Jean-Guy Moreau did his famous impersonation of Mayor Drapeau, or during Dodo and Denyse's sketches, the house came alive, laughter rang out, but it all subsided, fizzled pathetically, during the acts in English. Maybe we should have laughed out of courtesy, I don't know ... But I guess we were tired of being polite with people who are never polite with us.

During the scene with the little dress, heads turned towards my friends who swelled with pride because the sketch was nearly identical to what they'd done on the plaza. True, Dodo and Denyse were a lot funnier, but Jean-le-Décollé and the Duchess had good reason to be proud. And they were. As for Madame, she did her best to be amused, laughing constantly over nothing, applauding at the wrong time, perhaps because too much had gone wrong since the start of her birthday party, which she wanted so badly to be a success ...

If I think back, there were some very brief moments of happiness inside a very long hour-long show. In the end we gave a standing ovation to our idols, whom we were finally seeing in person, but with the others I think we were barely polite.

We left the theatre amid a murmur of slight dissatisfaction. We would have preferred a show all in French and one all in English. Two shows actually, and we could have chosen between them. That wouldn't have been so exasperating. For the tourists too, if you think about it. A bilingual show was ridiculous.

In the end it was Fat Sophie who best summed up our thoughts when she declared as she lit her first cigarette, "It's frustrating to only understand half a show. And learning English just to understand the other half is worse!"

A gorgeous sunset was unfurling its passionate colours over Montreal as we left the theatre. Blood-red and lemon-yellow streaked the sky, were reflected in the water of the river and daubed the undersides of clouds; Mount Royal seemed even greener with this sumptuous lighting and Place Ville-Marie whiter. Night comes quickly in August and the picture was constantly changing. Habitat 67, the new modern housing complex built in the middle of the St. Lawrence River on a peninsula called Cité du Havre, was already sunk in darkness far away on our left. It looked like a pile of gigantic cardboard cartons stacked up between the Old Port and us. We had the impression that we were on the deck of an enormous ship that was taking us to the end of the world, that we were in the midst of a dream journey that we would never experience. We stood silent for a long time, regarding all that beauty until there was no more light in the sky and the city lights began to come on one by one.

When it was all over and Madame had given the signal to leave, Greta-la-Vieille dabbed her eyes.

"You have to admit, that's one hell of a show! And it's free! The bad thing is, we never look at it!"

To which a sarcastic Nicole Odeon replied, "A sunset over the Main isn't a sunset over the St. Lawrence River!"

Behind us on the plaza outside the Canadian Pavilion, some musicians dressed like farmers from the early days of the French colony, insensitive to the beauty of the moment or simply earning their living as they did every night, were playing a hysterical jig and tapping their feet and playing the spoons. We raced away from them, Québécois folklore not being our cup of tea—especially not at a moment like this. With Montreal standing out on the horizon like a brilliant necklace laid down along the St. Lawrence, at the heart of this nascent night that promised to be glorious, the last thing we wanted was a rigadoon or a call-and-response song; we wanted South American music, a languorous tango, a shivering rumba, Carlos Gardel, Abbe Lane, Carmen Miranda—or at least our very own Gloria who, despite a blatant lack of talent, could nonetheless make us dream about tropical nights that we'll never see as she stumbles through songs in Spanish of which she doesn't understand a word—or the rhythms of the Caribbean, Cuba or … yes, or Jamaica, and that was where the boss was taking us for supper!

Madame, back on the arm of Monsieur Jodoin, who tested us by asking, with a straight face, "What would you say to a couple of theme pavilions before we eat, ladies?"

Protests on all sides.

"Forget theme pavilions!"

"We didn't come here for an education!"

"Right on! This is a party, not a funeral!"

"I'm too hungry, wait till after!"

"Is there a theme pavilion for fast food?"

I think we actually ran away from Canada's plaza.

And as the Duchess put it so well when we were leaving the site and she was straightening her daytime wig which had slipped over her ear, "After all, you don't go to a World's Fair to visit your own country!"

As the pavilion of our own country had been built on an enormous site completely surrounded by canals, to leave it we had to walk down little flower-filled paths disguised as bridges, which were pretty but impractical because they were so narrow. It was hard for traffic to move that night and bottlenecks had formed at the exit from the show. We waited our turn to cross the one that led to the western provinces' pavilion, impatient to sample food different from what we were used to, to the rhythm of exotic music that we sorely needed, when we heard a familiar voice in the middle of the crowd, "They're expecting us at the Mexican Pavilion! We're late!"

Denyse Filiatrault and Dominique Michel themselves were lined up just like us to get to the rest of Île Notre-Dame!

It would be hard for me to describe here the excitement that took over our ranks. Suffice it to say that the entire Boudoir, Madame included, used its elbows, arms and maybe its feet, as well, to catch up with the two actresses. But the crowd had divided in front of them like the Red Sea before Moses and they just managed to get away from us. We watched them run, looking neither left nor right, anxious to get to the Mexican Pavilion, I suppose, and unwind after a frustrating performance.

Babalu had stood on tiptoe to watch them disappear somewhere between the western provinces' and the asbestos pavilions.

"Denyse must be going to meet her boyfriend, he's a Mexican ... "

Some heads turned in her direction. She shrugged.

"If you read the right papers you'd know."

We were sorry that we'd missed a chance to tell our idols how much we admired them, but I was sure that it was just as well for them. They must be sick and tired of having strangers come up to them after their show. Signing autographs. Acting nice when they aren't in the mood. I would have thought that a limousine would be waiting to take them home every night ... But as Denyse herself had said, they had a date at the Mexican Pavilion, maybe they'd cancelled the limousine to go and eat ... And Babalu, who knew everything about the local and international stars thanks to the gossip sheets she'd been enslaved to since she was a teenager, had suggested that they might be on their way to meet the actress's Mexican boyfriend ...

The Jamaican Pavilion was nearby, just behind the one devoted to asbestos; once we were across the bridge we were there in less than two minutes, excited as fleas and hungry as fighting dogs. Musicians, not the same ones we'd seen earlier, were playing calypso, the crowd was swaying, legs tracing complicated arabesques on the cement, things were looking good!

Madame made the first move, tried to make herself look taller to be more impressive and asked one of the handsome Jamaican cadets who was still controlling traffic, in nearly incomprehensible English, how to get to the pavilion's restaurant.

He replied that there wasn't one.

Stupefaction.

Heaving a sigh that seemed to be the last one in her life, Madame brought her hand to her heart as if she'd been stabbed. She turned pale in seconds. The monochrome was now complete: she was truly white from head to toe. With her other hand she clung to the arm of Monsieur Jodoin, who patted her gently, most likely worried that she'd have another fit.

"I can't believe it! This lousy day is turning out to be lousy from beginning to end! We're going to finish it off at the Sélect, I just know! I'm going to celebrate my sixtieth birthday over a club sandwich! I wanted to dance the calypso to the sound of marimbas and I'm going to listen to Jean Ferrat tell us over and over that *c'est beau, c'est beau la vie*, as if he wanted to taunt me!"

Protests from all sides: it didn't matter, there were restaurants elsewhere, it was a point of honour for certain pavilions to serve their country's finest fare, and chefs had already had offers to stay in Montreal after Expo. But there was nothing to be done, it was in

Jamaica that Madame wanted to end her birthday party and she was sticking to her guns.

"I wanted palm trees!"

"There's palm trees in other places!"

"I wanted calypso … "

Silence.

She looked, damp-eyed, at the orchestra of handsome black musicians who were making the crowd dance.

"That's what I wanted! We aren't here to gobble hotdogs from a French-fry stand while we dance the calypso! I wanted things like fried bananas or mangoes or pineapples! A chicken with every tropical fruit you can imagine and a bottle of dark rum—that's what I wanted!"

Babalu had slipped in next to her while she was talking. Madame, though she'd kept an eye on her, hadn't spoken to her since the incident with the ticket-taker and the fake Brigitte Bardot was obviously scared. But she screwed up her courage and worked up the nerve to say, "Can I make a suggestion, Madame?"

The boss looked at her as if she barely knew her.

"Nothing can console me! Nothing!"

Babalu cleared her throat before going on, then looked at us one by one, as if she were getting ready to risk her life.

"Look … I heard … Actually, I read in *Échos-vedettes* … "

Madame, mocking, cut her off with insulting brusqueness. Babalu wanted to help her after all, why not let her finish and not interrupt her? But disappointment had robbed her of all politeness, all civility, "If it was in *Échos-vedettes* it must be cast in bronze! What have you got for us this time?"

Babalu swallowed the insult without flinching.

"All I wanted to say was, apparently the restaurant in the Mexican Pavilion is fantastic … And it's not far away … It's called Acapulco and I'm sure they serve chicken with all the tropical fruit you want … "

She coughed into her fist, smoothed her pink dress, looked down at the tips of her shoes.

"And since Dodo and Denyse just said that they were going there, I thought maybe we might see them while we're eating ... "

Everyone hastened to say that it was a wonderful idea, except of course Fine Dumas, who wanted us to go on feeling sorry for her for a while. She even dragged her heels before following the rest of the group, talking nonsense in a quavering voice, nonsense such as, "The rest of you go ahead, I'm not hungry. I'll just have some French fries with vinegar ... I'll stay here, I'll have a drink at the bar to toast my health and watch the people dance ... Go and eat, the rest of you, enjoy yourselves ... When it's time to pay for your supper come and get me, I'll pay and then we'll go back to Montreal ... Or I'll entrust my money to Céline and she'll pay in my place ... Can you do that, Céline, sweetheart, pay in my place if I give you the cash?"

When Madame calls somebody sweetheart it means that something's wrong: she's either mad at the person or seriously upset and you always have to be on the alert because the unexpected can jump out at you without warning. As well, it was most important that Madame not get it in her head to have a drink by herself—we all knew it was too dangerous and, once again, we overdid our enthusiasm a little for Babalu's plan, for the sole purpose of diverting her and dragging her with us for a real meal, far from the dangers of drink and its detrimental consequences.

True, we were hungry; we wanted to eat, and anything at all would have done. But the part of the day that was all wrong was the quest all over the World's Fair for a single thing: the happiness of Fine Dumas, which kept getting away from us because she herself—who was notoriously paranoid and convinced that everyone was against her—refused to be satisfied with what was going on. The atmosphere kept transforming itself, moving from light to heavy every fifteen minutes: all of that, in the end, was a burden to our systems and a strange kind of fatigue made up of nerves and anxiety was starting to be felt by each of us and to sap our energy.

As we made our way to the Mexican Pavilion, our progress grew slower and our voices more quiet. Fat Sophie was dragging her feet and fanning herself; the two Gretas were by themselves and exchanging remarks in a whisper; Jean-le-Décollé and Monsieur Jodoin were on either side of Madame, who was playing the exhausted woman with such bad faith that you wanted to slap her; and the rest of us, what was left of the Boudoir, were trying to take the initiative, show some vitality, but without much strength because we felt drained. Even the thought of eating in the company of Dodo and Denyse didn't turn us on.

It was a fairly morose group then that turned up at the door of the Acapulco restaurant located deep in a very beautiful tropical forest that had been reconstituted for a six-month period on the shore of the St. Lawrence River, though it's so northern and so cold.

The Mexican Pavilion was pretty and light, with an amazing shape—an open fan on the edge of the water; it was animated and colourful, and when Madame heard the first notes of the mariachi band strolling on the small plaza in their tight white costumes and their huge sombreros sitting on their heads or tied to their backs, she seemed to emerge from her lethargy for a moment.

In any case she found the strength to tell us, "I love that music so much, I just love it!"

Good, that was something, maybe the mariachis would cheer her up a little.

Panic nearly broke out though when they told us that it would be hard to find a table for twelve at this hour. Madame let out a loud and disappointed, "Oh, no!" and we thought that the end of our memorable day had arrived. But I think that a fairly significant sum of money was handed out, very discreetly, after Monsieur Jodoin had talked with the maître d' for a few minutes, because suddenly, to everyone's surprise, a long, well-located table, was found to be free, as if by magic.

Our entrance did not go unnoticed. We were all too exhausted or too much on edge to stay cool or show a semblance of decorum and after the period of despondency we'd just gone through, our true natures quickly resurfaced, our horse came galloping back, meaning that a group of noisy and no longer very fresh drag queens walked right through the dining room, making heads turn.

Even Dodo and Denyse, bending over what seemed to be *seviche*, a famous Mexican specialty, showed definite surprise at our passage and stopped eating. They gave us a big grin and Dominique Michel herself in person, waved.

Babalu couldn't get over it and tugged at the Duchess's skirt.

"Did you see? Did you see? They're here! And they're waving at us!"

The Duchess grabbed her wrist.

"Don't point like that, you'd think you're ignorant!"

"But it's Dodo and Denyse!"

"Even if it's Laurel and Hardy, control yourself! Act as if you don't even see them, it's classier!"

"I'm not here to be classy, I'm here to be a fan! And you know as well as I do, you are too!"

The Duchess shrugged and gave Babalu a shove to speed her up.

"I'm here to eat, little girl; just watch me dig into the *pollo* and the *porco*."

Madame had regained her haughtiness and was manoeuvring through the tables, a consummate actress who knows how to make an entrance. But because she's short and more than pleasingly plump, she looked like a fat white pouf being dragged along by Monsieur Jodoin, and some diners hid behind their napkins to laugh as she sailed by. For ages now I've been used to people staring at me in public. I've chosen to look straight ahead and ignore it, it's become second nature. As the last of the group, I had a good view of the commotion set off by our arrival and I worried a little about repercussions. We wouldn't be discreet, that was obvious, people were certainly aware of our presence here in the Acapulco, so I had to watch out if I wanted to avoid the panic that was liable to break out among this rather sophisticated clientele who probably wouldn't appreciate being disturbed by the grotesque plebeians from the Main.

Our young waiter, who was very handsome and quite tall for a Mexican, impressed us from the outset when he managed to keep track of all the drinks we'd ordered without jotting a single note. And we were a table of twelve! And they weren't all margaritas! When the Pink Ladies, Piña Coladas and Daiquiris arrived, every drink was placed in front of the right person and without exception made as requested, with the alcohol at the correct temperature, the ice crushed or not, the glass frosted if it was supposed to be. In fact he didn't make even one mistake all through the meal and the only scrap of paper we'd seen in his hands was the bill, no doubt hefty from Madame's expression when it was time to pay. I confess that I would never have been able to do what he'd done back in my days at the Sélect, especially with all the hubbub and comings and goings in a crowded restaurant. This waiter was exceptional, exceptionally good-looking, and his tips probably reflected it.

With great elegance, he let practically everyone in our group come on to him, from Fat Sophie to Mae East and Greluche and even Madame, who took advantage of the fact that Monsieur Jodoin was looking elsewhere to cast a languorous gaze in the waiter's direction. He had a compliment for each of us: a dress was lovely; he admired an accessory—even Babalu's kerchief which had seen better days found grace in his eyes. He was of the same allegiance as the majority at our table and wanted it known—at our table at least. At one point I even wondered if he was in a way the opposite of the Duchess, waiter by night and drag queen by day, he blended into our group so well: the same language, same sense of humour, same facial expressions. And the same impishness in his words. Quite casually and with tact and marvellous control, he created victims in our ranks as he'd probably done at the neighbouring tables where rich and unworthy women shamelessly made eyes at him beneath the absent gaze, complicit or not, of their husbands.

To me he said that I had the hands of a magician and I realized that he was resorting to mentioning what's most attractive about me so he could avoid the rest, and I was grateful to him for not leaving me out, not ignoring me as others before him had done because they couldn't think of anything nice to say. He'd thought of something; it wasn't much, but I was touched.

When he was came to the Duchess, she said, "In my case, young man, don't compliment one detail of my person, you find me *totally* gorgeous!"

The waiter bowed very low.

"Which is precisely what I was about to say, Madame Giroux!"

Chalk one up for the waiter, everyone laughed—including the Duchess who was always happy when someone compared her with her idol.

Drag queens aren't a breed that knows its way around grand cuisine; most of their meals consist of all sorts of fast food, shovelled in any time, any way: it has a taste, you can wolf it down fast, it doesn't cost much—that's what they're interested in. The drag queens I know often eat on the run because a meal that lasts too long is time wasted, and time wasted means less cash under the mattress or in the purse. (Need I add that they don't spend a lot of time in banks?)

That night though, the twelve of us, without exception, were eating—with delight and without rushing—some amazing dishes, exotic and new to us, that were served with utter refinement: chicken *mole*, that sauce made from among other ingredients chocolate and hot peppers; multicoloured varieties of beans we'd never heard of; shredded pork mixed with olives, capers and coriander (I asked the waiter) that would have brought an outcry from their mothers; the avocado dish called *guacamole* of which everybody took seconds; banana-shaped plantains that some thought were a dessert served prematurely. We marvelled at every dish and tucked in ecstatically.

The Duchess said between mouthfuls, "A year from now when I've moved to Mexico this food will be my daily fare!"

And Mae East said, "A year from now you'll be so fat they'll be serving *you*—with an apple in your mouth and parsley up your nose!"

To which the Duchess snapped, "You know perfectly well, it isn't up my nose that I want parsley! Besides, I've already got some!"

The meal progressed with deliberate slowness, the tablecloth had more and more grease and red wine stains; faces became animated and took on a fine brick red colour—a sign of congestion and a promise of slow and difficult digestion; tongues, as if they needed it, were loosened; voices rose; everyone was happy. Even Madame. Countless toasts were proposed to her health, her long life, her prosperity; she replied with a tear in her eye and a sob in her voice. The news spread quickly enough that we were celebrating her sixtieth birthday and—ultimate gift, unparalleled tribute—she received a bottle of champagne from Denyse Filiatrault, Dominique Michel and their escorts, two stunning guys who had absolutely no reason to envy our waiter. Babalu nearly went berserk. Madame took it as she had the other compliments, with grace, like a *grande dame*, raising her glass as a sign of gratitude.

At one point the Duchess said, between mouthfuls of *pollo* or *porco*, "Good God! There are twelve of us at this table! One more and we'd have to elect a Christ!"

Jean-le-Décollé took his time before replying, "With you there's always one more!"

Which created a kind of chill, because we hadn't caught just what he meant. Was he insinuating that the Duchess was always *de trop* with us, or had he just wanted to say something funny without beating around the bush, without thinking? Only the Duchess had laughed; maybe it was some message between them that we didn't get ...

The musicians, more timid or more cautious than the waiter, had been wary of us at first and had played at all the tables except ours. By dessert time though, perhaps attracted by the atmosphere of pure pleasure that we gave off, by the laughter ringing out at our table non-stop and the free-flowing alcohol, they seemed less reluctant and came up to us, singing. Conversations around the table stopped, all heads turned in their direction.

They sang "Malaguena"; not very original, but it was enough to turn certain cheeks red with emotion. They circled Madame who was pinned between a mandolin and a guitar. The picture was quite funny because her face was level with the instruments and seemed to be part of the orchestra. She closed her eyes, threw her head back. The singer, who wasn't much taller than her—or even me—stood behind her chair, both hands on the back, and sang at the top of his lungs the way the song deserved to be sung. His high notes, held for a long time on the third syllable of the word *Malaguena*, were true and very pure. He craned his neck to send the notes up to the ceiling, ears red with the effort, his ribcage properly open, arms raised like Christ on the cross. He was aware of the effect his voice had on the audience and unabashedly took advantage of it.

I had never heard a mariachi band from so close. It was at once unsophisticated—like everything that comes from a folklore tradition we aren't familiar with, and haven't had time to get tired of—and deeply moving, like everything that is truly sincere. At the end of the song the entire restaurant applauded wildly and, of course, asked for more.

Immediately the mariachis started another piece, this one for several voices, a ballad unknown to me, slow and beautiful, captivating—but aren't all love songs that come from the south and that talk languorously about unhappy love, about irrational suicide or bloody murders on the shore of a heavenly sea? I didn't understand a word but I could see it all: the beautiful but treacherous mulatto, the macho man devastated by the end of his love affair, the glorious sunset over the raging Pacific followed by a remarkable full moon and a pitch-black night with sticky caresses. All that—total masochistic joy in the most absolute adversity—summed up in a song four minutes long.

I'd stopped looking at the orchestra, I was about to close my eyes so I could concentrate on the music, on the false and pleasurable suffering it stirred in me, when a female voice, warm and voluptuous, was added to those of the mariachis, grafted to them, turning around them while following their modulations, a deep, magnificent voice that, while serving as counterpoint, added to the lament a hint of female suffering that broke my heart.

In the restaurant, all heads turned.

The singer was Fine Dumas.

She had her hands on either side of her dessert plate as if to support herself, she was bent forward a little, her eyes still closed, and you'd have said that she didn't know she was singing. Her voice seemed to well up from the depths of her soul, from a corner of her heart we had never discovered, maybe because she didn't know about it herself: it was as if she had decided all at once and without thinking to lay out her darkest pain to everyone for the duration of a song, to serve us her deepest and most private secret when it was least expected. A startling confession of fragility, surprising in this masterful woman who never allowed any weakness to show, this woman who was tough at work and tough in her relations with others. A sorrow that you could sense was unbearable rose up in the overheated atmosphere of the restaurant and dropped onto every one of the guests in little bits of painful, haunting music.

You would have sworn that Fine Dumas had been singing with this same mariachi band all her life, their voices went together so well: the style was the same, the language too, the owner of a Montreal whorehouse finding herself, by what stroke of fate, by what node in space or time, on precisely the same wave-length as a traditional band from Acapulco, at the opposite end of North America. Together they'd crossed every country in the world, they'd sung "Malaguena" before crowned heads and before notorious bandits, they'd known years of glory and periods of waning popularity when everything went badly, they'd triumphed in vast theatres and haunted clubs deep inside shady parts of unknown towns, they'd survived all of that to come here, tonight, to the Acapulco restaurant in the middle of the Montreal World's Fair to offer us their hearts one last time before disappearing forever.

The last musical phrase, a long lament that heralded a slow death from an agonizing heartache, was executed in unison, without modulation, and the final note stretched out to infinity. The song never ended, it died away without our realizing. The silence that followed was still part of it.

The ovation was unbelievable. *Bravo*s on all sides, food-stained napkins thrown into the air, feet stamped, hands clapped, encores demanded, everyone refusing to let it end. Mayor Drapeau with his restaurant where the waiters sang opera for strait-laced guests would have to get up early to compete, this was genuine emotion.

When calm was restored—relative, because you could still sense the excitement that hadn't had time to die away—Madame rose to her feet, cleared her throat as if she'd just made a superhuman effort and said in the tiny voice of a tiny little girl, "I had the voice. I didn't have the physique. I realized that soon enough."

And at that precise moment I knew that my destiny was linked forever with this woman's.

They asked for an encore. Demanded one. Madame consulted the mariachi players—did she speak Spanish too but hadn't told us?—before announcing, with an apologetic little smile, "I haven't sung outside the shower for a long time ... But we'd like to offer you 'La Golondrina,' one of the most beautiful songs from South America and my big hit way back when ... "

I had always heard that song in French, I didn't even know that it wasn't from France: *Tu vas partir, charmante messagèèèèère* ...; I didn't even know the title. I'd often heard it on the radio when I was a child and I liked the nostalgia that radiated from it.

As soon as the introduction began—four wailing guitars sad enough to break your heart—a religious silence fell over the restaurant. People stopped eating, the waiters stopped circulating, even the maître d' was glued to his spot at the entrance and did nothing to speed up service. Just before Fine Dumas began to sing, the trumpet player almost turned his back on the other musicians to tone down the acid notes from his instrument. And when the beautiful mezzo voice rose up in the air saturated with exotic perfumes and the lingering odour of alcohol, eyes closed, heads bowed—perhaps to hide too powerful emotions.

The rapture was complete.

The execution was even better than "Malaguena" because the musicians were starting to know the boss's vocal capacities and she had a better sense of theirs.

I looked at each of those sitting at our table in turn while Fine Dumas was singing. What their faces registered most, I think, beyond surprise or admiration, was pride at discovering that someone in this group of misfits, of costumed oddballs, of unsophisticates, was able to do it. To do something so beautiful. All this time a genuine talent had been hidden among us and we'd never suspected it. Madame had spent entire evenings watching some lousy show, knowing that she could have simply gone on stage and changed everything but had never done it! How she must have suffered at the idiotic songs massacred by drag queens not even interested in performing in public and who executed their acts any old way before going off to earn their living by doing what they do best. Where was she coming from? What had happened to her? What kept her from being the star of her own establishment? With a voice like hers, what hidden tragedy, what intolerable grief kept her from going on stage and having a resounding success in the spotlight instead of sitting at the end of the bar, worrying herself sick?

I read the same questions in the eyes of the others. Because along with pride at discovering that Madame had a talent that they didn't was shame at knowing that the next night, and every other night, they would be doing their stupid acts in front of her.

Did she have a superhuman ability to cut herself off completely from what was happening on stage at the Boudoir? Could she ignore the grotesque nature of the *Follies* she offered to an audience of strangers for the simple reason that she made a lot of money? Or was that show simply an act of revenge against fate: "You didn't want me, you don't deserve me, live with it! And pay the price."

The two persons at the table who were most surprised and most moved were, of course, the Duchess and Jean-le-Décollé. Even they, her friends, her guardians, her outriders, hadn't known! They had their arms around each other and were crying like babies. I could sense that before long a detailed explanation would be demanded and I hoped I'd be there for it.

But it was during the third piece, which Madame had stipulated would be the last, a "Guantanamera" happier and more upbeat than anything I'd ever heard, that I was struck the hardest blow.

I was singing along with everyone else, clapping my hands, starting to feel like getting up from the table to join the people who'd started dancing when I spotted, in a secluded corner, over a meal they'd barely made a dent in, my entire family, watching me wriggling on the chair where a phone book had been placed to raise me up to the level of my food.

My father. My mother. My two sisters.

I hadn't seen them for a year and a half. I hadn't tried to contact them after my hasty departure. Nor had they. They hadn't asked for an explanation, I hadn't offered one. The break was clear, final, I didn't miss them and I don't think they missed me either.

All four were in the same position except my sister, Carole, who had to twist around on her chair a little to look our way because she had her back to our table: they were leaning slightly forward, holding their forks, frowning and furious, so still they seemed to be posing for a portrait. I suppose that they'd just noticed me too, you could still see the stupefaction in their eyes.

You can say that there's no such thing as chance, that fate is a myth or an excuse for those who lack it, what had brought all five of us to that place, that night, especially after all that I'd gone through that day—don't forget that according to Madame's initial plans, I would have been eating at the Jamaican Pavilion—had to have a name! Coincidence, yes, sure, how else to explain the crossing of so many paths up till then divergent, of people who've been living in two different worlds for eighteen months and who all at once meet up without having planned it, without having even thought about it; but I prefer fate because only fate can reserve such surprises for its victims. There, it's out, we are victims of fate. A machination by some minor gods on an Olympus of secondary importance had meant that there was no restaurant at the Jamaican Pavilion, that my mother had been too tired for the family to go home before supper or that my father, for once, had been persuasive when he sang the praises of Mexican food; a poor man's Bacchus had guided our steps, laid traps and reserved this rather melodramatic ending right in the middle of a folksong—no doubt to the delight of the demigods for whom it had been set up.

My mother, you could see from the layer of thickish liquid that covered her eyes, and that we call in my family "bean grease," had been drinking. I sensed that the meanness was still intact, coiled up deep in her heart, and that it could burst out at any moment in waves of insults all the more wounding because they would be unjustified. I knew that she was capable of hurling insults at me in front of everyone if I made eye-contact with her for too long for her liking, which was the last thing I wanted, especially in such a unique situation.

My father had aged. That's all I can say about him because I didn't look at him for long: he was the only one who could have made me feel any guilt, and this really wasn't the moment. But I could see that time and sorrow had left their mark on him. I had known, I'd guessed, now I had the proof before my eyes and that was what upset me most.

My two sisters are now young women. I wouldn't want to lack generosity towards them, but let's say that they didn't become more attractive when they passed from adolescence to adulthood, that very ugly butterflies had unfolded from their cocoons. Carole is fat now and Louise has bleached her hair platinum blonde, which doesn't suit her at all. And at that moment both were displaying, deep in their eyes, the malevolence inherited from our mother, hardly diluted by their curiosity to find out what kind of world I now lived in.

It was that very nastiness, I think, that made me decide to hold out on them. On the three of them, actually, because my father, after meeting my gaze, had bowed his head like a man who's been struck down and is conceding to someone stronger. "Guantanamera" was nearly over, in a few seconds the table where I was sitting would explode in hysterical applause and shouts of joy, demanding more, the concert would continue or not, the other three women in my family would see, if they hadn't already, whom

I was with, what kind of people I hung out with, the world I'd come to after leaving them, and with nothing to stop them, they could give in to their natural tendencies, especially my mother: verbal cruelty and destructive slander. So yes, I decided to confront them in silence; I had no intention of speaking to them, I was going to show them how proud I was to be part of this group of happy clowns, this weird bunch of people, men dressed as women, women of easy virtue, and I began to follow the music, to clap my hands, to sway from side to side in my chair while I looked my mother squarely in the eyes. Let her dare to get up, to approach me and speak first, I'll show her what kind of person I am!

I taunted them with joy in my heart; true, it was joy mixed with sorrow, and it put a lump in my throat and had an aftertaste of bitterness, but joy all the same. My mother brought her glass of wine to her lips without taking her eyes off me; in them I could see all the negative feelings—contempt, rancour, loathing—that she'd had towards me since I was born, a compilation of everything that had made my childhood and my teenage years so miserable summed up within the brief minute that it took the song to end. A blend of "I knew you'd end up like that" and "You've driven me crazy to the end," a wreath of mute reproaches, a murderous silence. And absolute. A discreet duel that was fought even though it ended in a draw because neither of the duellists could boast victory. I looked away before she did, but only so that I could pour myself a glass of wine and raise it in a toast to her health.

The restaurant was in utter chaos. The Duchess was dancing with the handsome waiter who was obviously very happy to let her have her way; the other girls from the Boudoir had chosen partners from the restaurant clientele and were making an attempt at a mambo that didn't always work, but that was entertaining because of its clumsiness; Monsieur Jodoin was looking after one of the most beautiful women present while Madame, followed by the mariachis, had started to visit all the tables as if she'd been doing it all her life. Without realizing it, she'd resumed her role of boss and her regal manner was nearly as impressive as her voice. The song ended in an explosion of notes from the trumpet thrown out in a confetti of sound that swelled the musician's cheeks and brought shouts of joy and encouragement from Madame—and in Spanish, if you please!—that seemed to come from a real flamenco show.

The applause was indescribable and went on for several minutes while Madame, who you'd have said had grown a good six inches, distributed kisses, displayed false humility by covering her face with her hands and beamed with pleasure at the compliments that were lavished on her.

Then she raised her arms to ask for silence.

"Please ... Please ... Silence, please ... "

She coughed into her fist, straightened her white suit which looked a little the worse for wear and assumed the voice of a business owner, kind and in her element, to deliver her little speech.

"As you probably know, today is my sixtieth birthday and I'd decided to celebrate it by bringing my staff to visit Expo. It's been a day full of surprises, not all of them good, I admit, and I would like it to end on a high note. So I've decided to open my bar, the Boodwar on St. Lawrence Boulevard near St. Catherine, for the rest of the night and I invite you all to tempt yourselves in our company! Now I have to warn you that our reputation is far from inflated and that you won't forget your visit to the Boodwar for a long time. Particularly not what makes it surprising and unique."

Her frankness brought laughter and people at several tables said that they would follow her to the Main: after Mexico and its piquant cuisine, the spice of Montreal's illicit world seemed like a good idea.

Denyse Filiatrault and Dominique Michel had made their way to her to have a word, and Babalu had flung herself in their direction so she wouldn't miss the conversation that she recounted to me later, proud to have witnessed it and moved by what had been said.

After shaking hands with Madame, Denyse Filiatrault had said, "I saw you in the old days at the Mocambo ... "

Fine Dumas had smiled. "Good Lord, you must have been a child!"

"I was fourteen and I'd got dressed up to come and applaud you."

"That was so long ago ... "

"You were divine."

"I was grotesque. Short and fat and singing sexy songs, honestly ... "

"Alys Robi would have been green with envy if you'd stuck with it."

"No. She made *me* green with envy. She had everything, including the physique; I couldn't do a thing about it, all I had was the voice ... She cost me my career, but she paid dearly for it."

"So did you ... "

"No, I chose another way."

She had changed the subject abruptly, probably to avoid lapsing into nostalgia or bitterness that nothing could redeem, not even cynicism.

"Are you coming with us?"

It was Dominique Michel who replied, "No ... we have to do our show tomorrow! But thanks for the invitation, it's very nice of you ... We heard about your ... bar from Maurice Chevalier, who had a very good time there. We'll have to go there too one of these days ... "

The two women moved away after embracing Fine Dumas who, according to Babalu, had discreetly wiped away a tear.

As soon as Madame had finished her speech, and without even bothering to think it over, I made my way straight to my family's table. When my mother saw me approach, she gagged and shrank down on her chair a little, as if she were afraid that I would hit her. My sisters had their noses in their plates and everything on them was cold—the refried beans, the rice, the *pollo*, the *porco*. As for my father, he seemed to be asleep as he always is when something important is going on around him, true to his role of nonexistent father. I knew he was listening to everything and I wished he were really asleep, the poor coward.

With them sitting and me standing, I was level with their faces and in a few seconds I saw the countless meals that I'd served them over so many years because our mother "wasn't feeling well," but we still had to eat. I would serve the food and we would sit the way they were just then, hunched over slightly as if they didn't want to look at me, me humiliated, always humiliated, offering them their pittance which they wouldn't take the trouble to appreciate because, as far as they were concerned, whatever I did for them I owed them.

This time though I was running the show. I placed my hands on the table and asked them, with a sarcastic smile, "Are you coming with us?"

Stunned, glued to their seats, they couldn't say a word. My victory was complete but also frustrating, because it had been too easy. So I decided to add to it, to lay it on thick to let them know that they didn't impress me any more. And, of course, I got my comeuppance.

"You can't imagine how much fun I have at work! I'm the hostess in a transvestites' brothel—in case you didn't already know. I'm the one who introduces the whores to the clients. And the whores are men. I make a lot of money. A lot. A lot more than you'll ever see. In a world that's struggling to stay alive instead of letting itself die by inches from booze and bad luck. Are you sure you don't want to come and have a look? You could finally meet some people who aren't ashamed of me!"

My mother slammed her glass onto the table.

"Do you earn your living on your back too?"

I thought I glimpsed a way to shut her up for good: leave her with a vague idea, let her simmer away in doubt, not let her know for sure if her daughter had become a prostitute or not.

"You'll never know unless you come to the Boudoir."

She let out a bitter laugh which I can't deny went straight to my heart. She hadn't forgotten how to get to me at my weakest point—my pride—and she remembered how that kind of sneering mockery from her could hurt me.

"I'd rather die than set foot inside that place. I'd be too ashamed."

"You've always been ashamed of me anyway."

"Yes, but not to that point. Tonight is the end of everything. The final stop. I'm more than ashamed, I'm so embarrassed I don't know what to do. I'm frozen here. Go away now, go and join your gang, Céline, your presence soils our table!"

I staggered under the blow while removing any expression from my face. I certainly wasn't going to give her the satisfaction of showing her the wound she'd just inflicted! And I left their table after saying into my father's ear, but in a way that everyone could hear. "Don't worry, Papa. I'm very happy."

The signal for departure had been given and there was an indescribable commotion in the restaurant. Madame, followed by her court which I was about to join, for good, was giving instructions to those who'd decided to come along. Everyone agreed to meet at the Boudoir—they all seemed excited, including the restaurant staff and even the mariachi band who promised to provide music for the rest of the night.

Jean-le-Décollé was waiting for me next to my chair where I'd left my little purse.

"Your family?"

I applied a good coat of bright red lipstick before I replied.

"Those people? Not at all. Clients from the Sélect. Boring…"

On the little square outside the Mexican Pavilion, the mariachis were strumming their guitars and a bunch of tired drag queens were asking themselves how they were going to get through the long and exhausting night that lay ahead. Would it at least pay? Did Madame's invitation include *all* the services of the Boudoir—for *free*? Fine Dumas was hanging on the arm of Monsieur Jodoin and we could hear her humming to herself some unknown tunes from the other end of the world.

And a midget, her heart lighter but still heavy, limped along behind everyone else and looked up at the moon.

Legends of the Boudoir

V—Céline's Boudoir: A Dream

In a few minutes a new millennium will begin.

Céline's Boudoir is packed with party animals of every kind decked out in the latest, wildest style, all with coloured cones on their heads, confetti sprinkled on their shoulders, flutes of champagne in their hands. Everyone is bellowing songs from the hit parade—we've come a long way from "Ce soir je serai la plus belle pour aller danser," Michèle Richard has been dead for a long time—and they're twisting and swaying to rhythms that would have been considered barbaric in the long ago days when I was just the hostess.

Today, and for quite a while now, I am not only the boss I'm also the owner. When Fine Dumas retired at the venerable age of eighty, she sold me her business, for a steep price, and I changed it totally, tripling its area with renovations that were tremendous, expensive and very extensive: I bought the disused movie theatre and the dry goods store on either side, I had walls opened up and ceilings knocked down, I added a mezzanine from which you can have a good look at what's going on down below while sipping a drink if you don't want to join the fray; I put in plenty of deep, comfortable armchairs and low tables lit by discreet little lamps: in short, I turned it into the chic spot that it had never been.

The only thing I didn't change, aside from Fat Sophie's upright piano, is the long, fake marble bar at the end of which Fine Dumas held court for so many years, dragging on that ridiculous cigarette-holder of hers. I left it where it has always been, in front of what used to be the entrance, even though it gets in the way now, like an old animal you allow to sleep in the middle of the room because you suspect he won't be around much longer. I know I should get rid of it—in fact I'd intended to do so to celebrate the turn of the new century, but the image of Madame, draped in one of her monochrome outfits, straight-backed and watching everything like a hawk, stopped me. Even though it encroaches on the dance floor I've had set up in front of the stage, enlarged of course, better decorated now and equipped with a more sophisticated sound system, I've decided to keep it for a while. Which means, I guess, that it will be there as long as I'm the owner of Céline's Boudoir.

I changed the name of the bar strictly out of vanity, I don't deny it. So that people will know that the midget they'd known, who didn't have two cents to rub together and was undecided about her future, had become the boss and that now she is the one called Madame. That's right. They call me Madame. I don't insist, but I do encourage it, and my suggestions, like Fine Dumas's in the old days, are respected by a staff that is well-trained, polite and devoted. I know how to seem as generous as a real madam and like a real madam, I know how to be strict. I am respected because people are a little afraid of me. But I confess that I play my part without taking it too seriously and it amuses me because I know the source of all the tics that I've adopted and that aren't natural to me: in a way I'm an actor who has only played one part in her life, perfecting it over the years and enjoying it. I quite unashamedly enjoy perpetuating the memory of Fine Dumas and I'm very proud of it.

The vocation of the bar, you may be surprised to know, hasn't changed over the years, it has only grown: under my reign, Céline's Boudoir has become one of the most profitable houses in Montreal and it's still the most unusual. Lifestyles have evolved since Expo 67; prostitution is now practically legal, it's more than tolerated but not institutionalized, meaning that without being under the yoke of a government that would scoop up the whole take, my business is run under precise regulations and, of course, still depends on well-placed bribes and well-stuffed envelopes.

Guilda in her heyday would have been jealous of the drag queens who work for me; I choose them myself not just for their beauty but also for their talent. The shows I present are staged by popular directors, my prices aren't excessive and everyone can afford to spend an evening or a night at Céline's Boudoir without ruining themselves. And the men who spend the night in the arms of my girls always claim that they're straight ... Luckily for me, some things never change.

It's two minutes to midnight. I take an anxious look at the front door where Marilyn, a giant of stupefying beauty, a monumental Marilyn Monroe even sexier than the real one, stands guard while we wait for the great moment. I hope everything will go well. My heart is pounding, I feel as if I'm five years old and that a promise made long ago is finally about to be realized. Voices in the bar get louder, the hysteria is at its peak. At one minute to midnight, Marilyn gestures to me that everything's ready and I give her the signal she's been waiting for.

The doors open at precisely the moment when the world topples into the twenty-first century and a very odd procession makes its entrance into Céline's Boudoir. You might think that they're ghosts, and maybe they are.

All of Fine Dumas's former employees have survived the trials and tribulations of the past thirty-two years and all are here tonight.

A bouquet of aging drag queens makes its appearance first—shy, hesitant, neat and tidy in their old hookers' costumes. They form a compact group, walk with studied slowness, aware of everyone's interest in them, at once proud and ashamed. They look as if someone has directed them, as if they're the opener before a show about which nothing is known yet, or that the leader is about to step out of the chorus and start to talk, and that the first scene of *The Trojan Women* is going to be presented by some most remarkable women of Troy.

Babalu, who is my age, fifty-four, has never forgotten Brigitte Bardot, as shown by her peacock-blue dress with crinoline. Though she has eliminated the kerchief, her bright red wig makes her look older. And the crocheted gloves with one button still cover her hands—now to hide the age spots probably, something that prostitutes dread and that my girls call, with horror, graveyard flowers. She's been playing the ingénue for forty years, and it would never cross her mind to try anything else.

Nicole Odeon and Mae East are arm-in-arm, as if to give each other courage. They still live together in the apartment on Place Jacques-Cartier and have changed professions, now selling ladies' lingerie nearby. Some of my girls are customers there but I, as I long ago gave up any thought of dressing provocatively, have never set foot in their business for professional reasons, only to chew the fat with them—and God knows they have stories to tell! They have to wear what they sell, advertise it: they're well over sixty, yet they seem more undressed than dressed for this reunion and are liable to catch cold before the night is over. They're still beautiful and I imagine they want to prove it to us.

The two Gretas haven't spoken for at least ten years—something about a man, of course—and I hope to reconcile them before the party's over. They make a point of standing far apart, but something in the way they hold their heads, in the way they wedge their purses under their left arm, in their rolling gait too—in fact everything about them, everything their personalities project—proclaims how close they've been for a quarter-century; they could still be taken for sisters. The older sister from the boondocks who's been able to make a nest for herself in the big city, the younger one who's a product of the city, which she has never left. Though they're no longer on speaking terms, their genes speak for themselves.

Greluche hasn't changed, she's just a little wrinkled, and her name still suits her very well. She has opened a hotdog place very close to here and a perpetual smell of stale grease follows her everywhere. But she's the sexiest purveyor of hotdogs on the Main and suitors of every allegiance line up at her door and have ended up smelling just like her.

Mimi-de-Montmartre is the only one to feel sorry for: she underwent The Operation despite everyone's warnings; now she's a real woman, and not one of her old pals wants anything to do with her because, when you get right down to it, she's a man dressed as a woman they'd like to have sex with. She still works as a barmaid, but in some dump in the west end of town where they take advantage of her experience, while underpaying her because of her age. At sixty-six she still makes Pink Ladies and Cucumber Delights for a clientele that can't appreciate her or her clever mixtures, either. I offered her a job in the cloakroom a while ago; she turned it down. But I haven't given up hope of rescuing her.

With a cigarette stuck in her mouth, her gait still rolling in shoes that are comfortable and very ugly, Fat Sophie, one of the two real women in this picture, leaves her group as soon as she's in the door and heads for her piano, which I've placed prominently in a brightly-lit corner of the bar. She runs her hands over it as if caressing a loved one, bends over to drop a kiss on its polished surface. Fat Sophie hasn't touched a piano since she left the Boudoir and she lives alone now on a private income—people say she has money tucked away, hidden all over her apartment—somewhere far away in the east end of town. She drinks her beer on her balcony come summer, and in her living room in winter. I wish that she'd turn around so I could get a better look at her. Most of all I wish that she'd bring the piano back to life, that she would send up into the air of Céline's Boudoir her old honky tonk tunes or something from her inexhaustible repertoire of songs from the forties and fifties. But the piano is out of tune, has been for years—and maybe she is too.

All that—the procession of ghosts from my past—takes place in the bar amid cries, laughter, shouts of *Happy New Year* and *Happy New Millennium* on all sides and under a rain of confetti, balloons and streamers. I am the only one who saw them make their entrance without moving from my seat at the end of the bar. They spotted me quickly, then made their way towards me. Once level with me, the group split in two and in came the ones I was most waiting for.

The triumvirate together again. Undoubtedly for the last time.

Jean-le-Décollé is decked out as usual in rags of grey, brown and black found God knows where, that droop from his body; you could almost think they were the same ones he'd sported in 1967, so worn are they by the patina of time, so baggy and shapeless and faded from too many cleanings. The skirt gapes over his knees, the very low-cut blouse lets you see his bones, you'd swear that the nylons date from just after the war, the shoes are broken-down because of his bunions, and the excess jewellery—bracelets, chains, necklaces, earrings (all that's missing is a tiara)—make him jingle like the rich old ladies he used to think were so ridiculous and laughed at all his life. As for the jacket—a cheap Chanel knock-off purchased at a long-ago sale—it sags miserably around him: rheumatism has made him hunchbacked for some years now, and he walks bent over, accentuating even more the faded look of his outfit which is meant to be chic. He has lost weight and his flaccid skin drips down like melting candles; he has shrunk around himself, everything about him hangs down. And he has the waxy skin of a serious drinker. He lives off welfare, has organized a monk's life for himself in a room that he rents on Clark Street and, he maintains, is taking advantage of his old age to reread the great classics (cheap love or adventure stories) while sipping vintage wines (beer). He is still dressed as a woman and still insists being addressed in the masculine.

The Duchess and he often come to visit, and for hours at a time we go over with delight our shared history—so rich in events and amusing anecdotes. They settle in at the bar with me and we don't see the nights going by.

The first thing I notice about the Duchess is that tonight she is wearing her short, black wig that's so shiny and stiff it reminds you of a piece of pottery just out of a kiln. No more red wig à la Germaine Giroux for her—for a while now; the Duchess has been calling it her Zizi Jeanmaire look, saying it's easy to maintain and goes anywhere.

"You put it on your knee and that's that! And it goes with everything, a bathing suit or a floor-length gown! When it's too dirty you dump it in the washing machine and hang it up to dry ... I'm too old to give my wigs permanents ... Zizi, God rest her soul, saved my life! Don't forget, this thing is genuine ersatz imitation synthetic fake nylon! You can't stop progress!" She has nonetheless put on the most eccentric garments from her years of glory that she still owns: an outfit in lapis lazuli taffeta—or so she calls it—trimmed with cock feathers, scattered with multicoloured glitter that she still looks good in. A river of fresh-water diamonds—again, the Duchess's term—adorn her neck, which is beautiful, and overweight earrings that stretch her earlobes. She looks like a store dummy from the fifties and she spits on everything modern. She even claims that real fashion was over in 1967. Now past eighty, the Duchess is still hilarious, nasty, petulant and bitchy. And fat. Neither age nor illness has managed to do anything about her obesity. She still has the amazing pink complexion of a young girl, her chubby face doesn't have one wrinkle; in spite of her weight, she's so light on her feet it's as if she is inflated with helium. I don't know what she lives on, she won't tell me, but I suspect inordinate pride and deep poverty hidden under a heavy dusting of Yardley's powder.

At ninety-two and counting, Fine Dumas, though she now walks with two canes, still makes a powerful impression. She's smaller than ever, thin and weakened by numerous surgeries, but with her natural self-confidence, her tremendous control and her regal bearing—the rest of her body is going downhill but the head is still erect!—she is still the centre of attraction whenever she agrees to leave her home, which she does less and less often because, as she says herself, after so many years in the battle zone she enjoys her solitude. She has never abandoned her monochrome outfits and tonight's is lilac-coloured, like a Sunday in spring: everything is lilac, from shoes to earrings, even her hair which is still thick despite her age, though she must have dyed it for the occasion. Age has shrunk her to the same height as me: she's become a midget. And I, though I haven't grown, a Madame. She has intelligently invested the money I paid for her bar, and now her days are peaceful, if not happy, spent in a lovely apartment in the Plateau Mont-Royal, as far from the red light district as she could get. I would have thought that she'd miss the Main—her fast and furious lifestyle, her bar, her girls, the fray—but she claims not to when she comes to visit.

"I'm very fond of you, of the whole gang, but I've put up with you long enough."

She has become a delicate little thing you'd think was fragile, but as soon as she looks at you, you practically stop existing and she's the one, as in the past when we called her *boss* and she made people tremble with fear, who takes over.

The former staff of the Boudoir surrounds her, protects her, but we know perfectly well that, without her, we would cease to exist.

I embrace all three at length, I think that the eleven of us even shed a tear. The Duchess whispers in my ear, "The twenty-first century, Céline, think of it! Who would have thought we'd last this long!"

A gap of silence opens in the middle of the general rejoicing. All the guests present sense that something important is going on before their eyes and they register what they see and what they hear so that, some day, they'll be able to boast that they were there. They know that the group who've just made their entrance, who are together here most likely for the last time, are part of legend. They could put a name to every one of the characters, even recount some of their now-famous adventures because the stories have been told by generations of the Main's drag queens whose idols these are. Twenty-five years from now, when none of us will exist, they will tell those who'll have replaced us, "I was there when Fine Dumas's gang were together for the last time and I'm here to tell you, *that* was an event!"

With considerable difficulty and great sensitivity, we perched Fine Dumas on what used to be her stool at the end of the old bar. A knot in time. We were all at once several decades younger, the Boudoir was smaller, the air conditioning too powerful, a curtain made of cheap glass beads hung next to the men's room to hide what went on behind it, at any moment Fat Sophie would launch into the first song of the evening and a fake Marlene Dietrich or a gigantic Brigitte Bardot was going to climb onto the tiny stage to mock her to a crowd that wouldn't be listening.

And as if she sensed it too, Fine Dumas raised her head, took out her cigarette-holder, gestured to the Duchess to light one last one for her. She took a long drag, savoured it, then released the smoke towards the ceiling.

With tears in her eyes she said, "If you please, ladies, a little discipline! The clients will soon be here!"

(I know that this dream is illusory—who will still be around in the year 2000, who will be gone?—but to satisfy this new pleasure in fiction that I've just discovered, I have decided to invent for my group of queens whose days are over a happy ending that suits my need for harmony.)

Epilogue

Going there, we were twelve in the minibus; coming home, nearly twice that many piled in as best we could amid comical confusion and joyous cries: the waiters from the Acapulco and the mariachis had decided to travel with us instead of taking the last Expo-Express back to the city, it was simpler and more convenient. We had loaded some musical instruments, which were fairly cumbersome, onto the back seat of the minibus, men were sitting on the others and each had taken a woman, real or fake, on his knees. That was how I ended up on the muscular thighs of the little singer, not altogether by chance because, without saying a word, we had arranged for it to happen, using our elbows and weaving our way through the crowd. From close up, his face level with mine, he was even more handsome, his eyes greener and his smile more devastating. Unaccustomed to having someone come on to me, I took advantage of the prevailing darkness to blush without wondering if my friends could see.

They saw everything of course and there was an exchange of knowing looks, I saw them, between Jean-le-Décollé and the Duchess who, subtle as ever, actually said, loud enough for everyone to hear, "Jean! Mae! Nicole! I think you'll have another roommate tonight! I hope there'll be four, but there's one for sure!"

If the singer—I was positive he'd be a José or a Pedro, but as it turned out he was a Miguel—understood French, he didn't let on and kept smiling at me in all innocence, as if everything was perfectly normal. And went on holding me close. For my greater pleasure.

Babalu was already consoling herself over the loss of her ticket-taker in the arms of the trumpet player—the lightning stroke had turned out to be just the heat, once again, Madame had been right—and the Duchess was deep in conversation with our waiter. No sexual complicity in this case, though, just good old collusion between two individuals of the same allegiance who are happy to recognize one another and between whom a friendship can be born very quickly because they have the same interests. And I think that their shared interest at that moment was one of the guitarists who, to their dismay, was assiduously courting Nicole Odeon. Couples were formed in the dark of the minibus—Fat Sophie was courted by the maître d', Greta-la-Jeune by another guitarist, not handsome but very sexy—and the approaching night looked promising.

Madame had automatically taken a seat next to Monsieur Jodoin; I imagine she'd chosen to forget that she thought he was a moron. But it didn't matter, given how she hoped to use him a few hours later!

In the middle of the Jacques-Cartier Bridge, my devoted escort began to sing very softly something that his colleagues took up in chorus: it must have had to do with love, because a strange glimmer had lit up his eyes and a sly smile adorned his face. I let him woo me then, thinking to myself that for once I was going to put aside my fears and worries. Relax, Céline, let yourself go for once! I listened to my own advice.

As we were driving into Montreal along de Lorimier Street, the Duchess said to no one in particular, "We spent a whole day at Expo and managed not to visit a single pavilion!"

When the minibus, which was taking on a lovely bluish colour in the light of the streetlamps, started up the Main, Madame turned towards us and said, "It's past midnight and my birthday is over, but the rest of the party is still on me … "

To bring my red notebook to an end, now that I've told about those two extraordinary days, I would like to quote the last two sentences from de Maupassant's story "La maison Tellier," which I'm very fond of, and that are so appropriate for the end of this account—which resembles it a little:

"*And as they were surprised at such generosity, a radiant Madame told them: 'Not every day is a holiday.'*"